The only fate worse than death is life—in the hellish urban jungle of Christopher Fowler's imagination. . . .

BOX
A curious young messenger discovers that good things don't always come in small packages—sometimes bad things do. . . .

THE LADIES MAN
He has everything—including any woman he wants. But what fate awaits when the tables are turned, and *he* is seduced . . . and abandoned?

SHADOW PLAY
A game of hide and seek in the dead of night introduces a lonely boy to a band of playful street urchins—and a game that's played for keeps. . . .

. . . Plus nine more nerve-jangling stories of city life to read behind locked doors.

Also by Christopher Fowler
Published by Ballantine Books:

ROOFWORLD
RUNE

THE BUREAU OF LOST SOULS

Christopher Fowler

BALLANTINE BOOKS • NEW YORK

Copyright © 1989 by Christopher Fowler

"The Art Nouveau Fireplace" © Christopher Fowler 1989
"Box" © Christopher Fowler 1988
"The Ladies' Man" © Christopher Fowler 1988
"The Sun in the Sands" © Christopher Fowler 1989
"Hot Air" © Christopher Fowler 1989
"Lost in Leicester Square" © Christopher Fowler 1988
"Shadow Play" © Christopher Fowler 1988
"Deceiving the Lizards" © Christopher Fowler 1988
"Jumbo Portions" © Christopher Fowler 1988
"Safe as Houses" © Christopher Fowler 1988
"The Master Builder" © Christopher Fowler 1989
"The Bureau of Lost Souls" © Christopher Fowler 1989

All rights reserved under International and Pan-American Copyright Conventions. Published in the United States of America by Ballantine Books, a division of Random House, Inc., New York, and simultaneously in Canada by Random House of Canada Limited, Toronto. Originally published in Great Britain by Century Hutchinson Ltd. in 1989.

ISBN 0-345-37371-5

Manufactured in the United States of America

First Ballantine Books Edition: November 1991

For Sparky

Contents

INTRODUCTION

Mundane Menaces

Bear with me, this should only take a minute.

In a short story entitled "The Bingo Master," author Joyce Carol Oates introduces us to a lonely middle-aged woman named Rose, whose adventurous imagination masks her inability to confront real life. She lives in a small Alabama town where the only excitement is provided by the weekly visits of a handsome bingo caller. One day an opportunity to escape from her stultifying existence presents itself when Rose wins the bingo jackpot and, seemingly, the love of the charismatic bingo master. But all is not as it seems. Being sexually and socially naïve, Rose is the perfect dupe for an agonizingly cruel trick which robs her of her dreams and destroys her growing confidence in herself.

It's a horror story.

True, it's not in the traditional sense. There's no mad slasher with a penchant for pretty girls, no depraved three-hundred-year-old vampire craving fresh blood, no cannibalistic demon revived from ancient rites—yet the reader experiences an acute empathy with the unfortunate heroine, suffering growing discomfort and the pain of humiliation at her side. What else could such a tale be called?

Here's another one.

In the story "Seven Floors," by Dino Buzzati, an Italian businessman with a minor ailment is sent to a sanatorium for an overnight stay. The clinic is divided into seven floors. The patients are housed on each level according to the gravity of their illness. The top floor is for mild cases; the bottom for those with no hope of survival. Gradually, and to his increasing alarm, the businessman finds himself a victim of bureaucracy as he is bumped from one floor down to the next. Could the doctors be lying to him? If he isn't sick, why can't he get out? His inexo-

1

rable spiral continues downwards to a profoundly disturbing death. This, you must surely agree, is also a horror story.

Neither tale operates within the traditional boundaries of the genre. Both have mundane settings, ordinary characters and a distinct lack of supernatural paraphernalia. Yet the structure and style of each story are more gothicly haunting than a dozen chronicles of vengeful spirit-creatures or rabid werewolves. The everyday trappings of these stories, their basic believability, serves to escalate discomfort and unsettle the reader to a surprisingly high level. This is nothing new. Waugh and Monroe were both aware of the darkness lurking within everyday social situations.

Traditional Terrors

But horror stories based on vampires, ghosts and werewolves don't necessarily fail to excite. *The Howling* is a truly frightening book. Bram Stoker's *Dracula* still provides a powerful *frisson* of fear when read alone, tucked up in bed. And who could hope to sleep after reading William Hope Hodgson's *The House on the Borderland*, with its tale of demons tapping at the windows in the dead of night?

These days, traditional tales are often turned on their heads to reveal new aspects of their principal characters. Anne Rice's *Interview with the Vampire* returned eroticism to its rightful place in the Transylvanian legend. George R. R. Martin's *Fevre Dream* vampire was touching and sadly human. Frankenstein and Mr. Hyde have been presented as everything from hip playboys to song-and-dance men. Nobody, however, has had much luck updating the Mummy, probably because he didn't have too much of a personality to begin with.

Now there are new spectres.

Horror movies are filled with the Living Dead (who are beginning to wear out their welcome), Demons from Hell (many of whom seem to like heavy metal music for some reason), and Crazed Psychopaths who Prey on Young Girls in Tight T-Shirts (who are now deemed ideologically unsound). Horror novels have covered every Satanic sect, every form of possession, every radiated mutant insect that could be given sharp teeth and the ability to crawl up someone's trouser leg undetected. But still we look for new ways to scare.

Which brings me to these stories.

Dark Laughter

The most bizarre, upsetting and blackly humorous stories are inevitably the true ones. Recently, a farmer in Northern France was killed when a block of frozen urine fell out of a jumbo jet which was passing over his field. According to the *Las Vegas Sun*, an Austrian circus dwarf recently died when he bounced sideways from a trampoline and was swallowed by a hippopotamus. In Nottingham, the students of an evening class designed to help people cope with anxiety got locked in their classroom overnight.

These stories originate from local newspapers, not from the fevered brain of a horror writer. Compared to the daily news, most so-called "video nasties" seem lame and anemic. Why should the writer need to look further into the world of supernatural myth when so much raw material is here at his fingertips? Urban paranoia interests me. The stresses and strains of city life force fears to grow where none existed and provide a catalyst for strange events. Let's define the boundaries of this collection.

No vampires, werewolves or beasts. No traditional ghouls or ghosts. No Antichrists. No dolls that come to life. No brain-eating zombies. No misogynistic slasher sex. No demons from the bottoms of lakes. No malevolent spirits freed from their dwelling places after eons. No possessions or exorcisms. And positively no children locked in attics for generations.

Instead, twelve stories of desperate people in seemingly ordinary situations—workers in offices and friends in pubs, husbands and wives in apartments and houses. All of them the most unlikely—and therefore the most likely—people to find themselves trapped with their own personal, private visions of Hell.

Christopher Fowler

THE ART NOUVEAU FIREPLACE

A T NINE THIRTY-FIVE on a wet Monday morning a man tele-phoned Brockton & Shipley about a house. There was nothing odd in that. After all, Linnea Shipley was an estate agent. No, it was the manner of the man that was strange. He sounded vague and disinterested, as if he hardly cared about the house at all. He wanted it valued, today if possible, and as the property was situated in an extremely desirable location, Linnea decided to attend to the matter personally. She had already been at work for two hours, and felt like stretching her legs.

It was a very rare thing for a building in Rathbone Terrace to come on to the market. Usually a For Sale board only appeared there if an owner had died. Linnea brought the car to a stop and ricked up the handbrake, dipping her head to look through the windscreen as she did so. It was a curving, leafy road of pleasantly terraced red-brick houses. They had been built in a style which dated from the turn of the present century. The decorative scrollwork around the doorways, the carefully rendered window surrounds showed a craftsmanship rarely found these days, one which evoked memories of a forgotten era. Linnea was aware that every house in the street was a potential goldmine, and that their proximity to the new railway station added further to their value. In fact, she and Simon had been wanting to move to this particular part of North London for quite some time.

The front garden of number thirty-five was wild and overgrown with enormous nettles. Linnea stung her hand on them as she edged her way up the half-hidden path. The windows were dark and coated with grime, but the brickwork appeared to be in sound condition. And at least the bell seemed to work. She quickly checked her appearance, then unbuttoned the top of her blouse. Every little bit helped when it came to impressing a future client.

4

The man who opened the door was indeed as strange as he had sounded on the telephone. He was tall and dark and thin, all angles and elbows, and walked with a shuffle as he beckoned Linnea in. He wore spectacles with black plastic frames, and an old nylon shirt that was buttoned right up to the collar. As he showed the estate agent from room to room he threw out odd little gestures, as if suffering a minor affliction. Linnea had seen plenty of people like this on valuation trips, but they were normally old and had lived too long alone. This man could scarcely have been more than thirty-five.

The house was decorated in the worst excesses of mid-sixties taste. Orange-patterned wallpaper in the lounge, op-art swirls in the bedrooms, cheap fitted cupboards in white Formica, all showed signs of long-term neglect. Linnea smiled to herself. The owner was obviously penniless, and could be beaten into the ground when it came to settling the price. What little furniture there was appeared damaged and worn. There was also a very unpleasant smell emanating from the ancient carpet . . . but the walls were sound and dry, the floorboards strong, the ceilings unbowed.

And there was the fireplace.

She had noticed it the second she walked into the lounge: an art nouveau fireplace with curling, fluted columns, and long-gowned women standing on either side of the bricked-in grate. It was sculpted in the style of Alphonse Mucha—indeed, it could have been created by him. The women stood facing each other with their hands demurely folded together and their hair piled high. They were exquisitely detailed, with budding roses and climbing vines entwined about them in a complex Parisian motif. The fireplace had been sloppily painted over a number of times and was currently a sickly pea-green, but it was easy to see how extraordinary the thing would look cleaned up. It had to be worth a fortune.

Linnea studied the vendor, who was now drifting into the kitchen, muttering about having to sell up quickly and get out. The man obviously inhabited his own private world and knew nothing at all about selling a house. She asked her new client, whose name was Mr. Myson or at least something which sounded very much like it, how he had come to pick Brockton & Shipley as his estate agent. Myson pointed to the circular that Linnea's company dropped through letter boxes in the area, then resumed mumbling on about his reasons for wanting a quick sale—something to do with a dream he'd had recently.

It was then that Linnea knew she could undervalue the house, buy it for herself and make a killing.

She was quick to exaggerate the building's faults—the lack of central heating, the dangerous electrics, the medieval plumbing—and she invented a few new drawbacks of her own. She played down the good features and pointed out the bad, and finally, with much heart-searching and shaking of her undeniably attractive head, produced a selling figure so low that she shocked even herself. But the owner seemed unsurprised, and half-heartedly agreed to the terms, and Linnea shook his hand and left with a promise to draw up the details immediately and send them on.

She couldn't wait to tell Simon the news, but it was better not to mention anything until the sale had gone through. Linnea stuck to her original low valuation, typed out the description sheet within an hour of returning to the office, and then delivered it to Rathbone Terrace by hand. The sale that followed was one of the fastest she had ever made. She handled the documentation by using her maiden name on the forms. Naturally, it was important for Mr. Myson not to discover that she was buying the place for herself.

Seller and purchaser met just once more, on the day that Linnea arranged to collect the keys. Mr. Myson looked as if he had not slept for a week. He promised to collect the few remaining sticks of furniture which had been carelessly stacked at the back of the hall, then passed the keys to Linnea as if the ring to which they were attached had suddenly grown red hot in his hand.

It began to rain just as Linnea reached her car, but the young estate agent failed to notice. She was already thinking about the bottle of champagne she would open in celebration as soon as she returned to the office.

Two weeks later the builders moved into the now vacant house at number thirty-five Rathbone Terrace. A month after that, Linnea and Simon Shipley arrived and began to decorate.

They concentrated on finishing one room at a time, starting with the bedroom, and then the kitchen. Surprisingly, Linnea had trouble adjusting to the new house. Her sleep was disturbed by bad dreams, but she was never able to remember them when morning came.

One windswept autumn afternoon she stood in front of the fireplace and scraped at the curving mantelpiece with a pocket knife.

"God, Simon, it's gold underneath the pea, then purple, can

you believe that?'' She scraped a little more and checked the blade. ''Then it's black, and underneath that it's finally marble. White marble or alabaster, I think. But the figures are made out of inlaid bronze. Do you suppose we can take the paint off without scratching the metal?''

''There are all kinds of solvents. It shouldn't be too difficult.'' Simon knelt down and examined the floor. ''These boards are in good enough condition to varnish.''

''Then let's do it. I hate carpets, especially the one that was down in here. It smelled like someone had died on it.'' Linnea stepped back from the fireplace and admired it, her head on one side. The lounge had been painted white but still seemed cold and gloomy. The only way to make the place brighter would be to cut down the overgrown laburnum in the front garden.

''Perhaps we shouldn't sell the house once it's finished,'' said Simon, rising from the floorboards and dusting down his jeans. ''It's in such a great area.''

''I know,'' agreed Linnea, ''but we could make fifty grand on it, at least. I'll find us another one around here.'' She gathered her long red hair at the back of her neck and tied it up. ''Of course, we'll never find another fireplace like this so we'll have to take it with us.''

''Do you think that's fair?''

''Of course it's fair. Anyway, who cares? You've no business sense, Simon. It's not part of the original house, anyway. Someone imported it and installed it in the wall. Pity it's bricked up, though.'' Linnea ran her hand over the blocks which had been amateurishly cemented into place between the supporting pillars. ''I wonder why he did that.''

''Who knows?'' replied Simon. ''It sounds like he was a loony. It shouldn't be too hard to open up. Hang on a minute.''

He disappeared upstairs and returned with a hammer and chisel. After tapping at the mortar which surrounded the bricks for a few minutes, he rocked back on his heels and wiped his forehead with the cuff of his shirt.

''There wasn't much sand in this cement, I can tell you. I've barely left a mark, look.''

Linnea examined the wall of bricks and stepped back, worrying a nail with her teeth. ''Perhaps the whole cavity is filled in.''

''I don't think so. Listen.'' He banged the wall with the head of the hammer. The sound reverberated up the chimney. ''I'll get to it at the weekend, but right now I'm going to take a shower.''

As Simon left the lounge, shucking his shirt as he went, his wife crouched down against the fireplace wall and listened. It seemed to her there was a scratching from within, as if a bird had blundered down the chimney and was now flapping about in the darkness of the cavity, bloodying itself in a desperate frenzy to find the narrow passageway back to the light . . . She rose quickly, shivering, and ran from the room.

That night she remembered her dreams for the first time since they had moved into the house. She saw a man, tall and thin, dragging a woman's body across the floor of the lounge. The man pulled the corpse away to the side of the room, then darkness closed around them as he stepped through the wall, heaving his human burden in with him.

''Well, it's obvious, isn't it?'' said Simon when she described her dream to him the next morning. He pointed to the small portable television which stood on a pile of books at the end of the bed. ''You were watching that ridiculous horror film when you fell asleep. You know how susceptible you are. How many times does Doctor Hammond have to warn you about being influenced by such rubbish before you take notice of him? The last thing we want is for you to have a relapse.'' He slammed the hall door on his way out of the house, angry with her for revealing this glimpse of her former self.

Although her husband asked her not to, Linnea worked late the rest of the week. There was a big auction coming up, and the new office was due to open in a fortnight's time. That meant a lot of extra paperwork, and as Linnea had recently been made a partner she was now expected to shoulder more of the responsibility. Besides, she made more money than Simon ever did in his teaching post, so who was he to tell her when she should and shouldn't work?

Most nights when she returned home he could be found asleep on the couch cradling an empty wine bottle. He had always been a heavy sleeper after a few drinks, so she got into the habit of going to bed alone rather than trying to wake him. She turned off the portable lounge heater as she went, so that he would inevitably join her upstairs at some point before dawn, when the chill of the night finally penetrated his bones and forced him to wakefulness.

One night, letting herself in and finding Simon in his usual unconscious state, she did not go straight to bed but sat sipping the last of the Chablis bottle as she stared at the art nouveau fireplace, wondering if he would ever manage to finish the job he had started. Much of the paint had now been removed from the surround, revealing tantalizing portions of the lustrous bronze figures beneath. The grate was still blocked up. There were heavy scratch-marks over the brickwork, as if Simon had half-heartedly attempted to break through the wall to the cavity beyond. He would need a power drill, she thought, making a mental note to buy one tomorrow. God, how he hated her being in control of the purse strings. But, she thought bitterly as she drained the glass, he had no choice in the matter. She was the one with the buying power.

Half-asleep, she rose and walked over to the electric radiator to unplug it from the wall. As she bent down she heard the scraping sound again, as if something was trapped behind the fireplace bricks. Tucking her unruly hair behind her ear and pressing her head against the cool stone, she listened intently. There it was again. Faint and repetitive, a tapping and scratching, like the claws of a squirrel, or the dragging fingertips of a slowly reviving corpse . . .

That night she firmly locked the bedroom door.

"It's always the same thing," she said, pulling the dressing gown tightly around her as she entered the kitchen. "He's dragging a body through the lounge. It's in this house, and the room is decorated the way it was before we moved in, when Myson lived here."

"That's how you first saw it," said Simon, following her. "The scene left a strong impression on you, so you dream about it."

"He drags the body over to the fireplace with great difficulty."

"Why's that?"

"I'm not sure. I can't see too clearly. I think his victim is just stunned, or maybe drugged. Anyway, she's resisting. Then he pulls her into the fireplace and steps over her body, out of the hole."

"Then what?"

She looked at him as if the answer was obvious. "He bricks it up, of course," she replied.

She had to work through most of the weekend, but managed to find time to buy Simon the drill. When she presented it to him, however, he was reluctant to use it.

"Unsealing the hearth can wait until I've cleared away all the paintwork," he said. "I'm not going to rush things just because you're convinced you're going to find a body behind there. You've been warned God knows how many times about your overactive imagination." He sighed, exasperated with her. "Try to remember the way you felt before your breakdown. All the things you imagined were happening to us. Just keep that in mind, OK?" And with that he resumed rubbing a small patch of the mantelpiece, carefully removing layer after layer of the paint.

Upset, Linnea left the house and went for a walk to clear her head. At times she found the house stuffy and claustrophobic. And she was starting to feel uncomfortable when left alone in the lounge. Alone in the room with the fireplace, and its odd little scratching sounds that nobody else seemed to hear . . .

The next evening she came home from work at nine o'clock and found that he had finished removing the paint from one side of the fireplace. The effect was startling. The women were carved in glistening bronze, with sashes of inlaid copper strip tied around their waists. The stems of the twining lilies and roses were fashioned in green metal, the color of the deepest part of the sea. The piece was an extraordinary work of art, most likely unique. Linnea thought of what it was worth and her excitement overcame her growing fear of the object.

"I think we're going to find that it's signed somewhere," said Simon, wiping his brush clean on a rag. "Nobody could fashion this and not put their signature to it. Now do you see how silly your imaginings were?"

"What do you mean?" asked Linnea coldly.

"Well . . ." He sat down on the floor and crossed his legs. "Ask yourself, how could something as beautiful as this be hiding a corpse?"

"There are a great many beautiful tombs," she said, turning on her heel and leaving the room.

Simon sighed and threw down the brush. He would not go after her. Showing sympathy had no effect. He still remembered the time before. Linnea had been working until all hours, growing increasingly neurotic, and becoming so convinced that he was having an affair while she worked late that she managed to smash up the flat before the doctor finally arrived. One way or another he would have to see to it that the events of the past did not repeat themselves.

At Brockton & Shipley the auction was due to take place in three days' time, the new office was about to open and several members of staff were off sick with the flu. Linnea was the only member of staff who had a clue about the company's ongoing sales, and was consequently working harder than ever.

Halfway through the week she returned home late to find the house closed and dark. There was no sign of Simon. Angry, she let herself in, went straight to the lounge and poured out a whisky. Then she flopped down on to the couch to gather her thoughts. It took another few moments for her to notice the sheet that had been draped over the fireplace.

Standing her drink down, she rose and moved closer. Why had Simon covered the damned thing up? Two cans of paint pinned the sheet to the ends of the mantelpiece. Gingerly she reached out and touched the cloth, but could not bring herself to remove it. A cold draught seemed to move through the room, as if someone had opened the door to the garden. And there was a strange sour-sweet smell, reminiscent of rotting vegetables. Strengthening her resolve, she raised one of the paint pots and let the sheet pull out from beneath it.

Simon had succeeded in removing a large area of paint from the remaining covered column of the fireplace. Now the other woman stood revealed in magnificent detail, from the delicate tracery of her burnished hair to the tiny scrolled stitchwork of her bodice. And he had managed to remove one of the center bricks from the blocked cavity between the columns.

Linnea felt the draught brush her legs again and realized that it was coming from the neatly chiselled hole. She badly wanted to look into the wall beyond, but lacked the courage to do so. Obviously, there was nothing inside the fireplace. Simon had presumably removed the brick in daylight, and would never have left it open for her to stumble upon if there was anything un-pleasant to be found beyond. Slowly, she bent her legs and brought her eyes close to the opening. Cool air fanned her face. So, she thought, the chimney *is* open.

There was a muted sound from within, the light tapping she had heard before. It's the wind, she thought, lifting and dropping a desiccated, ancient piece of paper, or perhaps dry leaves, fallen from the blackened tunnel above. Moving closer, she peered into the dark oblong hole. For a few moments her eyes failed to adjust to the gloom. Then, in the faint light which filtered from the distant chimney opening, she found that she could just dis-cern the soot-caked far wall of the fireplace. All was quiet as she stared in, save for her own hesitant breath and the continuous faint scratching behind the brickwork.

Then suddenly she was looking into another pair of eyes, staring back at her from within the cavity, eyes in an ancient corpse-black face, rolling eyes, glittering and mad. She screamed and fell backwards, knocking over the paint pot of turpentine, scattering the brushes and scrapers as she fought to her feet and fled the room, terror still shrilling in her throat.

Simon did not return at all that night. Linnea ran to her room and stayed there, breast heaving, locked in with the lights on and the radio playing, until exhaustion robbed her of consciousness in the cold hour of dawn-light.

She heard him come in. He went straight to the kitchen and boiled water for tea, barely acknowledging the rumpled figure in the dressing gown who stood in the doorway and stared at him in silent accusation.

"I know what you're thinking," he said casually, filling the teapot, "but you're wrong. I got drunk last night and stayed at the school. The staff party—I warned you about it, remember?"

"I remember nothing of the kind," said Linnea icily. "I know you. I could see this coming, as soon as I began working late again. I've always been able to tell what you're about to do."

"Well, you were wrong last time, and you're wrong again," he replied with a sigh. "Call the school if you don't believe me. My energies are all taken up here, with you. I haven't the strength to see anyone else, believe me." He held out a cup of milky tea to her.

"Believe you!" she repeated, knocking the cup from his hand and storming out.

In the office later she considered the rashness of her behavior. She had accused him of starting an affair. The pattern was repeating itself. She had been wrong before. As the telephones rang around her, she buried her head in her hands and thought carefully. She would find a way of letting him know that there would be no repetition of last time. This was just an isolated incident. She was still a sane, rational person. She would apologize for flying off the handle. She would even leave the office a little early tonight and take Simon to dinner somewhere smart, just to show him that she was still in control.

Then she remembered the fireplace. How could she describe what she had seen without him thinking her mad? Of course there had been nothing within the wall. Her mind had provided an apparition because it knew she would be perversely disappointed if there was nothing to be found. She decided to treat the incident as if it had never happened.

She called Simon, then booked the restaurant. The rest of the day followed smoothly, until she opened the evening newspaper.

"It's not the same man," said Simon finally. "This one's name is Parsons, not Myson."

"And I'm telling you that it is," said Linnea, her voice rising. "He may have changed his name, but that is definitely the man I bought the house from. I'd know his face anywhere." She tapped the photograph with a bitten nail. "He's lying to the police about his identity."

"Come on, they don't even know if they've got the right person." Simon pushed the folded newspaper back across the table. "All it says here is that he's helping the police with their inquiries. Besides, that photograph's so blurred that it could be anyone."

"For God's sake, don't you see?" Several other diners at nearby tables looked up from their meals at her. Noticing their alarm, she lowered her voice. "It all fits. He's wanted in connection with the murder of a woman."

"The body was found in a railway siding, not a house," said Simon patiently.

"Who knows how many others he's murdered? He could be like that man who killed all those teenagers and buried them beneath his floorboards. He was scared when I met him, anxious to sell up and get out." She tried to recall the occasion of her meeting with Mr. Myson. She had been so intent on reducing the value of the house that she'd missed parts of his mumbled conversation.

"He said he'd been having bad dreams. He kept looking at the fireplace. I've been having the same dreams, only it's *him* I see!"

Simon pushed his glasses back up his nose and thought for a moment. "You can't possibly know that you've been having the same dream as him. You're building a case out of nothing. A few nightmares, a blurry photograph, it makes no sense." He reached across the table and took her hand. "Please, darling, listen to yourself."

"There's a body behind the fireplace," she said quietly. "I looked in, I could see it. I know it's there, I could smell it. He killed someone in our house, then he killed again and the police caught him. You took the brick out. Didn't you see anything?"

"No, I didn't," he admitted. "But I was in a hurry. I wanted to get through the cavity wall, just to make a start on the removal of the bricks. Then I remembered I had the staff function to get ready for, so I left everything where it was.''

"I want to go to the police, Simon." She drained the Chablis from her glass and refilled it, finishing the bottle. "I'll take the morning off and we'll go first thing.''

"That's stupid. We'll open the fireplace first, completely. We'll see that there's nothing inside and we'll be able to forget the whole ridiculous incident.'' He shook his head. "I'm beginning to sound as . . .'' He changed the sentence. "Like you.''

In the car on the way home she could feel him watching her as she drove. He had been about to say "as crazy as", but had caught himself. Could she be crazy, concocting conspiracies where there were none to be found?

That night he tried to hold her in bed, but she rejected his attentions, pushing him away to the far side of the mattress. She slept fitfully, winding stickily in the sheets until she became trapped by them. The fireplace and its grisly secret burdened her dreams until the nightmare once more replayed itself in full, as if the corpse in the wall below was forcing the images of its death upon her.

She saw the man again, dragging his stunned victim across the threadbare carpet to the fireplace, but this time she saw the details clearly. The room was different, brighter, as if the laburnum beyond the lounge window no longer obstructed the sunlight. The fireplace was unveiled now, and stood free of paint in full magnificence. Indeed, there was a fire burning fiercely in its bright copper grate.

This was not her dream but a variation of it, a bizarre off-kilter version where details were subtly altered. The light source in the room was different, the victim seemed much plumper than before, the room itself more gaily decorated. What was happening here? The murderer was dressed in clothes from an earlier era. Now he stooped over the sleeping body and slipped his hands beneath her broad, bare arms. Slowly he dragged her nearer to the blazing log fire. Decorative tiles were inlaid about the hearth. A coal scuttle stood to one side, an extravagantly designed poker and brush set to the other. She could even read the lettering on the side of the scuttle: Vulcain. The murderer raised his victim to a sitting position. The lace on her ample bosom rose and fell as he gently lowered her face into the searing flames . . .

Linnea awoke in a gasping fit, unable to catch her breath, the sheet twisted about her. Her head throbbed with the after-effects of the wine she had consumed at dinner. She turned to wake Simon but found herself alone in the bed. From downstairs came the rhythmic sound of metal on brick. The luminous hands of the wall clock stood at three thirty-five. Linnea swung her legs from the mattress, untangling the sheet as she did so, and reached for her dressing gown.

The lights were on in the lounge. She came down the stairs and pushed the door open. Simon was kneeling before the fire-place, his forehead beaded with sweat. He was wearing a short-sleeved sweater over his pajamas. He lowered the hammer and chisel, and twisted around to face his wife.

"I couldn't sleep," he said with a shrug. "You were tossing and turning so much. Anyway, I knew I wouldn't get any peace until I opened the damned thing up . . ." He turned back to the brickwork and continued striking at it with the chisel. The second brick was loose now, nearly ready to come out.

"I know about the fireplace," she said, her mind still heavy with sleep.

"What do you mean?" He hammered at the brickwork. A shower of cement fell to the newspaper which wreathed the hearth.

"I know who built it." She raised her hand to her head, feeling dizzy once more. Already, the nightmare was fading.

"You've been dreaming again. You were talking in your sleep." He checked the cynicism in his voice. "So who built it?"

"Henri . . . Henri Désiré . . . something . . ." The name blurred and vanished, erased from her slumber-ridden mind. "I can't remember any more."

The chisel bit deep into stone and dislodged the second brick. Simon carefully removed it and began on the third. Outside, rain began to spatter the windows.

"Simon, don't take any more out," she cried suddenly. "I'm afraid."

"Look at it from a logical viewpoint," he replied, hammering rhythmically at the brickwork as he spoke. "If there *was* a corpse behind here, it couldn't hurt us now. It would hardly be likely to leap out, would it?"

"There is danger here. The most terrible danger."

She barely recognized her own voice. Behind her, the rain fell hard against the glass. She could hear it falling on the roof, drumming distantly at the top of the chimney. As she inched closer to Simon he removed the third brick and started on the fourth. The rest came away easily, and soon a pile of bricks had formed on the newspaper beside the fireplace. The black hole which gaped before them was ready for investigation.

"Pass me the torch." Simon held out his hand, not once removing his eyes from the terrible dark space between the engraved pillars.

"Don't go in there. Please, Simon, listen to me." She stood behind him as he switched on the torch and shone its beam into the cavity. Linnea could not bring herself to look.

"Well, there's your corpse all right." He turned and gently removed her hands from her face. "Take a look."

Slowly, Linnea raised her eyes to the spot where the torch shone. The cavity within the fireplace was completely empty, save for a large dead rat. The plump meatiness of the rodent's body suggested that it had died not long before.

"It was probably what you heard scratching at the wall. It may even have been what you saw. No ghosts, no murder victims, just a poor bedraggled old rat."

"Oh, Simon." She felt like crying with relief—and yet the feeling of dread was still there. After a moment or two, it began to grow again, stronger and stronger.

He took her hand and brought her close to the fireplace. "Such a beautiful object." His voice sounded far away lost in dreams. She looked down at the carvings of the women who posed resplendent in bronze and copper raiments, at the delicately curved roses and lilies which grew in profusion about their feet, and the small patch of peagreen paintwork still to be removed at the base of the column.

"You've forgotten a bit," she heard herself saying, as if she had intoned the same remark a hundred times before. She pointed a wavering finger at the patch.

"If I'm not mistaken," said Simon jovially, "that will provide us with the last piece of the puzzle."

He switched off the torch and the soot-covered corpse of the rat jumped back into darkness. Removing a palette knife from a tin filled with methylated spirit, he wiped the blade and began to gently lift the paint away in small strips. She leaned forward, her curiosity overcoming her fear. Inlaid letters were appearing beneath the paint. Simon picked delicately with the knife, gradually revealing an extravagantly scrolled signature. Linnea's hand flew to her mouth as she read the name with mounting horror. The room dipped beneath her and tendrils of darkness swam across her vision, removing the scene from view and thrusting her into a void of blackest night. She fell heavily to the floor.

The dream closed in again, but this time she was a part of it, cast in the role of the murderer's victim. She felt herself being dragged across the carpet, then pulled upright into a sitting position, in preparation for her interment within the wall. The dream grew dark as all sensation faded.

She awoke from the nightmare to find herself crouched in a tight, dark space with her hands tied painfully behind her back. It took a few moments for her to realize that she was inside the fireplace. Her worst fear realized, she tried to scream but the cotton rag tied across her mouth prevented her. She was still wearing her nightgown, which had somehow become hitched up about her thighs. At her back, the cold furry body of the rat pressed against her bare buttocks. Far above, a dim luminescence showed at the top of the soot-encrusted chimney. Droplets of rain lightly touched her face.

Before her terrified eyes, Simon was patiently cementing the bricks back into place. His face appeared sheened in sweat through the shrinking gap in the wall. Behind his spectacles, his eyes were blank and unseeing as he labored at his task, fulfilling his prophesied role. She longed to tell him of her mistake, of how she had confused past, present and future to arrive at this inevitable conclusion.

Henri Désiré Landru, the signature had read, the signature of Bluebeard himself. The insane mass murderer had spent his childhood years at the Vulcain ironworks in Paris, where his father was a fireman. He had disposed of at least ten women in his fireplace, macerating them in flame and destroying them so thoroughly that no trace of their bodies could ever be found. Even after his capture, he had remained silent and unrepentant.

Myson had been aware of the fireplace's influence, had grown fearful for his sanity, and although he was able to escape the house, had eventually succumbed to his terrible destiny.

As Simon eased the final brick into position and patted the surrounding mortar into a smooth finish, she knew that it was now too late for either of them to break the unending pattern.

Alone in final darkness, she provided appeasement to the stone and metal thing which made up her prison. The fireplace fed on her terror, just as it would eventually rob her of her life.

BOX

"I'VE GOT A Beauchamp Place, a Beauchamp Place, wait and return, a Beauchamp Place anyone? Anybody coming free out there? Beauchamp Place, come on now, gentlemen, there must be someone . . ."

Tony reached forward and unclipped the radio mike with his free hand. "Seven five, I'm at Cambridge Circus. I'll take Beauchamp Place." Full of smart shops and restaurants, Beauchamp Place, thought Tony. Elegant ladies with expensive tastes and immaculate diction, could be worth a bob or two. The radio mike crackled in reply.

"Go to Brasserie Gourmet and collect an envelope from a Mr. Ramirez. It's going to West London. He'll give you the correct address."

"I'm on my way."

Tony pushed the last piece of hamburger into his mouth and tossed the wrapper into a nearby litter bin. Glancing up at the gathering clouds before he wheeled his Honda into the road, he began to wonder if it would snow after all. The sky had turned to the color of greaseproof paper. He zipped his leather jacket right up to the top and adjusted his crash helmet before swinging himself on to the motorbike. Throughout the day the city traffic had been light, despite the approach of Christmas and the shopping spree which usually accompanied it. He hoped that the delivery would not take him too far out towards the airport. It was nearly four thirty, and he wanted to be home by six.

He reached Kensington in surprisingly good time, and collected the envelope from Mr. Ramirez. Pushing open the door of the brasserie, Tony found himself surrounded by middle-aged women with bobbed noses and winter tans. They sat sipping coffee and chatting to one another, their glossy fur coats casually draped across the backs of the high white chairs scattered

Box   19

throughout the restaurant. The air was rich with the aroma of cooking pastry and subtly expensive perfume. The women eyed the gangling leather-clad kid with distaste before returning to their cappuccinos.

Tony was relieved to return to the crisp odorless air outside. Perhaps the job had made him so, but just lately he had begun to feel claustrophobic in crowded offices and restaurants. He loved the freedom of being able to climb on to his motorbike and take off through the underpasses and over the bridges of the city. Where others carped about the noise and pollution of the roads, Tony found little cause for complaint. For six months now he had been working as a messenger, and was finding it a much more enjoyable job than he had anticipated. He had given himself a year to build up some financial resources before returning to college. The work paid a reasonable wage, the hours were adaptable, and the only boss to whom he was answerable remained a disembodied voice crackling over a two-way microphone.

As the Honda shot beneath the road at Hyde Park the warmth from the cars filling the underpass suddenly enveloped him. When he roared up the slope and out of the other side a blast of icy wind swept from St. James's Park across the road to ram the bike side-on and fill his helmet with fresh bitter air. By the time he reached Piccadilly Circus the surrounding buildings and buses had trapped the city air and warmed it once again. Tony had dropped off the envelope in Hammersmith, and was now returning to Cambridge Circus to see if any of the other messengers were about.

As he headed along Shaftesbury Avenue, past chubby young executives hailing cabs and elderly American couples clutching maps as they searched the theatre signs, he remembered the previous evening, when a South London delivery had taken him across Lambeth Bridge just as the setting sun was flooding the sky with rusty light. He had stopped the bike in the center of the bridge, sitting back on the pillion to watch the slabbed sides of the city's banking blocks transform from an insipid concrete grey to a searing oxidized orange. Even the sluggish tide below reflected swirling amber. Tony knew then, as he always knew, that London was his city.

Pulling up at the motorbike rank behind the Cambridge theatre, he stood the Honda down on its stand and turned to the young punk sprawled across the seat of the next bike along. He sported shaggy, dyed hair twisted into tufts, and regardless of the cold, lay reading a library book.

"What are you on now, Ace?" asked Tony, pulling off his gloves.

"It's still bloody *Bouvard et Pecuchet*, isn't it?" replied Ace without lifting his gaze from the page. Behind him, the bike's radio mike emitted electronic scatter. "Bloody night school. I'll finish this if it kills me."

"It just might," said Tony. "You've been reading that for weeks. I'm going for coffee. Do you want one?"

"Yeah," grunted Ace, still engrossed. The cold afternoon air ruffled his fluorescent hair.

Tony leaned across and tapped the back of the book. "Listen out for my mike, will you? Oh, and by the way . . ." He dropped his voice to a confidential whisper. Ace looked up.

"*Bouvard et Pecuchet* doesn't have an ending. Flaubert never finished it."

"Oh, thanks a bunch!" shouted Ace after him, throwing down the book. "Stupid bloody frogs."

After polystyrene cups of bottom-of-the-pot coffee, Ace set off to deliver a film can in the Paddington area, and Tony decided to do one more run before heading home. He was about to put in for a Red Star delivery at Waterloo which could take him part of the way home, when the call came through.

"I've got a pick up and deliver in Great Titchfield Street, Great Titchfield Street anyone."

Tony unclipped his microphone and answered. "Seven five here. I'll take Great Titchfield Street. Over."

"Roger rog, seven five. Where are you now?"

"I'm at Cambridge Circus."

"Seven five, contact a Doctor Stan Kennifer at seventeen Great Titchfield Street, collect a package and deliver."

"I'm on my way."

Dodging along the backroads behind Oxford Street to avoid the taxi-only routes, Tony entered Great Titchfiled Street from the top end and pulled his machine into the curb to check the building numbers. Below, in Oxford Street itself, the buses queued at the traffic lights, preparing for the rush hour ahead. Tony searched the doorway of the nearest building for a number. Seventeen turned out to be a squat glass block constructed in post-Festival of Britain style which appeared to be some kind of medical unit or clinic. Removing his crash helmet, he entered the reception area and approached a pale young woman seated

Box   21

at her desk reading a magazine. She raised indifferent eyes to him.

"Can I help you?"

"I'm collecting a package from a Doctor Stan Kennifer . . ." Tony consulted the piece of paper on which he had written his instructions.

"Oh, it must be this," said the receptionist, reaching under the desk and pulling up a neat square parcel wrapped in brown paper and sticky tape. The sides of the box were roughly equal, each one being slightly smaller in size than a record album.

"Here's the address it's going to," she said, handing him an envelope. "On the front. It's to be delivered along with the box."

Tony read the address and slipped the envelope into the pocket of his jacket. He left the building with the box wedged awkwardly under his arm. The destination was a street in the center of Soho. When he reached the bike he unclipped a pair of elasticated straps and fastened them around the box to keep it securely tied to the pillion rack. The weight within the package was unevenly distributed, as if whatever was inside had been loosely packed. He flicked the side of the box with a forefinger. Cardboard. There were no identifying marks or labels on it at all. The only clue to the identity of the sender was concealed within the accompanying letter. With a sigh of frustrated curiosity, Tony mounted his bike once more and headed out into the now bustling traffic for Soho.

By the time he arrived the sun had almost set. In contrast to the previous day, the sky was a grimy darkening slate, a foreboding of the snow to come. Pedestrians were turning up their jacket collars and heading home from their offices as he drew the bike to a halt in Meard Street. The street itself was a curious mixture of private apartments and seedy clubs. Scaffolding and wet piles of sand obstructed the roadway ahead. Checking the door numbers against the address on the envelope, he paused before a gloomy trash-covered doorway next to a Chinese restaurant. Unclipping the box from its place on the bike rack, he withdrew the envelope from his pocket and examined it again. Across the front was scrawled:

STAN KENNIFER
DNA Research Inc.,
c/o 42 Meard Street, W1
FRAGILE!!!

The corners of the box were reinforced with heavy-duty card, and one side was definitely heavier than the other. Gingerly Tony turned the box over. Something within fell with a thump. It had a heavy, fleshy weight, as if the box contained a dead codfish, or something similar. Shrugging, he headed for the door. It was unlocked, so he was able to push his way inside. Before him, the sloping stairs rose into darkness. Knowing that he would have to find someone to sign for the receipt of the box, he climbed the stairs carefully, feeling his way in the increasing gloom. He set the box down on the landing and struck a match. Locating a door handle just ahead, he entered a small dingy office with orange plastic seats and scruffy government-green walls. It looked like a doctor's waiting room. A bell was located beside a service hatch in the far wall. He pressed it and stepped back. After a moment, an old man slid back the hatch and stuck his head through. He seemed annoyed.

"We're closed. What do you want?"

"I need you to sign for this." Tony reached forward and passed the delivery form through the hatch.

The old man scratched the stubble on his chin and slowly shook his head. "I can't sign for it. This has to be signed for by Doctor Kennifer, and he ain't here."

"Wait a minute," said Tony, "there seems to be some confusion. I thought I was collecting this *from* Doctor Kennifer."

"I dunno, mate. All I know is, we got nobody by that name here."

"This is DNA Research, yeah?"

"That's right, but we got no Kennifer."

"What about at your other office? The one I just came from?"

The old man thought for a moment, then consulted a typed list of names. "Nope. Nobody by that name at all."

"This is ridiculous. I collected this just a few minutes ago from your other office, to come to this address."

The old man was adamant. He pushed the box back towards Tony. "Well, you can't leave it here. You'll have to take it back to head office."

Sighing, Tony hefted the box beneath his arm and headed back out of the depressing little office as, behind him, the old man closed the hatch door. Outside, he strapped it back on to the pillion rack and prepared to return to the far side of Oxford Street. The whole set-up bothered him. For a scientific institute, the place had been pretty run down. It looked more like the sort of building which housed a strip parlor than a research labo-

Box   23

ratory. Darkness had descended completely now, and it was without surprise that Tony discovered the office from which he had collected the package was closed for the night. As he sat back on the bike, staring at the box which nobody seemed to want, it occurred to him to open the envelope which came with it.

Carefully ungluing the flap, he withdrew a single typed invoice. It was headed:

DNA RESEARCH INC.
Splinter Group C

A gift from the lads in Falconberg Mews . . . .
        Item: Remains of
        "SPIRAL" Project #B26749

Next time, check your halides! The whole damned thing became halophilic!

Tony turned the invoice over. That was all there was. Puzzled, he slipped it back into the envelope and resealed it. He knew where Falconberg Mews was, but he had no building number. No matter, the mews was a tiny turning behind the Roman Catholic church in Soho Square. It wouldn't be difficult to locate the place. What the hell were "halides"? Perhaps he should just go home with the box and deliver it in the morning, but something bothered him. He decided to radio in for advice, and unclipped his microphone.

"Seven five, this is seven five. I've got a problem with this delivery, rog. Over."

"Seven five, what sort of a problem?"

"The delivery address is on night service, and they're denying any knowledge of the person the package is addressed to, over."

"Hang on, seven five. We'll give the sender a call for instructions."

"Their office is shut for the night."

He sat by the mike, listening to the pops and crackles from the speaker as sleet began to fall.

"Seven five, suggest you hang on to the package until the morning, when we'll sort it out."

"OK, rog, over and out."

As Tony drove back to Cambridge Circus the falling sleet forced him to stop and wipe the condensation from his helmet visor. He steered the Honda through Soho, along Broadwick

Street, past a Liberty's still thronging with Christmas shoppers, and glanced up at their huge baroque clock as it rang six thirty. As he pulled into the bike rank at Cambridge Circus, he saw Ace wheeling his bike from the stand.

"Hey, wait!" Tony called the boy back, and together they ducked under the glass canopy surrounding the theatre as the sleet grew heavier. Tony darted out to his motorbike and brought in the box, setting it down beside him. Further along the wall, scenery shifters were unloading props from a truck, setting down heavy-duty nylon sacks and leaning them against the wall, ready for transporting backstage. Ace shouted over the scenery men.

"You got any free tickets, then?"

"You must be joking," one of the men laughed, pointing at the canopy above the theatre. "It's a load of rubbish, this is!"

Ace turned to Tony and scratched his dazzling scalp. "Here, why don't you open it? Could be something really good, coming from a laboratory. Might be nerve gas, or a highly combustible explosive, or a cobalt-saturated, extremely volatile . . ."

"Shut up, OK? Read this invoice." Tony withdrew the pink sheet of paper and handed it to Ace. Beyond the messengers, sleet fell on the props and sacks awaiting delivery to the theatre, pooling icy water around them.

Ace read the invoice and began chuckling to himself. Tony snatched it back in annoyance.

"What's so funny?" he asked irritably.

"Well, it's a joke, isn't it?"

"What do you mean, a joke?"

"It's an anagram."

"What is?"

"The delivery name. Stan Kennifer. It's an anagram of 'Frankenstein'. Someone's pulling your leg."

"You're kidding." He reread the invoice. "Someone's still got to pay for the bike, though," he said grumpily as Ace took the invoice once more.

"This word here—'halophilic.' It's a biological term. I know what it means . . ."

He looked over at the workmen as they continued unloading in the falling sleet. His eyes fell on the sacks propped against the wall.

"That's it!" he said. "It's to do with salt. If something is halophilic, it stays alive by thriving on salt."

"How the hell do you know stuff like this?"

"Studied biology at night school, didn't I?"

Box   25

"Finish the course, did you?"

"Almost."

"I see. Thanks, Ace, you're a regular mine of useless information."

"Hang on," called Ace, "where are you going?"

Tony was striding off towards his bike. The sleet fell heavily as he adjusted his helmet and turned back in the direction of the theatre.

"I'm going round to Falconberg Mews, to see if there's anyone there."

"Blimey, what's so important about a bloody box?"

"I've got nothing better to do," said Tony, "unless you're going to buy me a drink."

"Can't, mate, I got me sociology class tonight."

"OK, then, see you tomorrow."

"Here." Ace brought over the box and passed it to Tony. "Mind out, the bottom's all wet."

Tony slid his hand beneath the package. The cardboard was soft and soaking.

The front wheel of the Honda caught a large pool of muddy water and threw it on to the pavement as Tony turned into Soho Square from Frith Street with the box once more strapped firmly on its rack. The entrance to the mews was framed by the back of the Astoria theatre and a filthy warehouse which had been converted to offices but not, it seemed, cleaned up for the occasion. The narrow alleyway formed a T shape, one arm of which ran beneath an arch and out into the Charing Cross Road. Huge circular steel canisters filled with rubbish lined the walls, and the whole area was lit with sodium street lights, giving the road an old, neglected feel. Tony was constantly surprised by the way in which London's modern main thoroughfares quickly gave way to Victorian backstreets. The end of the mews was a dark rubbish-strewn cul-de-sac, and it was here that Tony kicked his bike up on to its stand and unclipped the package from its platform. The underside of the box had turned mushy from the puddle it had stood in outside the theatre, so he carefully held his outstretched palm beneath it.

It was as he was doing this that he felt the contents of the box move. Puzzled, he pressed his ear to the cardboard. A faint shuffling sound emanated from within. Something inside the box was alive. Yet how was that possible? He had been carrying it around for the best part of two hours, and had felt nothing move before now.

"This is crazy," he said to himself, raising the box to eye height and shaking it. Sure enough, there was the sound of something shifting from side to side, moving as if in straw.

"Whatever you are in there," said Tony warningly, "you're going back to your owners, right now." Supporting the box with both hands, he set off along the curb, searching for doors in the long blank wall which formed one side of the mews.

In a couple of minutes he had covered most of the possible offices in the road, which was little more than an alleyway. The box felt still and heavy now. At the far end of the mews, in the darkness of the rising walls, he found a small building entrance with half a dozen companies listed on its steel registration plate. One of the companies was called DNAC. It had to be the name of the splinter group responsible for sending the package. The door to the building was locked tight, and the place was in darkness. Tony turned on the steps and looked for the mailbox. He found it in a recess beside the bottom step. Kneeling down, he pushed his hand through the metal slot and felt around. His fingers closed around a letter. Carefully withdrawing it, he tried to read its typed address in the dark, but was forced to strike a match. On the step beside him, the box shuddered. The light from his match confirmed the address on the letter. This was the right company, all right. He tore open the envelope and removed its contents.

Back at the bike with the box at his feet, Tony unfolded the letter. It read:

PROJECT SPIRAL

All experimentation under this heading is now terminated. All by-products produced with the aid of radical halides should be destroyed in accordance with British safety regulations. May I remind you that failure to comply with this ruling is an offense punishable by law.

 Seriously, chaps, this has gone far enough. The genetic strains produced by B Group have a bite like a rabid dog, and are twice as infectious. Get rid of whatever you're holding. There are no exceptions.

Signed
Doctor Stan Kettner

So that was it. The guys who had packed off this parcel fooled around with the good doctor's name as a little inter-office joke. And whatever they were sending to him was the end product of

Box   27

a failed experiment. Tony wondered if DNA Research Inc. was some kind of rogue American agency operating under the sanctions of the Ministry of Defence, tampering about with genetics. He turned the box over on its side, pulled off his gloves and tore at the soggy brown cardboard base.

Inside, the whatever-it-was thudded from one side to the other. He realized now why the little critter had returned to life in its cardboard prison. It needed salt to live, Ace had said so. The box had become soaked outside the theatre, where men had been delivering tons of the stuff, great sacks of rock salt for the stage set. It had been sitting in a salt water solution. It had been revived. Now it craved more.

Tony knew that he had to open the box. Leaving the bike on its stand, he ran to the brightly lit pavements of Charing Cross Road, crossing over into Denmark Street where there were fewer people, and sat on the steps of a music shop as he tore at the hole he had made in the bottom of the box. Once he had made it big enough to see it, but not so large that the thing could escape, he put his face close to the hole and looked.

Inside, all was blackness. Then, in the corner, through layers of straw, he made out a shape the size of a smallish rabbit, but thinner. It seemed to be breathing, faintly and hoarsely. Tony moved his face closer. Just then the thing threw itself across the box and needle-sharp teeth bit into his face. He felt a hot, searing pain, and screaming, threw the box to the ground, clutching at his burning cheek.

Blood from the wound filled the palm of his hand. He turned to the glass doorway and stared at his face. The creature had torn a small deep strip of skin from his left eye to the tip of his nose. He looked down at the box and saw the thing pushing its way from the cardboard container. For a moment he stood transfixed, horrified.

It was small, grey and hairless, with short legs but no arms or tail. Its skin had a sickly wet sheen, the color of oatmeal. There was no head to speak of, rather a broad stump in which was set a wide mouth filled with tiny narrow teeth, and above this a cluster of black spider-like eyes. It was an abomination, a sad, cruel mistake of science, a creature which should not even have existed. Tony saw the salty fresh blood running from its mouth and knew that he had to prevent it from getting away. With one hand over his face he reached down for the box just as the thing tore itself free and shot off down the street.

"Jesus Christ!" Tony staggered after it, his long legs gaining on the creature just as it scuttled into an alleyway and vanished into the piles of trash lining the walls. Tony dived into the rubbish-filled boxes and bins, hurling them aside as he searched the ground, knowing that he had no chance of ever finding the creature here in the dark. He stood up and tried to control his ragged breathing, wiping his bloody cheek with the sleeve of his jacket. Then he heard it, rooting around under a stack of thrown-out music sheets.

A moment later it reappeared and Tony upturned a metal trashcan and dropped it on top. It took him a while to transfer the creature to a plastic sack, but he managed it. His face felt as if it was on fire. He knew he had to get to a doctor and at least have the wound cauterized, but he wanted to leave with proof of his assailant. It occurred to him that there could be damages to claim.

Walking back to his bike with the creature struggling in the tightly wound bag, he decided to make for a wash and brush-up place, where he could bathe his cheek and examine the damage. Parking the bike outside Euston station, he headed for the public washroom, taking the bag with him.

The mirror revealed a livid red gouge which was even now beginning to fester. Mike turned pale when he saw how seriously infected it had become. Other people in the washroom took one look at his face and moved away quickly. He had begun to feel sick and dizzy. It occurred to him that the creature could have been subjected to radiation in its creation, and that right now he could be suffering from some kind of blood poisoning. Clutching the bundle, he climbed the stairs from the washroom and entered the station snack bar.

"Are you all right, love?" asked the Pakistani lady behind the counter.

"I, uh, got attacked outside," he replied, not untruthfully. "You haven't got any aspirins, have you?"

"We don't sell them, but I might have one in my handbag, hold on a sec." She hunted in her bag and withdrew a piece of silver foil.

Mike withdrew to a nearby table and rinsed the tablets down with tea from a plastic cup. The heat from the sweet powdered beverage burned his throat and made him feel drowsy. Sweat formed on his forehead and fell into his eyes. All he wanted to do right now was sleep. Behind him, the station announcements boomed indistinctly as commuters ran across the concourse to their trains, and the glass doors of the snack bar banged open

Box   29

and shut. He may only have lost consciousness for a few seconds, but that was long enough for him to jump when he felt the body brush by his shoulder. His head swimming, he looked around, then down at his feet, and found the plastic bag gone. He jumped up with a shout. Everyone in the snack bar turned on their stools to look at him.

Outside, as the glass doors started to close, he saw them. Three skinheads, making off across the concourse with the bag, heading for one of the departure gates, laughing.

Mike half ran, half staggered after them. His body felt as if it were made of clay. He tried to keep pace with the skinheads, heard himself call out, but fell back further as they passed through the gates on to the platform and the guard blew his whistle. The last thing he saw before he fell to the ground was the train slowly pulling away from the buffers on the start of its journey to the north. He felt something heat within his body and burst, and knew that he was dying, and as he fell to the concrete, leaking warmth from every pore, all he could think of was that it was a terrible, depressing place to die.

"We should have got a private carriage, you wanker!"

"There wasn't time, was there? Come on, we can change at the first station."

The carriage was an open one, and was virtually empty. This was the slow train to York, stopping at just about every town which had a station. The three skinheads fell back in their seats and put their cherry-red Doctor Martin's boots up across the aisle.

"Come on then, show us what you got."

"Yeah, open it up and lessava look!"

The third skinhead grinned back at the other two. He had a roll-up wedged behind his left ear, and a snake tattooed across his forehead. He was barely fifteen. Carefully, he unwound the plastic bag and peered inside.

When he withdrew his face from the bag he was not grinning but screaming, and a large slug-like creature was hanging by its teeth from his right cheek. There was an awful sucking sound as the flesh tore away, exposing the boy's teeth and gums, making him look like a medical cutaway diagram which had suddenly sprung to life. In the ensuing chaos, the other two ran swearing through the length of the train, leaving the creature to gorge blindly on the warm salt blood of the unfortunate teenager.

Once it had feasted, and the young skinhead's body had rolled beneath the seat, it tacked its way along the carriage, rolling with the movement of the train as it searched for somewhere warm and dry to sleep. It found such a place in the luggage rack above one of the few other commuters in the carriage.

The passenger was a broad, craggy-faced gentleman with cropped dark hair, definitely military and probably American, who sat reading a copy of the *National Geographic*. He had left work early this evening to head for the north, where he would be spending his Christmas with friends.

As he began to doze and the magazine started to slide gently from his lap, the creature in the luggage rack climbed over his briefcase and squeezed its sickly grey-green body through the opening of a loosely packed Christmas gift, presented to the American by the women he worked with. The gift was labelled DO NOT OPEN UNTIL CHRISTMAS in large crimson letters. The creature snuggled into the woollen sweater which lay folded inside, and prepared to sleep off its bloody saline feast.

Below, the passenger started to snore peacefully as he dreamed of a Christmas spent with his wife and children in the beautiful city of York. The weatherman had warned that they were expecting snow, and he had made a mental note to put plenty of salt down on the pathways this year.

As the two warm-blooded beings were united in sleep the train thundered on, over the points and into the night. Above in the rack, the cheerful holly-leaf wrapping paper concealed the box which had become a new home for the satiated parasite. It would sleep for eight or ten hours now, to awaken in time to provide its latest owner with a grisly yuletide surprise.

THE LADIES' MAN

CLICKING HIGH HEELS on wet concrete, they strut and sashay down the darkened street, their light summer skirts rippling and rustling in the warm night air. As they pass one of them spins in an impromptu dance step, and another laughs softly into the sky. Dressed for the night, these three women are out to have fun, out to celebrate, out until dawn floods the city skyline. Their hair is braided with gold, their long gloved arms are clattering with bracelets of amber, coral and topaz. Now all three of them move into a dance step, treading on each other's toes, swinging and swaying and looping their arms together as they try to keep pace with one another.

One of them doubles with laughter, the other two scooping her under their arms and lifting her high until the neon above catches lipstick, earring, diamond, chain and buckle glancing, sparkling in the city night. Their exhilarated shouts leap to the walls of the buildings and reverberate into the glistening brickwork.

They climb into the shining black taxicab and it takes off at great speed, leaving behind the smell of burnt rubber drifting lazily in the air like autumn smoke as it slowly mixes with the faintest trace of bitter perfume . . .

"What's the worst thing that could happen?"

"Oh, Mum . . ."

"Come on, what's the very worst thing that could happen?"

Her mother tugged the blue plastic comb through her hair as she talked, bending to catch Margie in the dressing table mirror. She believed in confronting her daughter's fears head on. Wasn't that how she had cured Margie of her childhood stutter?

"I don't get the . . ."

" . . . get the job," completed her mother, pulling on the

31

comb. "Now let me look at you, child." She turned Margie
around on the fleecy swivel stool and surveyed her handiwork.

"Pretty as a picture. I've ironed your blue skirt. You want to
look smart, don't you?"

Margie stood up and smoothed out the creases in the white
cotton shirt, brown hands passing over a boyishly flat chest. Her
reflection reinforced her fears. She looked too young. Too awkward. Too short. Too . . . everything.

"And try not to be so nervous this time. When he asks you
questions, answer plainly and in truth." Her voice softened as
she reached for her daughter's hand. "You've nothin' to lose by
speakin' out clear and simple. Just remember that I'll be with
you in my thoughts." She raised Margie's chin so that the girl
looked up into her eyes.

"I worry 'bout you so much, Margie. But I know you can do
it this time. You just have to prove it to yourself, that's all."

She watched as Margie slowly finished dressing, her eyes cast
downward once again. It pained her to have to lecture her daughter so, but the child was so agonizingly shy that without her
mother's help she would never be likely to find herself a job.
Since she left school Margie had been for five secretarial interviews, and each time her averted gaze and barely audible answers had persuaded employers to hire bolder, more outspoken
girls.

Margie was keenly intelligent, of that her mother had no
doubt. In the company of her own friends she could be strong-
willed, articulate and even vivacious. But cast into the cold,
bright world of big business she became a different person. She
felt inferior, tongue-tied—and very Jamaican. Margie lived with
a mother whose working hours brought her home late and tired
every night of the week. Both of them knew that she had to find
a job, and find one quickly. Margie felt that she was only good
enough to apply as a traffic warden or a supermarket clerk, but
her mother knew better, and the importance of finding decently
paid work before the end of the summer made each interview
more tense than the last.

At the front door Margie kissed her mother goodbye and
stepped out of the council flat in her plain, smart shoes and her
matching blue tam o'shanter. Her mother had scraped back her
hair and secured in a tight knot, held in place with a tortoiseshell
slide that matched her spectacle frames, the lenses of which
made her ebony eyes appear large and soft.

"You're sure you know the way? When you get out of the station . . ."

"I'm old enough to find my way around, Mother, it's all right." Margie smiled. "I'll be back in a couple of hours. Keep your fingers crossed."

The large black woman obeyed, and stayed on the doorstep until her daughter was out of sight.

The reception area of the advertising agency was not immediately recognizable as having been designed for such a function. It consisted of angular multi-hued wall panels sweeping in bold arcs around an arrangement of oriental shrubbery, pale sticks which sprouted from white plastic pots filled with black glass marbles. Behind a bare acre of desk sat a Sindy Doll receptionist, vacantly thumbing backwards through an Italian fashion magazine.

Margie sat awkwardly on the low leather couch with her handbag perched on her knees. She was afraid that if she sat back on the seat she might slide into the hide interior, never to be seen again. She was waiting to be collected by the personal assistant of Richard Templeton, the agency's creative director. His letter in reply to her application for the post of "Girl Friday" had been witty, full of charm and to the trained eye definitely not written by him. About the coming interview Margie was hopeful but uneasy, her palms sweating as she perched amid the ephemeral designer bric-a-brac.

Her previous interviews had all taken place in the dingy offices of insurance salesmen and estate agents. Here everything was spotlit, spotless, bright and bursting with primary colors. Deep inside, Margie knew that she would never get the job. She was duller than the furniture, for a start. Every few minutes someone would bustle through the smoked glass doors carrying television storyboards. Messengers with crackling headsets lumbered past in their motorbike leathers like spacemen on delivery errands. Margie looked at her watch. The appointment had been set for 2:00 p.m. The huge brushed-steel clock above the reception desk now read 2:40 p.m., and there was still no sign of Mr. Templeton or his personal assistant. Margie needed to go to the toilet, but did not like to disturb the receptionist again. Butterflies fluttered in the pit of her stomach.

Finally, an attractive middle-aged woman marched into the reception area with a sheaf of papers pressed to her bosom. She apologized to Margie for the delay in the proceedings, and suggested that she came upstairs to wait for the creative director on the seventh floor. As Margie followed behind her she could not help noticing how drably sensible her clothes appeared against the other women passing in the corridors. Their garish designer outfits seemed to announce to the world how creative and stylish they were.

Margie was shown into Templeton's office and told to wait. The walls of the large, airy room were smothered with samples of photographers' work, including a disturbing picture of phallic red peppers covered in salad cream, and a woman walking into a Venetian restaurant with her bottom exposed. Broad windows overlooked a beautiful garden square which had been sealed from public pillage by locked iron gates. Margie looked up. Colored paper kites hung from drawing pins in the ceiling. Each one was emblazoned with an advertising slogan for a unit trust company. On the far wall a calendar promoting private health schemes displayed a photograph of a glistening young woman, large breasted and tanned, lounging on a sunchair by an ice-blue pool. She was holding an outspread share portfolio. Moist pink tongue poised between crimson lips, she was studying the figures with sexual intensity.

To Margie the room looked like a film set, not an office at all. She half expected Blake Carrington to walk in. Removing the crumpled reply to her letter, she smoothed it flat on her skirt before slipping it back into her coat pocket, keeping it handy in case she was suddenly asked to produce it.

The outer office door slammed open. She jumped to her feet, then thought better of it and sat back in her place as Richard Templeton strode into the room. Tall, broadly built and artificially tanned, Templeton was an archetypal media man from the tips of his chunky gold cufflinks to the toes of his tasselled loafers. A somewhat snugly fitting pair of Armani slacks stretched across his ample buttocks, and a striped Paul Smith shirt made for a younger man struggled to contain a hefty pudge of stomach. Although he was only thirty-four there was something much older and rather unhealthy about the way he looked, as if he had spent the last few nights locked in a nightclub without any sleep. One ringed hand contained a large Havana cigar. The other held a heavy tumbler filled with Scotch, and from the way he dropped heavily into his desk chair it was certainly not the first of the day.

Templeton stood down his glass and removed his absurd red

plastic-framed spectacles with a weary sigh. As yet, he had failed to acknowledge the presence of anyone else in the room.

To Margie he seemed like some larger-than-real symbol of a better life. All Templeton saw, when he finally managed to focus, was a small black girl perching nervously on the edge of the favorite chrome-and-leather beanbag seating unit. He snatched the cigar from his mouth and stood up.

"Who's this?" he shouted indignantly to the office next door. Still totally ignoring her he stalked back out of the office.

The palms of Margie's hands had started to sweat. She pressed them against the sides of her skirt and concentrated on the carpet.

"But what's she doing in my bloody room?" She heard him ask the middle-aged woman who had ushered her in.

"She has an appointment to see you, and it's in your diary," came the hushed reply. "About the vacancy for an assistant."

"Oh Christ, that's all I need today."

Templeton reappeared in the office, slamming the door shut behind him, obviously annoyed. Margie remained motionless, her handbag clutched tightly on her lap.

He crossed to the big leather armchair behind his desk, collapsed into it and began to make a telephone call, glancing at her as he punched out the number. From the softened tones he used speaking into the receiver Margie guessed that the call was personal, and tried hard not to look as if she was listening.

When he had finished he replaced the receiver and turned his full attention to her, eyeing her clothes with barely concealed distaste.

"If it's inconvenient . . ." she began quietly.

"You want to be my Girl Friday, then?" He said it in a way which suggested total disbelief.

"I . . . yes, sir."

"So what qualities do you have which you think I cannot afford to be without?" He paused, then sat back. "Sell yourself to me."

"Well, sir . . ."

"Can't hear you, love."

"Well," she began again, clearing her throat and speaking louder. "I'm prepared to work very hard . . ."

"Still can't hear you."

"I'm prepared to work very hard, and I think . . ."

"I wouldn't be paying you to think." Templeton's voice cut across hers, blowing smoke everywhere. "A lot of kids are prepared to work hard these days. It's a buyers' market. You should see the letters we get. Advertising is one of the most highly paid professions in the country, and we're right at the top of the tree. I mean, who honestly wouldn't give up one of their kidneys to work here? I was doing breakfast TV the other morning—perhaps you caught it—and that's what I said to Anne, why take the shit when you can have the best working their guts out for you?''

He seemed to lose the thought, gazing off into middle distance. Margie felt her confidence ebbing as she pulled herself forward to speak.

"I'm a very good organizer. I can type and do shorthand, and . . ."

"Yes, lovey, I'm sure you're totally fab but I'm afraid you can't just stroll in fresh out of school and start at the top, no can do. You're what, how old?''

"Nineteen." Margie had pulled a Kleenex from her shirt sleeve and was kneading it between her fingers.

"Bit old to be starting out, aren't you? I am assuming of course," this Templeton said with a smirk, "that you haven't been pursuing a particular interest at university. So what've you been doing all this time?''

"I have been studying, but I've got to give it up because . . ." Her voice started to soften as she lost her nerve. "I just need to work now.''

The leather chair creaked ominously as Templeton leaned forward and spoke with his cigar still clenched between his teeth.

"Darling," he breathed, "I hate to disillusion you, but you can't swan straight into some cozy little job and spend your time bouncing on the boss's knee waiting for Mr. Right to come along.'' His voice had risen and although Margie did not notice, he was slurring his words. He drained the whisky tumbler and banged it down on to the desk with a sigh of irritation.

Silence fell in the room as Margie began to gather up her belongings. A caul of hot tears began to form over her eyes. She tipped back her head in an effort to stem the flow. Templeton ran his fingers through highlighted hair and rose from behind the desk.

"Well, Miss . . ." He consulted his desk diary but failed to locate her name. His voice softened slightly when he saw that he had upset her. "If it's any consolation, I've turned down graduates for this job. They just can't take the heat. The position has responsibilities. There's the mail to be sorted, coffee to make, calls to be answered when the group secretary's on her lunch break, plus it's very important—both for me and my clients—that you look good every minute of the day.''

Templeton looked down at his Scotch and was annoyed to find the glass empty. He crossed over to the window and beckoned Margie to follow.

''Look down there,'' he said, pointing to a custard-colored Porsche parked with two wheels on the pavement in a space provided for the handicapped. ''The best way to judge a man is by the price of his toys. I had to work my balls off for that. Long hours and late nights. This isn't a job, it's a vocation.''

He turned to Margie and placed an arm around her shoulders, enveloping her in a warm haze of cigar smoke, sweat and Scotch fumes. ''I'd love to help you but believe me, I've seen too many girls like you leave here in tears. I know you'd be far happier in a quiet little insurance office, really you would. They're not so fussy about qualifications, and the work's not too demanding.'' He guided her slowly towards the door. ''Now, off you toddle. Think about what I've said. And don't worry about having wasted my time because I enjoy setting kids on the right path. It's a perk of the job.''

Suddenly Margie was outside the office with the door closed at her back. Her vision began to blur so heavily that she was obliged to pull off her spectacles and wipe her eyes.

''Jesus Christ.'' She heard the muffled explosion of his voice through the door as he slammed around the office, furious at having his afternoon schedule interrupted.

As she ran down the corridor, the tears coming easily now, she felt people turning to stare after her. Finally, standing alone in the elevator trying to close the old-fashioned trellis doors, she felt her handbag slip from under her arm and watched helplessly as it scattered its contents across the floor.

Her face streamed wetly as she swept a few cheap cosmetic items back into the bag. As she stood, a woman's hand, slender, pale and covered with rings, reached into the elevator and touched her on the shoulder. Tears suddenly stemming, she looked up in surprise.

The air in the saloon bar of the Captain's Cabin was blue with cigar smoke, and vibrated with talk of copydates, airtime, halftones and media schedules. Against the bar were leaned as many executive briefcases as businessmen. The pseudo-Dickensian theme of the pub was echoed to some extent in the ruddy faces of the advertising men who filled it, as if someone had updated a Cruikshank sketch with pocket calculators and fruit machines.

As Allbright returned to the table with his pint he was surprised to find Templeton massaging the bottom of a pretty young woman who stood uncomfortably wedged between the creative director and the unlit fireplace. As Templeton's free hand roamed her posterior she vacantly sipped a rum and coke.

"Sexy little bitch, isn't she?" said Templeton, as if the girl next to him was either deaf and dumb, deranged or invisible. "Her father's the caretaker of our building. She often helps him out." He said this meaningfully, turning to the girl and chucking her beneath the chin. The girl smiled back lazily, a little drunk.

Allbright was perplexed. "I fail to see the significance of her father's occupation."

"God, Graham, you're so pigshit thick sometimes," muttered Templeton, his hand creeping over the girl's thigh and slowly disappearing up her dress. "She has her father's night keys." He grinned at the account executive and gave a lascivious wink. "Dabbling below stairs. Tampering with servants. Spanking the maid."

The girl pulled herself free of Templeton's meandering hand and stood down her drink. "I'll see you later, then," she said, slipping her shoes back on, then standing on tiptoe to give Templeton a peck on the cheek.

"Ten o'clock, on the dot. If you're not there on time I'll start without you." Templeton nudged Allbright as the girl pushed away into a sea of suits.

"I've been thinking of offering her a job as my Girl Friday. What do you think?"

"And you're conducting an interview with her in your office tonight? You dog!" Allbright grinned excitedly. He was a balding, boring accounts man who lived vicariously through Templeton, lapping up the details of his more salacious adventures with disturbing enthusiasm. But at least he was an appreciative audience.

"It's going to be an in-depth interview, I can tell you. She may even get the job. Randy little tart's been after me for months. You can tell that she's begging for it, just by the way she stands." Templeton imitated the stance, adding an extra little crudity to the pose. He drained his whisky and pointed at Allbright's glass. "Care for one at the Morocco? You're not doing anything special are you?" Before Allbright had time to answer, Templeton was shoving his way towards the door. He called back over his shoulder. "Leave that drink. We'll switch to their nasty house champagne, I think."

Outside, Templeton pulled on his leather jacket and walked briskly ahead so that Allbright had to run to catch up.

"You've been advertising that job for months," he said. "Aren't you ever going to find someone who can fill it?"

"I'm not sure I want to," replied Templeton as they crossed the road. "It's such a great way to meet women. If this one tonight asks me if she can have a job, I'll tell her to let me sleep on it for a while."

The Morocco was an expense-account cocktail bar, a post-modern chromium-plated hangout of artists and models, and therefore latterly infested with advertising folk, who slipped between the studio people with bottles and clusters of glasses as if hoping that a little uncompromised creativity might rub off on to them. Here portfolios replaced briefcases and champagne stood in for whisky. New-age jazz played discreetly from wall-mounted speakers.

"Take the glasses." Templeton lowered several into All-bright's outstretched hands. "Better to spend out on some decent fizz rather than drink the piss they're passing off as the house shampoo."

"Can you claim it back, then?" asked Allbright, hoping to pick up some new tips on fiddling his expenses.

"Oh, I should think it'll fit nicely on to somebody's photo-graphic bill. Although I'm quite happy to take it out of my own pocket these days. Beats letting it all into the hands of The Bitch."

"Ah yes, the alimony. I honestly don't know how you get away with it." Allbright dutifully set the champagne glasses upright and waited for them to be filled.

"I pay up eventually, of course. But God, I make her wait. I've got it down to a fine art now. I know just how long to delay, how far to push. Here, take another one."

"Three glasses? Is someone joining us?"

"You never know, Graham, you never know."

As he opened the first bottle of the evening Templeton turned to acknowledge the presence of his colleagues, and to be acknowledged in turn by them.

"You're incorrigible," sad Allbright enviously. "I thought you had arranged to meet that girl at ten."

"Yes, but there might be something a little more substantial floating around. The one at ten is a slag. She's really only good for a twenty-minute knee-trembler. I want something that'll keep me up all night.''

He stopped suddenly and looked over Allbright's shoulder. ''And I do believe I've found something. Look.''

Allbright followed the direction of the pointing finger and settled his eyes on a tall blonde girl who stood nervously sipping a fruit-juice cocktail in a corner of the packed lounge.

''She's stunning, absolutely stunning,'' he mooned, jealous of the guiltless manner in which Templeton conducted his affairs. To be fair, he could not exactly tell if the girl was stunning or not. She leaned half in, half out of the shadows thrown by the neon bar sign high on the wall above her.

''So I'm right. She's that good, huh?'' Templeton's eyesight was little more than adequate, but his vanity refused to let him wear glasses and he hated the idea of contact lenses. Besides, he was sure that women found him more attractive when he narrowed his eyes.

''I've never seen her in here before. Looks like a model.''

''A new face, eh? Pass me that spare glass.'' Templeton filled it with Bollinger and moved into the crowd which surrounded their table. ''See you in a little while, old sport.''

He slipped between the chattering actresses and executives, pushing forward until he reached the clearing where the shadowy blonde stood drinking alone.

''Hi there. Thought you looked as if you needed a little glass of champers. What's your name?'' He moved in a little and inclined his head to catch her reply.

''My name is Inge.'' Her voice had a melodic, accented trace.

''And you are from where, Inge?''

''I am here from Norway.'' She sounded nervous. ''I work as model.''

''A model, eh? Not nude modelling, for the girlie magazines? I've heard about you Norwegians.''

The girl smiled politely. ''No, no. I model swimming clothes for big studio, just near here.''

''I'd love to see you model a swimsuit, Inge. I bet you have a great body.'' Templeton leaned closer still.

She accepted his proffered glass, the shadows crossing her face to reveal blood-red lips against the palest skin he had ever seen. She smiled again, her eyes lost in the darkness. Templeton was astounded. Her tall, slim body was encased in an outfit of shimmering blue satin. Elbow-length gloves sparkled on long white arms. Her shoulders were touched by curls of blonde hair. She smelled faintly of lemons, with a hint of spice.

"Can I be as frank with you as you people are in Norway, Inge?" he asked, resting his arm on the wall beside her.

"Please," said the girl as she moved forward from the shadows to reveal large electric-blue eyes. In the background a solo saxophone climbed the scale. Templeton was intoxicated. She was like a Greek statue come to life.

"You are very beautiful. Big breasts. They really turn me on. You know what that means, turning you on?"

Inge thought carefully for a moment, then gently shook her head.

"That's what we say in this country when we are attracted to someone. We say, Wow, she's a real Turn On. And that's what you are. It's a big compliment. You should be flattered." Templeton sucked in his stomach and knocked back the rest of his champagne in one gulp.

Across the room Graham Allbright was becoming bored. Nobody ever came and talked to him when he stood by himself. They only ever came over when he was with Templeton. Thirty years ago the same thing had been happening to him in school playgrounds. He drained his glass and looked at his watch. How he wished that he could be like the creative director! Fancy keeping three girls on the go at once, even to the point of being engaged to one, as Templeton was! Divorced after being caught with his trousers down, on their wedding anniversary of all nights, Templeton had left his wife exactly one year after they had been wed. Now he played the field as widely as possible— not that he'd ever allowed his marriage to get in the way of his philandering.

Allbright knew that he'd have to leave in a moment if he was to catch his train. He had already telephoned his wife to say that he'd be late. Now he looked up to see Templeton heading back towards him with the tall blonde girl in tow. His free hand was cupped around the neck of a fresh bottle of champagne.

"Graham, this is Olga . . ."

"Inge."

"Yeah, right. Inge, this is Graham Allbright, one of our account men." Templeton refilled his glass as he spoke. "Now we can get down to some serious partying." Inge looked quizzically at him, her head tilted. "Party. Get down. You know what that means, Inge?"

"No, I do not understand."

Templeton reached forward and ran a nicotine-stained index finger down the front of her dress. The fabric glittered and shimmered in the neon-pink half light.

"I'd love to show you what it means . . ." Allbright noticed the softness of speech which usually indicated that Templeton was becoming drunk. "Why don't you come back to my office and we can discuss the problems of translating Norwegian together?"

"Richard, haven't you got another appointment at ten?" Allbright waved his watch about, a child with a secret.

"Don't be such a wet blanket, Graham. S'only eight thirty . . . plenty of time. Don't you worry about us." He turned to face Allbright with a new malicious tone in his voice. "Shouldn't you be scurrying back to the little woman? She'll have the curlers in and the rolling pin out by now."

Allbright felt his face burning as Templeton slid his arm around Inge's narrow waist and began to chuckle.

"Perhaps you're right. I should be off. Nice to meet you, Inge." Allbright motioned Templeton to one side and dug him in the ribs. "Have fun, old sport. Don't forget to wear a condom, eh?" He released a schoolboy snigger.

Templeton gave him a withering look. "Fuck safe sex," he said. "You wouldn't have caught Hemingway wearing a noddy."

Allbright picked up his briefcase and moved out as the couple slid on to the couch behind the table.

"You sit here, darling, and help me finish this bottle before we go and play. Here, I've got a joke for you. What's the difference between True Love and AIDS? Don't know? AIDS is for ever."

Inge looked blankly at him, then smiled sweetly.

"You've got no idea what I'm talking about, have you? Good." He topped up her drink once more.

The building was dark and silent.

"There is no night watchman?" asked Inge as the Porsche slurred to a stop in front of the advertising agency. She dipped her head and peered up through the tinted windscreen at the building before them, suddenly apprehensive.

"He finishes at eight and locks the building up tight. I have my own keys 'cause I'm normally here working late. Advantage of being in a position of trust. Look." Templeton rummaged in his jacket pocket and produced a huge bunch of keys attached to a large gold Porsche medallion. He slid his free hand over Inge's stockinged thigh. "Follow me."

Weaving his way from the car to the front door of the building, he turned the keys over in the lamplight. "S'one of these . . ."

"Here, let me help you."

Inge sorted out one of the keys and slid it into the lock. At the top and bottom of the huge glass doors, bolts slid back. She pushed on the door and slipped inside, her ice-white legs catching the light of the overhead lamps, topaz glittering from a bracelet.

"Where are you?"

"Over here. By the . . . how you say? The elevators."

"S'right, Inge. You learn fast, don't you?" Templeton giggled to himself as he followed the direction of her voice.

When they reached the seventh floor he pulled back the trellis door of the lift and stepped into the corridor, which was illuminated only by a dim red exit sign above the door to the stairs. Inge stepped daintily out, pulling the steel latticework closed behind her. As she bent to straighten the hem of her dress Templeton smacked her sharply on the bottom. Inge gasped and turned around reproachfully.

"Oh, don't play coy, lovey," he said, pulling his shirt out of his trousers as he walked towards her. "You Norwegians like a bit of that, don't you?" He began to impersonate the pattern of her speech. "*Out* of the *sau*na and *in*to the snow, then ve *smack* each other wiz the *birch* branches, yah?" Inge stepped back into the dark as he advanced. "For God's sake stay in one place for a minute. Now where are you?" Templeton stumbled forward, feeling his way along the wall of the corridor. In the shadows, Inge released a musical laugh.

"You Engliss are so funny." She laughed again.

"When I catch you I'm going to tan your backside red, you little pricktease, then we'll see who's laughing. Where's the bloody light switch?"

Behind him the elevator hummed away up the shaft. Templeton stopped and listened. In the darkness, satin rustled.

"Richard."

Inge stepped forward in the weak red light. Her bare shoulders shone warmly against the glinting turquoise fabric of her dress. She was temptation personified.

"There you are! Come over here." Templeton lurched forward and planted his wet lips squarely over her mouth, squirming his tongue around her closed teeth. He withdrew after a minute or two, wiping his mouth on the back of his hand. Suddenly lashing out his arm, he caught Inge's neck and gripped the base of it in the palm of his hand.

"Now," he hissed, bringing her face around until it was directly beneath his, "I want you to tell me how much you want it." Tightening his grip, he forced her slowly down. "Tell me."

"You're hurting!" Inge suddenly pushed back up, breaking his hold on her neck. For a moment anger flashed across her face, then the emotion was smothered in darkness and replaced with a smile.

"First we drink. Then we do something special." The smile grew wider. White teeth flashed. Templeton grinned back and straightened himself up, stealing a covert glance at his watch as he did so. Inge felt around in the darkness and produced a hip flask, seemingly from nowhere. Along the corridor the glass walls of the office reflected the lights of the city below.

"Is very special. Is brandy from my home country. Very 'spensive. I know you will like it." She smiled once more, unscrewing the cap of the flask and taking a swig.

"Give me." She was obviously tougher than she looked. He liked this turn of events. She'd give him a run for his money. "Give it here." He outstretched his hand and beckoned with his fingertips. Inge passed him the flask and he drank deep without removing his eyes from her face. "It's very good. Think I'll hang on to this." He slipped the flask into his back pocket and stepped towards the smiling girl.

Something wrong . . .

The thought had vanished.

"Let's go to my office," he said huskily. "I have a couch and . . . stuff." He made a grab for Inge's hand but failed to connect as she moved back into the darkness of the corridor.

"Oh, I have a much better idea." She turned and walked away.

"Not again, no you don't." Templeton lunged for her hand and missed once more. There was another rustle of satin. And a sound below that, harder to place . . .

He staggered and fell heavily against the corridor wall, his head spinning. Jesus, he thought, that drink was strong. Brandy, from her home country? *Norwegian* brandy, for Christ's sake?

He couldn't see Inge now. He concentrated hard, trying to collect his thoughts. Funny girl . . .

She knew which key opened the front door.

She knew where the lifts were.

He felt sick.

"Sit down. You'll feel better." The accent from Inge's voice had disappeared. Suddenly she stepped out into the light.

"Give me your hand."

Templeton slid down the corridor wall and thudded on to the floor with his legs out straight. He could see and hear everything around him, could feel the floor beneath his touch, but he could not control his legs. His right foot had begun to twitch uncontrollably. Suddenly feeling very tired, he allowed Inge to take his hand. She raised it up, then removed her hand from his, leaving his palm high and outstretched.

"Don't you think I have lovely eyes?"

"Whassat? I don't . . . Yes, you have luv'ly eyes." His voice was slurring heavily now. Speech was becoming a great effort.

"Well, if you like my eyes that much, you can have them."

Templeton felt something brush his hand. He slowly brought it to his face. In the center of his palm lay a pair of bright blue contact lenses. Inge tipped up his arm, sending the lenses to the floor. Then she brought it close to her face and ran his helpless fingers through her hair.

"You like my hair, too?"

She released his hand. He found himself holding a long blonde wig. Now there were other distinct voices, whispering in the crimson murk. Two of them, both women by the sound of it.

"Are you okay?"

"Yes, I'm fine, just about."

"We'll take over now. You did great. Sit down and get your breath back."

"Yeah, you deserve it. Want a cigarette?" A red tip glowed and zig-zagged in the dark.

"Who's there? Inge, 'zat you?" He was so tired, he had never been this tired, ever. It was impossible to think clearly. There was movement before him. A rustle. A cough.

"Can we have some light around here before somebody falls over? Ta."

There was a click. The neon ceiling panels buzzed into life. He tried to focus his eyes. Before him stood three women. One of them was Inge. The other two looked familiar. On the floor between them was a black nylon sports bag. Inge's blonde tresses had been replaced by a short frizzy mop of black hair. Her eyes were now brown. He realized that this was the first time he had seen her in bright light. Her skin was a ghastly chalky white, lighter in some patches than others. Her arms, up to the elbow, were a deep ebony. She had taken off her evening gloves. She smiled down at him as she stepped out of her high-heeled shoes and became several inches shorter.

"You know, the padded look really suits you," said one of the other women. She reached down and rummaged around the sports bag. "Here, try using this."

Inge accepted something in her hand and began to apply it to her face. "Ta, ever so. Oh, that feels much better. I've only been white for two hours and I'm already fed up with it."

Inge was rubbing the damp swab over her face, which seemed to be coming off in her hands. Her cheeks and forehead were growing darker by the second. Templeton could only stare in amazement. Beneath the thick white stockings and the make-up "Inge" was the little black girl he had thrown out of his office the month before. She looked proudly to either side of her. The three women shook hands with each other and started to giggle. Templeton passed out.

He was woken by a nagging pain across his throat. He quickly discovered that he was unable to move his head in any direction. His mouth was burning with the taste of the brandy he had drunk earlier. Brandy mixed with—what? His whole body ached. He opened his eyes. Before him, the grimy drop of the elevator shaft swam into view. Templeton's head had been wedged through the bars of the lift's trellis door at a point where a small section of latticework was missing. Trying to move his hands, he found that they had been tied behind his back, and that he was kneeling on the floor of the corridor with his head thrust through to the shaft beyond. A leather gag had been strapped across his mouth.

"He's awake."

"Turn him over so he can see."

Hands grabbed him, lifted, then turned him over with difficulty. His neck sawed against the steel framework of the trellis. He grimaced with pain and attempted to cry out, but no sound emerged through the gag.

"You're hurting him. He's too low."

"Here, put a cushion under him."

"Give me the rope. He's trying to wriggle out."

Nylon cord was wrapped around his body and threaded through the bars of the old lift door, firmly securing him. He was now sitting against the door with his head tipped back through the gap in the bars, his neck resting on the steel V shape of the hole. Lifting his head as far as it would go, until his forehead touched the oil-smeared bars, he studied the three women before him.

The first was short and blonde, extremely attractive. He remembered that she used to work in the typing pool, but that was a while back. He'd given her the old come-up-to-my-office-tonight routine. There was some trouble—an argument? After that he had no memory of her. Presumably she'd moved on to another job.

"Hello, Richard. I think you know all of us." It was the blonde woman speaking. "I'm Sarah, remember? You should do. I slapped your face pretty hard. It got me fired, didn't it? In the middle we have Margie, who you interviewed—we'll come back to her—and on the end there is Laura. Raise your hand, Laura."

"Allo there darlin'," remember me?" Laura's cockney accent stood out in marked contrast to Sarah's refined tones. "I worked under you for a few weeks. Literally, as it turned out. I was temping, remember? I'm sure I left an impression on you, cause you left an impression on me. Stretchmarks. I turned to you for a clue as to what the 'ell to do, and you chose the occasion to tell me that you was married. I wanted to kill myself. Them was difficult days to go through alone, Dicky boy." Laura crouched down in front of Templeton and let her smile fall. "That's why we're here, y'see. To take revenge for us, an' all the other women you've tried to screw or screw over." Her voice lowered. "Time to start sweating, big boy."

"Richard, your fate seems to be in our hands," said Sarah cheerfully. "You're probably wondering how young Margie here got involved in all this. Well, Laura and I met a couple of months ago. She remembered seeing me at the office, and you became the subject of our conversation. How your ears must have burned that day! A short while later, I came here to meet a friend of mine, and she told me that you were behaving more badly than ever. Blackmailing the typists into sex, refusing to pay your wife's alimony. We thought it was high time that something was done, but what? Arrange to have you publicly accused of sexual harassment? We felt sure you'd wriggle your way out of that one. So we decided to take the law into our own hands, if we could just find a way to do it."

"And while Sarah was here, guess who she saw?" continued Laura. "Margie, flying out of your office in tears."

"You destroyed what little confidence she had," admonished Sarah. "So we decided to restore it for her. We devised a plan.

It took quite a while to talk Margie into joining us, but it's been worth the effort. Because we've proven to her that she *can* get the better of a man . . ."

"Even a pig like you."

"Now, Laura . . ."

Templeton tried to slide forward, to clear his head from the hole, but only succeeded in painfully twisting his neck. The gag across his mouth was cutting into his gums.

"To cut a long story short," said Sarah, "Margie fitted the part perfectly. We needed to lure you up here, and what better way to do it than with a woman? You'd have recognized either of us—or so we thought—but we knew you'd scarcely remember a girl you saw over a month ago, and then only for a few minutes."

"There was just one snag," said Laura, pointing over to Margie. "She was the wrong color."

"We all know what an appalling racist you are, Richard." Sarah slid her hands through the bars of the trellis and forced Templeton to raise his head again. "So we had Margie made up. We knew she'd never pass close inspection, but with careful lighting . . ."

"And a few drinks . . ."

"You shouldn't have drunk from the flask, Richard." Margie spoke for the first time. She peered through the bars into Templeton's eyes.

"Strong stuff," said Laura. "I'm training to be a chemist, y'know. You'd be amazed at the stuff we keep on our shelves. I mixed you a chemical cocktail. Courvoisier and something a little like curare. Sort of paralyzes you. Probably won't wear off for days, the amount you drank."

"Take off his gag," Sarah instructed. "Go on, Margie, you can do it now."

Margie looked hesitantly at Templeton as he squirmed angrily on the floor, still trying to pull his head free of the bars. Finally she stepped forward and gingerly tugged at the strap until it fell free. She jumped back as he snarled, trying to bite her.

"Now, Richard!" Sarah said, wagging a finger at him, "That's not very friendly. We thought you'd enjoy the gag. We found it in your office, in the bottom drawer of your desk. Can't imagine what you use it for, although—like you—we have some pretty rough ideas."

"Wait until I get out of this!" shouted Templeton, pulling and twisting at the bars with his shoulders. "You bitches are dead!

Dead, do you understand? You'll never work again, anywhere!''
His legs sprawled uselessly in front of him as he struggled.

"Let's get one thing clear, Mr. Macho," said Sarah, dropping
to her knees beside him. "We're in control of this situation.
We're going to stop you from fooling with other people's lives
just to please your adolescent sex drive, you got that? One shout
and the gag goes back on. Tighter.''

"Or what? What can you do?'' Templeton spat at them, then
turned his attention back to struggling with the bars. Margie
looked nervously at her companions.

"We can leave you here until morning, when someone will
use the lift," said Sarah. "Look up.''

Templeton threw back his head. Above him was the cabled
base of the elevator, stopped at the next floor. His eyes widened
in alarm as he remembered the girl he was due to meet at ten
tonight, here on the seventh floor. The caretaker's daughter, the
girl who always carried her father's door keys . . .

"What time is it?'' he croaked.

Sarah looked at her watch. "Ten minutes to ten," she said,
puzzled by his sudden change of manner.

"Oh Christ," he murmured sickly, raising his head once
more. "Untie me and I'll let this whole thing drop. I won't touch
you, I won't even call the police. You have my word. I promise.
Just untie me, then get the hell out of here.''

"I think we're reasonably familiar with the validity of your
word," said Sarah. "Thanks anyway, but we're going out on
the town tonight, and 'Inge' still has to take a bath.''

"I'm going back to basic black," said Margie.

"He'll be all right here until the morning.''

"I won't . . . you've got to let . . .''

"Okay, we were teasing about the curare," admitted Sarah.
"You should get the use of your legs back soon after midnight.
You'll be free well before anyone calls for the lift. Provided
Laura knows her cocktail recipes, that is.''

"There's someone coming here tonight!'' shouted Templeton
finally. "She'll be here any minute now!''

"What do you mean?'' asked Laura. "Who's coming here?''

"A girl! I arranged to meet a girl here! She'll be here at ten
and she'll call the lift! Undo the ropes!''

Sarah stood up and folded her arms across her chest.

"Well, ladies," she said coldly. "I guess he just gets worse.
He was going to dump you before ten, Margie, dump you and
get straight down to business with another one . . .''

"He doesn't deserve to be set free," said Laura, quite serious now.

"But he'll be killed." Margie bit her nail and turned to Sarah. "We can't let him die."

"Why not! We could get away with it. Who knows we're here? They've only seen you, and that was while you were in disguise. I say we leave him to his own fate."

"Oh God, it must be ten by now! For Christ's sake, untie me!" Templeton writhed desperately, his back banging against the bars.

"Put the gag back on." Sarah pointed to the leather strap in Margie's hand.

"I can't." Margie stopped before Templeton, watching him twist and strain.

"Then I will," said Laura, taking the strap from Margie and forcing it across Templeton's saliva-spattered mouth.

"Two minutes to ten," said Sarah, checking her watch. "Say goodbye to the world, Richard. It's time for you to make your peace with God, and I hope for your sake She's listening."

Laura and Sarah took Margie by the arm and together the threesome headed for the stairs, clicking out the lights as they went. Behind them Templeton writhed frantically against the lift doors, the whites of his eyes showing above the gag as he continued to scream into it. As the girls clattered down into the concrete stairwell they could no longer hold back their laughter. Even Margie dissolved into a fit of giggles.

"Here, who's got the key?" asked Laura.

"What key?"

"The key to the emergency switch that turns the lifts off, of course."

"Oh, hang about, I've got it." Sarah held up the caretaker's master key to the cupboard which contained the main power switches to the building. "Perhaps we should leave it where someone will eventually find it. Here." She tossed the key into the stairwell and listened as it dropped to the basement floor with a distant clink.

"I hope he doesn't get free before his date turns up. Imagine him trying to explain what happened, he'll be really embarrassed."

"And fancy telling him he was paralyzed."

"Don't worry, Margie," said Sarah. "It did the trick. We scared the hell out of him. And he can't get back at us. That's the great thing about male chauvinists. They can never remember women's surnames.''

By the time they reached the bottom of the stairs they were all laughing again.

As they crossed the marble hallway they could see a young girl standing on tiptoe, using her key in the outside front door lock.

"Hey, that must be her."

"Pretty in a tarty way, I suppose," sniffed Laura.

"Evening." Sarah passed by the girl in the doorway. "You must be on your way up to see Mr. Templeton. You've got a long climb."

The girl blanched. "I . . . I'm getting something from upstairs," she said in surprise.

"Oh," said Sarah, smiling to the others. "We thought you were having a late-night meeting with the creative director. He told us how he almost lost his head over you." Collapsing with laughter, the three of them staggered out into the night.

The young girl shook her head and pushed the glass door shut behind them, locking it at the top. Her heels clicked on the marble as she crossed to the elevator bank and summoned the lift.

Nothing happened.

She pressed again, then tried to peer up inside the shaft, but could see nothing. She was about to head for the stairs when she remembered that she had her father's spare keys with her. Pulling the ring from her jacket pocket and sorting through it, she located the correct key and unlocked the door of the cupboard by the side of the elevator bank. She switched on the overhead light and saw with annoyance that someone had turned off the elevators at the emergency switch. Turning it back on was a simple enough matter. She reclosed the cupboard door and returned to the elevator bank.

Her manicured finger hovered before the lift button as she raised her eyes heavenward.

"God," she sighed, "it would make a bloody change if a man really did lose his head over me."

She pressed down hard on the lift button.

High above her there was a hum of machinery. Suddenly the sound rose sharply in pitch, and abruptly stopped. The lift juddered, then moved smoothly on as the hum resumed.

The girl stood staring vacantly through the trellis doors. As she waited in hope, something round and heavy shot past in a furious crimson spray on its way down to Hell.

THE SUN IN THE SANDS

"IT'S ALL RIGHT, I'm back on the right road. There's a signpost right in front of me. No, no, I won't make it back to the office tonight. Just remember to lock up when you go home. We have Councillor Harding in on Monday, so make sure you're there by nine."

Neil Hawkley clipped the car-phone receiver back into its illuminated cradle and pulled over to the side of the road.

Ahead, barely visible through the deepening gloom of the early evening drizzle, stood an old-fashioned country signpost with two white wooden pointers marking off distances to the villages of Elveden and Brandon. Neil leaned forward and peered up at the sign once more before checking it against the instructions in the smart calfskin Filofax lying on the seat beside him. He scratched his nose thoughtfully. This was definitely the right route for Teakwield, not that he would have recognized it even in broad daylight. He hadn't been back here since the funeral three years ago.

For the past half hour Neil's silver Porsche had been nosing through the rain-bloated lanes of Breckland, three hundred miles of lonely heathland scarred with military airstrips and battle-training territory in the heart of the eastern counties. Before long he hoped to reach the small village which lay marooned within the stained marshes scalloping the Norfolk coastline. With a pudgy finger Neil flicked his headlights up to main beam, illuminating a path through the effervescent downpour, and turned the car in the direction of Teakwield. By the side of the road an unbroken line of beeches twisted in the wind, the tops of their branches hidden in rippling sheets of rain.

How typical it had been of his father to settle in this part of the country. If only he had chosen to spend his declining years in London he would at least have died in a property which had

53

kept its resale value. Instead, Neil had had the devil of a time getting rid of the old house. As a property developer he had always believed that any plot of land, no matter how inhospitable, could be put to good use of some kind, but his father's leaky, ramshackle Teakwield Cottage had nearly defeated him. The old man had loved the place so much that it still gave Neil a *frisson* of pleasure to remember seeing it knocked flat by the bulldozers just weeks after the funeral and days before the preservation order came through. In fact, if he had been alive to see the home freezer center Neil had built on the site of the house, the shock would probably have killed him.

Several miles further on Neil was able to pick out a white-painted stub of stone set in the grass verge. Carved into its side with a single word: Teakwield. He smiled smugly, running his hand lightly over the carefully arranged strands of hair which concealed his bald patch. The Porsche splashed on past a handful of cheaply finished modern houses, unlit and unlived in—a housing project which had failed when local businesses were forced to close—on past tiny whitewashed cottages set back from the road among rustling birches, and around a sharp bend to the Wretling farm.

He removed the ignition keys and settled back in his seat. The rain seemed to have eased off for a few minutes. Listening to the ticking of the engine as he cooled, he contemplated leaving the car to take a look around but quickly rejected the idea. On his approach, the driveway to the main farmhouse had dissolved into gravel, then mud. He had no torch. Besides, he was wearing expensive Italian shoes with gold buckles. Neil liked gold. It was such a tangible symbol of wealth. Heavy gold links pierced his crisp shirt cuffs. Two thick chains lay hidden in the matted grey hair of his chest. His wedding ring was a golden initialled slab. He was successful, after all, so why shouldn't everyone know it? Turning on the interior light, he reached over into the back seat and withdrew the plans from his briefcase. He traced the layout of pale blue lines with his fingers, then looked out of the window, trying to equate the low brick building which stood in darkness ahead with its two-dimensional form on the paper. From here the place seemed bigger than he had imagined, even though he had been aware of the square acreage involved from the start.

Councillor Harding had first mentioned the possibility of obtaining the property over lunch a few months ago. Staring wistfully into the dregs of his port while Neil reluctantly summoned the waiter again, he noted the likelihood of a particular farm in the Teakwield area being sold in the next few months. The owner was frail and ancient, though currently enjoying stable health. It was a property to keep an eye on, Harding had suggested with a wink as the ruby liquid tumbled into his glass once more. Neil was not a patient man but he took the councillor's advice. He waited and he watched, but the property remained tantalizingly unavailable as old man Wretling seemed to show no signs of shuffling off his mortal coil.

Then, thankfully, an unpredicted downturn in the weather caught his exhausted kidneys by surprise and he suddenly passed on, leaving the farm in the calloused hands of his long-suffering wife.

With little money to pay the farmlands and no way of ever being able to cope on her own, for the Wretlings had no children to share the burden, she had caved in to the constant pressure being put on her to sell the property, and tearfully moved out to live with her sister in Norwich. With no other takers in sight, Neil was able to win a spectacular reduction in the asking price. He did not feel badly about this. On the contrary, he looked upon himself more as a benefactor. He was helping a widow in her time of need by buying up a near-derelict nineteenth-century farmhouse, just as he would soon be bringing to the community a valuable new service. Wretling farm would be pulled down to make way for another CrownMart DIY Hyperstore, the twenty-ninth in England. Neil slipped the plan back into his briefcase with a satisfied smile. OK, so he had wasted far too much time worrying the old woman into selling. And he'd promised her that the farmhouse would be restored, not demolished. But the agreement had been a verbal one. On paper all that appeared were the clinical details of a business transaction, and that was all that counted.

He looked out at the ramshackle barn and across to the flooded, windswept fields. The end of the property was marked by a desolate barricade of Scots pine. Tear down those trees and you could get a decent-sized car park in there, he thought. He twisted his key in the ignition and noisily revved the motor, pulling away in a spray of stones.

He had only travelled half a mile back the way he had come when the engine inexplicably idled into silence at a crossroads. For a moment he sat looking out at the deserted road ahead. Then with a sigh he tried the ignition. At first the engine seemed within a whisker of turning over, but his impatience caused him to flood it, so that there was nothing to do but wait. Releasing the brake, he allowed the car to coast over the intersection and across the gentle camber of the road to the verge on the far side. As he sat waiting, the rain vigorously renewed its drumming on the roof. Angrily he punched out the telephone number of the office. No answer. That was typical, his employees sneaking off home the second his back was turned.

Beyond the smeary windows of the car the village of Teak-wield was dark, dead and virtually invisible among the trees which led down to the barren Norfolk coast. He tried the engine once more. The low grinding sound which came from beneath the hood told him there would be no chance of starting it without the use of a pair of jump leads, leads that his wife had borrowed some weeks ago to start the Alfa and had never replaced. Neil thumped the wheel with the heel of his hand and swore aloud. He had not passed a garage for miles, but the village lay just a short way ahead. He would have to walk, even though it meant risking damage to his new shoes. He glanced at his watch. Ten to seven. With any luck a pub would be open by the time he got there.

On his way into the village he passed not another living soul. The inclement weather was certainly keeping people within the shelter of timber and brick. No cars splashed by on the narrow curving streets. The few shops he passed were barred and shuttered with old-fashioned linen blinds. A priest appeared around a corner and hurried on without looking up, his cassock flapping wetly around his ankles. He turned into the gatehouse of a large flint-walled church and disappeared beyond rustling trees.

At the end of the high street was a low concrete wall over which the wind whipped sprays of seawater. Beyond this lay miles of marshy salt flats, eroded and reformed by the unending assault of an icy gray sea. The pub sign of The Sun in the Sands depicted a deep yellow sun with a grinning Victorian face slowly slipping behind amber dunes. Similar colors shone through the curving lead-light windows on either side of the low red door, which stood no more than five and a half feet high.

By the time he reached the small whitewashed public house Neil's clothes were thoroughly soaked. He unlatched the door and stooped into a welcoming lounge. Wooden trestle tables covered the flagstoned floor, at the far end of which was a large fireplace filled with blazing logs, complete with copper kettles and hanging muslin bags of smoked meats. There was a darts board, and skittles, and a red-faced barman polishing glasses who looked up and smiled, and the crackle and pop of wood settling in the grate. There were no other customers.

"Nasty night out there," said the barman. "What can I get you?" His voice had the softly lilting tone of a local.

As Neil approached he removed his coat and dropped it to a nearby bench. "I'll have brandy. Better make it a double."

Propping an elbow on the bar he surveyed the room, noting the corn dollies tied over the entrance to the saloon bar. He coughed lightly. "My car's conked out about half a mile up the road."

The barman remained with his back facing Neil as he unclipped an optic and changed bottles.

"I think it's just a flat battery. Is there a garage around here?"

The barman turned around and stood the brandy glass down before him. "Won't be open this time of night, I'm afraid," he said. "But Willum will be in for his regular shortly. He never misses, even on a night like this. Works at the garage, he does. He'll be 'appy to give you 'and, you can be sure."

Neil thanked the barman and headed for the overstuffed armchair in front of the fireplace. He hated the idea of being stuck in this God-forsaken hole any longer than was necessary, but if he had to suffer a delay this at least seemed as good a place to wait as any. The rich smell of brine-dampened wood assailed his nostrils. Carved into a blackened beam above the fire was a date: 1844. Farming and fishing implements, none less than a century old, hung from the walls.

The brandy tickled fingers of fire at the back of his throat. Dreading the thought of stepping back into the cold tonight, he allowed his eyes to close, and listened to the rain pattering at the window like showers of needles, backed by the persistent distant roar of the sea.

How ironic that his father's death had brought about such a change in his own fortunes, he thought. The old man had been penniless all his life. A patient, methodical craftsman, uninterested in personal gain, he had been deeply ashamed of his son's frenzied dreams of acquiring wealth. What would he have thought to see the ludicrous freezer center that had been built on the site of his beloved house? Neil had carefully built up the business and sold it for a fortune. He'd be able to do the same thing, too, with the Wretling farm. Put up his final DIY supermart and sell the chain off at the peak of its profitability. All it took was a clever idea to make money, and Neil had hit upon a winner. He built vast stores in small towns, undercut the local competition, then let his rivals know that he could be persuaded to sell up for the right amount . . .

The door banged, and Neil turned to see a bull of a man in an oil-stained sweater stride to the bar.

"Ev'nin,' Willum," said the barman, already drawing up a pint of best bitter. "There's someone wants to 'ave a word with you." He nodded to the portly city gent drowsing in the corner armchair, his raincoat steaming by the fire. "Needs to borrow your jump leads by the sound of it."

Willum lifted his pint in a meaty hand, drained a third of it and strode over to the fireplace.

"Car won't start, eh mister?" Neil sat up and faced the speaker, who pulled a sodden wool cap from his head and tossed it down next to the grate.

"That's right, it's . . ."

"The flashy Porsche, just past the crossroads?" The big man grinned broadly. "Very nice, too. Still, not much good if it doesn't go, eh?" He took another swig from his pint and watched Neil's face with amusement. "Now the problem, see, is that I'm not in the truck tonight. One o' my mates has borrowed it. But don't you worry, he'll be along in a minute and then we can go and fix your flashy car." Willum settled his huge bulk on to a stool which barely seemed capable of taking his weight. "Mind, I'll 'ave to ask you for a little something." He rubbed his thumb and forefinger together. "For the inconvenience, like, on such a nasty night."

"Yes, of course," agreed Neil, nodding his head vigorously. He had concluded his business in the village, had seen for himself that the Wretling property was indeed now empty, and just wanted to get the hell back to civilization.

"We don't get many of your lot around 'ere at this time o' year," said Willum. "Smart city types, I mean."

Neil noticed that he had drained his pint pot and was now staring intently into it in a crude hint for a refill.

"Here, let me get you another." Neil rose and took the glass from his fist.

"Thank you kindly. Very nice of you."

As Neil returned with fresh drinks the door opened again and two farm laborers entered. They were followed by a wizened old man in an enormous dripping plastic mac who was immediately hailed by Willum and beckoned over to a stool. As Neil distributed drinks, Willum laid a heavy hand on his arm.

"This 'ere is Mick. Could you maybe get him a pint too?"

"Of course." Irritated, Neil crossed back to the bar and dug for his wallet once more. Upon his return, Mick and Willum abruptly halted their conversation as if they'd been discussing him.

"I seen you before," said Mick once they were all settled.

"Could be," said Neil in a carefully noncommittal manner. "I'm sometimes in these parts on business." The old man eyed him thoughtfully.

"I was telling Mick 'ere about your little problem," said Willum, already well into his second pint.

"That's the trouble with them cars," said Mick, suddenly brightening. "They'se all very well for impressing the girls, but give 'em a dose of country weather an' they're buggered. Fools' cars, I call 'em." His hooded grey eyes stared mirthlessly at Neil as a log dropped in the grate.

"Well, we better get the gen'leman fixed, Mick," said Willum, tugging at the old man's arm. He held out a broad palm and grinned at Neil. "Give us the keys and we'll be back in a jiffy. You stay here. Don't want you ruinin' your fine suit in the rain."

Neil reached his hand into his pocket, then hesitated. "I think perhaps I ought to come along with you."

"Now where's the sense in that? Stay here in the warm and we'll bring the car around to you."

Neil handed over the chunky gold key ring and Willum slipped it into his pocket with a wink and a nod to Mick.

"Are they to be trusted?" Neil asked the barman after the two mechanics had ventured out into the night.

"Mick and Willum? Oh, they're as honest as the day is long. Mind you, I wouldn't want to get on the wrong side of 'em. Willum has a terrible temper. See that?" He pointed to an oak beam which formed part of the doorway to the public bar. A section of the wood had been shattered and repainted at some point in the past.

"Willum did that with his fist," said the barman. "Can't remember why now. Over a girl, I think." Neil lowered his eyes to his drink, disturbed that such a neanderthal should be in control of his car.

"I know you, don't I?" A hatchet-faced woman was leaning forward from the next bar stool and examining his face. "You're old Mr. Hawkley's son. You was at the funeral." The woman appeared to be the resident barfly, judging from the fact that her gin glass had a name engraved on it. Martha, it looked like.

"Your father told me a lot about you," said Martha, her voice rising as the recollection grew. "I knew about you." She took a swig from her glass and slowly turned her back on him.

For his part, Neil was surprised that anyone remembered him. He was always careful to keep a low profile in the towns where he had dealings, particularly here, where his father had lived.

"That right?" said the barman, picking up on a fragment of the conversation. "Old Man Hawkley was your father?"

"Er, yes, he was." There was no point in Neil denying it.

"You heard they pulled his house down to build a store, then?" asked the barman, his eyes narrowing. "Awful it was. They had no right to do that, no right at all."

"Yes, I did hear something about it," admitted Neil, carefully studying his glass. "Perhaps you'd care to join me in a drink?"

"No, thank you sir, too early for me." The barman returned to his glass polishing as Neil headed back to the quiet corner by the fireplace. He felt suddenly tired, the hours spent on the road today beginning to catch up with him. After a few minutes in the old armchair, he fell fast asleep.

"You flooded that engine good and proper trying to start it, didn't you?"

Neil awoke with a start to find Willum standing before him wiping oil-tipped fingers down the front of his filthy sweater. For a second he could not recall his surroundings, the amber grate, the murmuring background, the chink of glasses. Everything seemed alien and distorted.

"We've had 'er goin' once or twice, but she won't stay turnin' over." Willum looked across to Mick for corroboration and found the old man more interested in his fresh pint.

"Well, what would you recommend that I do?" asked Neil, annoyed. His face was slick with sweat from sitting too close to the fire. He ran his fingers lightly over his hair to make sure that the strands had not fallen out of place.

"You're goin' to have to give it another 'alf hour or so at least. Your engine's in a terrible state. Don't know much about cars, do you?"

"Where is it now?" Neil's temples throbbed. His mouth was dry. He needed a drink, something cold and refreshing.

"It's around the back, where it's nice and dry."

"And I'll be able to start it in half an hour?"

"Not without this, you won't." Willum dangled the distributor cap in his hand for a moment, then snatched it away and headed for the bar.

"What . . . !" Neil rose from his armchair and followed the mechanic to the end of the counter where he had begun to strike up a conversation with Martha, the gin-soak. Pushing between them he turned to face Willum, whose friendly face now bore a distinct trace of anger.

"What do you mean? Is there something else wrong with the engine?"

"No," said Willum, suddenly grinning at Martha as if sharing a private joke. "I just don't think that you should be leaving until we've settled a price."

Neil was about to point out that Willum had really done nothing to fix the car, then thought better of it. He reached his hand into his jacket and withdrew his wallet.

"All right," he said with an air of resignation. "How much do I owe you?"

"How much do you got?" Willum beamed down at Mick, who released a wheeze of laughter. Neil was unable to decipher the look which passed between them.

"Well, it was just a stalled engine . . ."

"Still stopped you from getting anywhere tonight, didn't it? There'll be an overtime charge o' course. Don't worry about cash. You can write out a check."

Neil began to wonder just what kind of a bill he was in for. He dug for his checkbook.

"Just make it payable to me. William Wretling."

Neil's heart skipped a beat as the smile began to fall from the young mechanic's face.

"I didn't think . . ."

"That the Wretlings had any children," completed Willum. "Well, mister city gent, you thought wrong, didn't you?" Willum stepped closer. He towered above the businessman, breathing beer fumes down into his sweating upturned face. From the corner of his eye Neil saw the barman slip from behind the counter to the front of the pub and discreetly draw a wooden bar across the door.

"I told you I knew about you," said Martha, tapping him on the shoulder. Her words slurred into one another. "I used to run the corner store near your dad's place. Till we went out o' business."

"We know what you're up to," Willum cut in. "You're going to tear down our farm. I knew it were you, soon as I saw the papers you left in your car."

Neil silently cursed himself for leaving the blueprints of the

Wretling place lying open on the passenger seat of the Porsche. It meant that this bumpkin standing before him had seen his plans for the DIY center. But all was not lost. These were simple people, and his guile was more than a match for them. He could run rings around yokels like Willum, even if they were physically more powerful than he.

"Now look," he said with a tentative smile. "I can understand your sadness in losing the old farm, but I promise you that things will work out fine for all of us. If I can explain my plans for your property . . ."

The rest of the pub had grown silent now, the customers lowering their drinks to watch him. Neil could feel the sweat beginning to trickle across his forehead, but before he could raise a hand to wipe it away, Willum thumped him in the chest with a meaty fist.

"I'm not listenin' to your fancy words. You already talked my ma into sellin' the farm. I couldn't run it—I got my own business to attend to. I never expected her to sign it over, just like that."

Willum stopped, his reddened face halfway between anger and sadness. Neil could see that he was confused. Now was the time to strike back.

"But Willum, may I call you that? Willum, you have to understand that times are changing. People can't afford the upkeep of these big old places any more, so they sell to us. We are the benefactors of your kind, providing you with capital . . ."

"Lies. Just like the lies he told his own father." The barman cut into the conversation. "He was a good man, old Hawkley. He hoped that his son would settle here one day. Guess he thought the surroundings might make a better person out of you."

"Now look." Willum pressed Neil back against the bar, prodding him in the ribs with a thick forefinger. "You've already hurt us once with your damned redevelopments. I'm not lettin' you leave 'ere until I have your promise that nothing will happen to the Wretling farm."

Neil breathed a sigh of relief. He could lie to the mechanic, lie to everyone in the pub if necessary, leave in a hearty hail of promises and conduct his future plans for the Wretling place through local agents. After tonight, he need never set foot in this blighted spot again.

"I'm a reasonable man," he said, smiling at the assembled group. "I understand how you feel. Believe me, if I'd had any idea that Mrs. Wretling had family still interested in the property . . . Perhaps you'd be interested in buying the place from me?''

"He can't do that," said Mick. "He hasn't enough money to pay for the garage, let alone the farm."

"I want you to promise that you'll not knock it down, that's all." Willum was beginning to realize the weakness of his bargaining position.

That's better, thought Neil, he's starting to smarten up. "I'm willing to enter into negotiations," he offered, raising his glass. "Of course, I can't promise . . ."

"On paper. You'll promise on paper. Or you don't leave here." Willum grabbed Neil's hand and closed it over his brandy glass.

"Now, Willum . . ." the barman cautioned, moving nervously forward.

"Promise." Willum's grip tightened. Neil could feel the glass warping in the palm of his hand as the mechanic's fist crushed down.

"Now look, I don't respond to physical vio . . ." The glass shattered, cutting Neil's palm wide.

"You maniac! You bloody maniac!" Neil clutched his palm as blood began to pool and flow. Somebody to the left of him reached forward and checked his hand for shards of glass.

"Look, I'm sorry about this. You'd better leave." The barman offered him a wad of paper napkins. Willum looked away, ashamed and stupid.

"You're damned right I'm leaving," shouted Neil. "Bloody peasants, stick to something you understand, like digging the ground." The blood from his torn palm was beginning to blossom through the layers of napkin. "You know what's going up in place of your farm? A hypermarket. I'll run your crummy little businesses out of town."

Drawing himself to his full height, he passed through the group and collected his overcoat. Behind him an argument broke out between Willum and the barman. The mechanic had obviously overstepped the mark this time. He'd probably be banned from the pub. As Neil reached the door the barman caught up with him. He's probably going to offer me an apology, Neil thought.

"I'm sorry, Mr. Hawkley, but we can't let you leave." Neil stopped in his tracks, stunned.

"He's right, is Willum. You must sign the paper. It's our livelihoods, you understand."

"I won't make any such promise," Neil said, attempting to reduce the quaver of anger in his voice. "How dare you threaten me! I'll have that gorilla up for assault if you don't get out of my way."

"You *have* to sign."

Neil spun round. Everyone in the bar had turned towards him. Looking from one to the other, he could see in their faces the beaten contours of a lonely, hostile land. He knew then that they needed him to sign, not for personal gain or pride, but to hold together the threadbare skein that allowed their daily survival.

"Ned, what do we need to draw up a legal document?" called the barman, gently moving Neil away from the bolted door.

Ned, an elderly man seated in the center of the bar, rubbed his unshaven chin thoughtfully. "Any piece of paper'll do. Must be dated and signed by witnesses, though. Then you got to get it stamped, legal-like."

"I'll take it down to solicitors in the mornin'," said Willum, carefully filling a sheet of ruled writing paper with block letters.

While those at the bar checked the document they had drawn up, Neil was held in his armchair by the two labourers. He could not believe what was happening. He certainly had no intention of signing away his rights to the farmhouse, but how could he avoid it? He looked around the cozy lounge, with its floral drapes and oak beams, its ploughblades and hoes in their place on the walls, and realized that something was missing . . . Two hooks and a blank space on the wall above the fireplace indicated that an object had been removed in the last few minutes. But what?

"You're wanted over here, mister city gent," called Willum, beckoning. "Your signature, please."

The two laborers hoisted Neil from the chair and brought him to the bar. Mick slid over the sheet of paper and shoved a Biro into his blood-crusted palm. All eyes turned to him.

"I can't write properly like this—my hand." He affected a look of pain and splayed his fingers to the assembled group.

"You'll just have to do the best you can," said the barman sternly.

"Can I go to the bathroom and wash it first?" he pleaded. "It hurts."

Willum moved forward to grab at his lapel, but Martha pushed him back. "Let him go for a minute, it's all right."

As Neil walked unsteadily towards the toilet, the unmistakable thrill of triumph began to grow in him. Willum had returned his car keys. The fingers of his good hand closed around them in his jacket pocket. The toilet sported a large opaque window which opened out on to parking spaces in a shed at the rear of the pub. And hadn't Willum conveniently moved his car back there?

Once inside the cool, tiled lavatory he crossed to the sink and, kneeling up on it, slipped open the catch on the window casement. As slowly and as gently as possible he pushed the lower half of the window up. It rose about two feet then jammed, but Neil could see that the gap was easily wide enough for him to climb through.

Hauling himself up on to the sink, he lifted his legs out of the window, then his torso, and finally pushed off into the darkness.

"He's been gone a long time." It was Willum who broke the uneasy silence in the lounge bar.

"Will you stop worryin'?" said Martha. "He'd not get far, even if he had designs of leavin'. I made sure o' that." Her eyes brought Willum's attention to the empty space above the mantel.

The height Neil fell was no more than three feet, but the excruciating shock he suddenly experienced in his left leg at first suggested that he had fallen a much greater distance.

Through a haze of pain he looked down and saw that an ancient animal trap had been primed and set just beneath the window. Its rusty square jaws had slammed shut on his skin, biting their way through the expensive material of his suit, through flesh and veins, down into bone. He stifled a cry as he reached down and tried to prise the jaws apart, but the trap was too large and the strength was already ebbing from his arms. Pieces of bloody shattered bone stuck up from the crushed teeth of the trap as each move he made caused the jaws to close tighter.

His foot grew numb, the pain receding as the steel teeth bit through the nerves of his leg. He looked wildly up, now desperate to reach his car before the others came looking for him. If they were capable of doing this, they were surely capable of anything. The Porsche was nowhere in sight. Unless there was an extension to the shed, Willum had lied to him.

Ahead was the sea wall, and beyond that a low arc of dark sand leading to the lighted homes at the far side of the bay. He had to get away from these people, but how? Pulling himself forward with a scrape of steel on concrete, he released a scream as the movement cause the trap to chafe and dig its way deeper into the bone of his shin.

Against the sea wall lay the severed branch of a tree. He tried to sweep the clouds of pain from his head and think. Could he use it to lever open the steel maw encompassing his leg? Falling gratefully to the wall he sobbed as he pushed the branch between the steel jaws. Fresh blasts of rain swept down on him as he strained with all his might to prise the contraption open. He pushed again, the palm of his injured hand searing as the branch bit into it, but slowly the steel teeth rose away from his leg, first by an inch, then two. As the pressure on his shin lessened, the relief it afforded was blessed beyond all measure. Then with a crack the branch snapped in half and the jaws slammed shut, biting deeper even than before, almost shearing the bone in two, causing him to scream into the biting rain-laden wind.

Behind, the regulars of the Sun in the Sands appeared around the corner of the building.

"Bloody hell, Martha, you weren't muckin' about, were you?" said Willum, his eyes widening in fright. "You gone and done it now. We'll go to jail for this."

"I was right, though. Slippery devil was trying to get away, wasn't 'e?"

"Better get that damned thing off his leg before it cuts right through," said the barman, slowly approaching.

"You get away from me!" screamed Neil, lifting himself over the wall and dropping down on to the sand. It was his only hope. If he could just make it over the marshy flatland to the houses on the far side, he'd find someone to take him in. Then he swore there'd be hell to pay.

"Stop him!" shouted one of the laborers. "Before he gets out too far!"

The group gathered at the edge of the sea wall, shouting in confusion and watching helplessly as Neil limped out over the sand, his shattered leg dragging the heavy steel trap behind him.

The pain in his shin was receding, only flaring up when he rested his weight on the damaged leg, which had now grown as numb as a stick. In the distance the sea boomed mournfully, a thin band of grey on the horizon. What was it they were all shouting? Why weren't they coming after him? Were they fearful that he could be seen by the occupants of the bay's overlooking houses?

Yard after yard he painfully hauled himself over the sand, the animal trap clumping behind him, never loosening its hold. Neil was aware that the bitter driving rain was the only thing preventing him from losing consciousness. Soon he was more than halfway across, and the group by the pub could no longer be heard. The sand sucked at his shoes, finally pulling one free and causing him to stumble to his knees. The pain in his shattered leg suddenly began to increase. Neil turned, long strands of hair flopping into his eyes. The trap was being swallowed by the sand. Already, half of it had vanished beneath the slick, cold surface of the beach. Quicksand? He hadn't heard of such things in this area, but that was what it most assuredly was. Along this stretch of coastline a man would have to be extremely heavy for the tidal currents beneath the marsh to succeed in sucking him down. But the deep tramlines cut across the sand by the steel trap attested to his newly increased weight. Slowly, inexorably, the trap continued to disappear beneath the sluggish grey sand, its shining moon-reflected surface fractured by the falling rain.

Neil felt himself being pulled sideways as the trap hastened in its descent. His only hope was to sever his leg completely before the contraption dragged him under. Flinging his whole body forward, he slammed his fists down on the jaw of the trap, encouraging it to bite deeper and deeper into the bone, tearing and grinding until his leg was a mass of tattered flesh. Screaming until his lungs were raw, he hammered at the device, but still it held fast. The bone was surely broken through, but still the skin and muscle surrounding it refused to tear apart. He ripped at the leg with his bare hands, digging his fingers deep within the flesh and tearing the muscle out in strips. As the sand closed over him, his struggles increased the angle of his descent and he slowly slipped from sight, the grey mud choking and filling his mouth, his windpipe, and finally his eyes, until all that remained on the surface of the beach, thrusting up from the sand, was a tuft of lacquered hair and a raised little finger bearing a smart gold ring.

"We'd better go back inside," said Martha. "We'll catch our deaths out here."

"Oh Lord," said Willum, wringing his huge hands as he turned away from the grisly scene on the beach. "We can't never tell a soul 'bout this, not till the day we die."

"Oh, don't take on so," said Martha. "You got yourself a nice new car."

"Better not drive it for a while yet, though," said old Mick. "Better do some work on it first."

As the group turned away and slowly trooped back to the warmth of the lounge bar, the barman hung back for a moment and surveyed the rainswept beach.

"At least Old Man Hawkley got his wish," he said to Willum's retreating back. "His son finally settled here. In the sands."

For the rest of the evening it was doubles all round.

HOT AIR

"**H**E'S DRUNK," SAID Paula. "Listen to this." She passed the headphones over to Karen, who removed her hair-band and slipped them over her ears. "How am I supposed to decipher that?"

Karen listened for a moment, then returned the headphones with a grimace. "I wouldn't bother," she said. "You know why he gives you dictation late on a Friday. It's not got a lot to do with encouraging British exports."

The two typists laughed softly together. Two desks away, Miss MacKendrick swivelled around and stared sourly at them before returning to the wads of computer paper besieging her desk.

Both girls had recently turned eighteen, and were newly employed by Symax & Co., a monolithic Japanese-owned city corporation which exported British components to the Germans with the aid of American finance. Neither girl knew much about the company beyond the fact that it had been featured in a series of glamorous TV commercials, but Paula, the more ambitious of the two, was determined to move up from the typing pool at the first available opportunity.

Reluctantly, she began the sisyphean task of deciphering the area manager's drunken dialect and transposing it to paper. Karen was supposed to be coordinating the reports in readiness for the company's traditional Monday morning meeting, but she sat with her chin on the heel of her hand, idly snapping a stapler and staring across the vast open-plan office to where Mr. Felix sat.

Unaware that he was being observed, the tall, blond-haired accounts manager sat running his fingers lightly over the touch-panel of the adding machine. His dark eyes matched the blue of his suit. Occasionally he would pause and look up, absently flicking his hair over the back of his jacket collar, lost in thought.

"He plays squash, you know," said Karen. "I saw the handle sticking out of his briefcase."

"If you're that crazy about him, you should go over and have a word," said Paula.

"It's no use, what would he see in me? I can't play squash."

"You can't type, either," said Miss MacKendrick, suddenly looming between the desks like a tanker coming into port. "I assume this reads 'rental agreement' rather than 'rectal agreement'. Amend accordingly, please." She dropped the page of type back on Karen's desk.

"Good night, Mr. Felix," called Karen as he walked by on his way to the elevator bank at five thirty. "Have a nice weekend." The accounts manager paused to tuck a sheaf of papers into his briefcase, then turned and smiled with surprise, a sapphire twinkle playing in his eyes.

"Thanks . . . ."

"Karen."

"Thanks, Karen. You have a good one, too."

"He spoke to me!" screamed Karen moments after the lift doors had shut. "I really think he's interested."

"On the basis of your conversation so far I'd say that was a little difficult to judge," said Paula, switching off her typewriter and searching the floor for its dustcover.

"It's all right for you, you already have a boyfriend."

"Had, Karen. He's changed his mind again. He says he's feeling pressurized."

"That's what men always say when they want to dump you," said Karen carelessly. "Well, just remember that I saw Mr. Felix first."

"Don't worry, Karen," said Paula, irked, "I wouldn't want your Mr. Felix if I needed him for a bone marrow transplant."

She swung her bag on to her shoulder and left the office just as the first drops of rain began hitting the windows.

"I wonder how he is," Karen sighed, looking over at the empty chair on the other side of the room. "That's three days he's been off work now."

Paula irritably abandoned the Dictaphone and turned to her friend. "I heard he's sick. It's this new kind of flu that's going around."

"Not another one! People are always getting ill in this office. I'm sure it's the air conditioning. Did you know you whistle while you're typing? It's very irritating."

"I'm trying to work."

"Don't you think he's gorgeous, though?" asked Karen, lifting her chin from her hands. "I mean, honestly."

"Who, Mr. Felix? He's a bit of a smooth mover." Paula flicked strands of long, black hair from her eyes and removed the paper from her typewriter. "I think I prefer someone a little more rugged. Mr. Clarke, perhaps." She crouched forward over the sheet and dabbed away at it with her Tipp-Ex fluid.

"Oh no," laughed Karen, wrinkling her nose. "Mr. Clarke looks like a child molester. And that awful hand."

Mr. Clarke was a strange, sour-smelling accountant who shaved badly and wore ill-fitting brown suits. One of his hands was badly deformed as the result of an unspecified accident which had occurred in his childhood. The girls in the pool treated him as a figure of fun, but in truth they were all slightly disturbed by his unflinching gaze. Short straws were drawn when he requested someone for dictation.

"He hates Mr. Felix, haven't you noticed?"

Paula lowered a sheaf of papers into a drawer and slid it shut. Office politics bored her. "No, I hadn't. Why would he hate him?"

"Because he got passed over when they promoted Mr. Felix."

"I'm not surprised," she murmured, glancing at her watch.

Suddenly, Karen sat up and raised her hand. "It's twelve thirty, Miss MacKendrick," she called in a sweet voice. "OK to go to lunch?"

Outside the rain fell from a blackened, sluggish sky, staining the brickwork of Symax & Co. to a dirty grey. Paula peered suspiciously over the collar of her mackintosh as Karen struggled with her umbrella.

"You could be right, you know, about the air conditioning. It's so hot and stuffy in there. The change in temperature can't be good for you."

"Everyone's been off with something at some point this winter," said Karen vaguely, raising the umbrella above their heads. "And now Mr. Felix. You wait, it'll be exactly the same in the summer. These new buildings, the windows are sealed tight. No fresh air from the street."

"There was never much fresh air in this street to begin with," Paula pointed out.

The girls fell in step on their way to the cafeteria, carefully avoiding the damaged paving stones which had filled with murky

rainwater. Overhead, the pregnant clouds held little promise of
a pleasant afternoon.

The following Tuesday morning was as dark as night and
heavy with veils of misty rain, but the office windows of Symax &
Co. shone with bright, false light. The overhead fluorescent
panels of the third-floor typing pool were turned on at 7:30
a.m. by the janitors and succeeded in clearing the enormous
room of any lingering shadows. As Paula stepped from the lift,
her coat dripping, dry heat enveloped her and warm artificial air
filled her nostrils. She tried to pretend that she was alighting
from an aircraft into the tropics, but beeping telephones and the
steady tacking of word processors quickly dispelled the dream.
As she pulled the plastic cover from her IBM she again noted
Mr. Felix's empty chair and bare desk, visible through a single
partition of fluted glass on the other side of the office.

"Apparently," said Stacy, a young West Indian girl who would
have made a better gossip columnist than Dictaphone typist,
"he's not coming back. He's gone yellow, he's that sick."

"What's wrong with him?" asked Paula, wondering where
on earth Stacy garnered her information. As they spoke, Karen
was removing her raincoat at the next desk and shaking it out.

"Nobody knows," Stacy whispered mysteriously. "But apparently, it's catching. That's why somebody's come and taken
his things away. I'm told they had to burn everything that was
infected."

Together the three typists stared over at the empty chair.

"Now there's been a lot of silly talk in this office about Mr.
Felix," said Miss MacKendrick in her best schoolmistress voice.
She reminded Paula of the woman at the birth control clinic, all
open air and common sense. The typists had been called to
attention by their supervisor halfway through the morning. As
they had all been wearing headphones, Miss MacKendrick had
been forced to shout at them until someone looked up. By way
of revenge she stood at the back of the room, making everyone
turn around in their seats.

"Most of you are aware that Mr. Felix has been taken ill, but
I am assured that his illness is not contagious, and has certainly
posed no danger to any members of the staff. I really don't know
where these rumors start." Miss MacKendrick looked as if she
were about to come down amongst them with a ruler and whack
a few ears.

"I'm sure you'll join me in wishing him a speedy recovery.

Meanwhile I trust you will appreciate the reduction in your workload until his return.''

''He won't be back,'' whispered Stacy despondently. ''Not if they've cleared out his desk. We'll be lucky if we even hear about the funeral.''

''He looked fine the last time he was in the office,'' said Paula. ''He was planning to come in the next day, because I remember he was taking work home with him.''

''That's what I mean. It's these new germs. They creep up on you without warning. I read about it somewhere. One minute you feel fine, the next—bingo, you're on the way out.'' Stacy gave a shrug of resignation. ''Medical science is baffled by new germs, it was in the paper.''

After this, the rest of the day seemed to pass in a cloud of gloom.

Wednesday was not a good day either. In the morning the sun surprised everyone at Symax & Co. by actually appearing in the sky from 9:06 a.m. until 11:42 a.m., at which point it retreated behind a wall of cloud like a frightened gazelle and remained hidden for the rest of the day. Karen arrived late with a glistening nose and a cardigan bulging with tissues, and Paula was summoned for dictation by the appalling and sinister Mr. Clarke.

The accountant's office was full of the smells Paula associated with old men—pipe tobacco, smoke and sickness, sour and indefinable.

Mr. Clarke, hair scraped greasily across his bald patch, was a study of unrealized potential, full of irritated tutting and bitter little asides. Although only in his late forties he walked with a stoop, moving with the reactions of a much older man. There were no framed photographs on his desk, no childish drawings pinned on his wall. It was obvious that no woman cared for his clothes.

Paula positioned herself as far away from him as possible when transcribing his letters. Sometimes he would stop in the middle of a sentence and she would look up, only to find him staring at her breasts with narrowed eyes. Then he would quickly lower his gaze and continue with the dictation. As he ushered her out of the office, he stood in the doorway so that she would have to pass beneath his outstretched arm. He rarely said anything complimentary. In fact, he seemed to have trouble managing to maintain a common civility between them at all. Paula found this paradoxical in a man who so obviously lusted after her. On the way out of the room he allowed his deformed hand to brush the top of her thigh. For a second she felt the damp heat of his twisted fingers through the cotton of her skirt.

Back in the typing pool she laughed about the incident with Karen. It was the only way she could prevent herself from shivering with disgust. She knew that it was wrong to be disturbed by a physical abnormality, but sensed that Mr. Clarke had found an unhealthy use for his handicap, enjoying the look of fear on the women he touched.

On Friday morning they were told that Mr. Felix would not be coming back to work.

"What did I tell you?" hissed Stacy conspiratorially. "He's dead, but nobody will admit it because they're scared it'll cause a panic."

"Rubbish," said Paula. "If the truth be known, he was probably caught fiddling and asked to resign. Here, have one of these." She passed a box of throat lozenges over to Karen, who had recently developed a hacking cough.

"Maybe you've got what *he* had," said Stacy gloomily. "You should ask Miss MacKendrick to move you away from the ventilation system. It's blowing hot air over you all day. You don't know who's been breathing it before you. Haven't you noticed the funny smell it has?"

"Stacy, you obviously have a minimal grasp of modern science," said Paula, irritably squaring a stack of folders and sitting down. "The air's recycled, like on a plane, so even if Mr. Felix *had* died of something—which I'm sure he hasn't—you wouldn't catch it from the air." She waved her thumb at Karen. "Honestly, you'll have her wearing garlic around her neck next."

Deflated, Stacy returned to her desk.

"I really don't feel well at all," said Karen. She coughed and spat discreetly into a handkerchief as Paula looked on, her face creased with concern.

At five twenty-five, just as the lifts had begun to fill with homebound passengers, Stacy returned from her dictation with Mr. Clarke. "I'm going to have to see the supervisor about him," she said, straightening her skirt. "He's getting worse with his touching. And so pleased with himself. Apparently he's been officially appointed to take over from Mr. Felix. He's even using Mr. Felix's old briefcase, if you please."

"You must be mistaken," said Paula absently. She pulled the

cover over her typewriter and switched off the desk light. "Mr. Felix took his briefcase home with him the last night he was here."

"Gold initials, two leather straps?"

"That's right."

"Then I'm not mistaken. Wait, hold that for me!" Stacy ran for the lift as the doors began to close.

As the office lights were turned out Paula looked back at the bare desk beyond the glass partition. Thunder rumbled somewhere overhead, rattling the darkened windows. Shuddering, she grabbed her overcoat and left.

"There's obviously some kind of bug going around," said Miss MacKendrick the following Monday. "I really wouldn't let it worry you."

"I'm sorry," said Paula from the other side of the supervisor's desk, "but I can't help wondering. Karen's off sick now, along with four other girls, and they're all from this department."

"It's the sort of thing that happens every winter, Paula." Miss MacKenrick adjusted her spectacles to the end of her nose. "You girls go around with hardly anything on. You have to be sensible and wrap up warm in weather like this. A hat guards against ear infections. Try eating an orange occasionally."

"You're missing my point, Miss MacKendrick. It all seemed to start when Mr. Felix was taken ill. Something's making us sick. If he did have a contagious disease then I think we should be told."

Miss MacKendrick removed her spectacles and looked up. She thought for a moment. "You seem a sensible girl," she said quietly. "If I tell you something in confidence will you promise not to let the others know?"

"Yes, Miss MacKendrick, of course," Paula lied blithely.

Miss MacKendrick's ample frame leaned forward in a confidential posture. "Mr. Felix was not actually taken ill," she said finally. "He went missing. The police have been in. I understand that he was under some pressure at home. It was not deemed necessary to inform you girls at the time." She leaned back in her chair. "So you see, there's absolutely nothing for you to worry about."

On Wednesday Paula developed a migraine that, despite a variety of remedies, would not go away. It seemed at its worst towards the end of the afternoon, clouding her perceptions and fragmenting her concentration as she stared at the stack of paper on her desk, massaging throbbing temples. Strange new faces surrounded her, temporary secretaries filling in until the sick full-time employees returned. None of them were familiar with the workings of the company, so Paula and the other long-term girls were forced to spend extra time explaining procedures and operating the advanced-technology copiers and word processors.

It was only at home later in the evening that the thudding pain in her head subsided and she was able to sink into a deep and merciful sleep.

On Thursday morning the migraine returned, so she excused herself after lunch and went to visit Karen, who now seemed much better and ready to return to work.

"I'm not coming back to Symax though," she said firmly. "That's where I got sick in the first place."

"But there was nothing wrong with Mr. Felix," said Paula. She explained what the supervisor had told her.

"I don't care what she told you," said Karen. "The man wasn't well. I'll go temping for a while. I don't want to go back into that building. You couldn't be a love and collect my wages for me, could you? Oh, and hand this in for me, too." She dug around in the pocket of a coat which hung on the back of her bedroom door, then passed Paula a long-barrelled key with a label attached to the end of it.

"What's this?" Paula turned the key over in her hand. The writing on the label was barely legible: FIREDOOR 3.

"I think it belongs to old Clarke. I found it down the back of the seat when I was taking dictation. I meant to give it to him myself."

"But you thought you'd let me do it. Thanks a lot, Karen."

Paula slipped the key into her pocket and left.

It was not until Friday evening that she remembered where she had seen it before.

Since Karen had the better typewriter, Paula took over her desk. She had dealt her ever-present migraine a hefty blow with the ingestion of four large headache pills and was now working on a report that Mr. Clarke required for a presentation the following morning. The old accountant remained in his office, waiting to check the finished document before leaving the building for the night.

For Paula, the overtime pay made it worth staying on late. Besides, since she had broken off with her boyfriend there really wasn't anything to rush home for. The clock at the end of the room read a quarter past seven. The building was quiet now. Even the steady hum of the air conditioning had dropped to a faint murmur. As Paula tapped at the keyboard she began to whistle tunelessly, the blank pages filling with type before her eyes.

She stopped and looked up. A distant sound, electronic. Gone now. She continued typing.

There it was again. A series a faint beeps. Now it had stopped.

Experimentally, she whistled a few bars. The beeping, hollow and distorted, recommenced. It seemed to be coming from the air-conditioning unit. She reached up and pressed her ear to the plastic ventilation grille, where warm, slightly scented air lifted the ends of her hair. Each time she whistled, the beeping resumed. The shaft attached to the unit ran down the wall and into the floor. Odd, she thought, rising from her chair and stretching. She peered through the grille but could see nothing.

Clattering down the metal stairs that led to the boiler room she began to ask herself if she wasn't being a little irrational. It was stupid, pointless and yet . . . There in the gloom of the lower stairwell she fitted the key to the lock and turned it.

The bright red door swung slowly open. Reaching to the inside wall, her fingers made contact with a battery of light switches. One by one, she clicked them on. Strings of bulbs illuminated a place of vast metal ventilation shafts and pipes. Square tunnels of burnished steel ran from a central boiler seated behind a wall of white-painted breeze blocks. The basement was a hot-house, an inferno of hard, dry heat. Paula took a few steps forward, her shoes clicking on the white concrete floor.

Mr. Felix had been the fire officer for the third floor. She had often seen the large bunch of safety keys on his desk. They were supposed to stay in the office at all times, but he had been forever losing them. That was, until he had bought himself one of those plastic key rings that gave an electronic beep when you whistled.

She walked further into the basement and gave a tentative whistle. Concealed somewhere within echoing sheets of metal, the electronic beeper answered.

The sound was coming from a wide, angled pipe in the dingiest corner of the room. Paula approached it and crouched down beside the large metal screwplate fixed over one side of the pipe. She pursed her lips and blew. The key ring sounded as if it was just the other side of the panel, which appeared to be removable for maintenance access. Mindful of her nails, she carefully unclipped the heavy grey metal catch and allowed the plate to fall back into her hands. It was nearly three feet high, and heavy. With a grunt, she dragged it away across the concrete floor and leaned it against the nearby wall.

Returning, she peered into the pipe, but it was too dark inside to see anything.

"This is no good," she muttered, straightening up and dusting down her skirt. "I need a torch."

A search of the basement failed to locate anything more than a half-empty box of matches. Holding her skirt to her thighs so that she would not snag it on the edges of the square hole, she bent down and stepped inside the vast pipe. A strange smell, sweet and cloying, instantly filled her nostrils and permeated her clothes. She struck a match, shielding it with her hand to protect it from the rush of air. In the flickering light she began to carefully stand upright. Above, a horizontal tunnel ran across the standing pipe to form a T junction. Paula's head and shoulders poked up into the tunnel, which stretched away into pitch black on either side. An eerie whistling filled her ears as the warm air flowed around her and up into the offices above. Every noise she made became magnified, booming mournfully through the maze of hidden shafts. As she stood, she whistled once more and the key ring answered. It could not be more than a few feet away now.

The match went out.

She struck another, lifting her hand as much as she dared into the crossbreeze of warm draughts. There, lying flat on the floor of the horizontal pipe about three feet away, was the key ring. In order to reach it Paula had to pull herself up into the tunnel. At least the floor seemed clean and dry, thanks to the constantly circulating air. Sitting on the edge of the tunnel dangling her legs into the standing pipe by which she had entered, she lit another match. On the third try, it actually stayed alight.

Inching forward, she reached for the key ring, which she instantly recognized as the one belonging to Mr. Felix. There were at least ten keys still attached to it. The bunch had fallen or been tossed beside a pile of rags in the conduit.

But what were they doing here?

Why would someone try to hide . . .

The body fell on her. In the guttering match she saw the rotted face of the corpse as it pressed down against her own, squirming maggots dropping from its eyes into her hair and screaming mouth. The dry air of the ventilation system had half-mummified the once handsome features of the accounts manager so that his teeth were bared in the grinning rictus of a smile.

Her cries echoed and distorted as they thundered through the tunnels above. She fell back to the metal floor of the conduit as the body followed down on top of her. She fought to push it off, but its sheer bulk made it impossible to move in the confined space. For a few seconds Paula laid still, desperately trying to calm herself. Her skin prickled stickily with wriggling larvae. She freed her hands and thrashed at her face and shoulders, sobbing.

The stomach of the corpse was touching her own. It felt as if there was something moving inside it. Her hands reached down and pushed it up and away from her. Suddenly, Felix's jacket opened and his abdomen burst over her in a mass of reeking, writhing life. The hot air had rotted his intestines and filled each bloated cavern with bacteria, germs which had risen through the pipes, wafting in the stinging, disease-laden air, out of the grilles and into every breath she took . . .

She passed out.

"I know you're up there."

Paula slowly raised her throbbing head as a fresh wave of nausea assailed her senses. The horror of her situation came rushing back as she realized that the leaking corpse still lay half-sprawled across her chest and waist.

"I'll have to leave you there if you don't answer."

The voice, there was no mistaking the voice. Mr. Clarke's nasal tones rang in the pipe. He thrust his head up into the hole and surveyed the scene in the tunnel. There was a sudden shaft of torchlight.

"Oh, it's you," he said with a distinct lack of surprise. He reached out his deformed hand and gently touched the top of Paula's head. Then he looked at the body spreadeagled on top of her.

"I thought it would dry out in here. Doesn't look as if it has, though." He ran a finger through the sludge which had pooled around Paula's pinned shoulders.

"There must have been too much liquid in his stomach." He wiped his fingers on the tunnel wall. "I didn't think anyone would find him here. Pity it was you. I rather liked you." He began to descend into the standing pipe.

"Don't leave me here!" screamed Paula. Clarke stopped and

considered for a moment, his greasy hair glinting in the beam of his torch.

"Sorry, but I have to. You'd only go around telling people about me if I let you go. How old are you, my girl?"

"Eighteen," Paula gasped, desperately trying to slide out from under Felix's body. Her legs were free. If she could just roll his chest away from her, she might be able to disentangle herself completely. But how could she get out, with Clarke blocking the exit?

"Eighteen," the accountant sighed. "So young. Well, this is what I'll do. To make things less unpleasant, I'll chloroform you. Then we'll play round a little, you and I. And after that, you can sleep in here with Mr. Felix for the rest of your damned life, you little teasing bitch!" His voice rose into cracked hysteria. "Take a good look at your handsome friend now. He's rather lost his looks, hasn't he?" And with that the torch beam snapped off and Mr. Clarke was suddenly gone, presumably to get the chloroform.

With an agonized shove, Paula pushed against the corpse. There was a sharp crack like a rotten branch giving way, and her fist broke through into its ribcage, her arm sinking deep into the viscous mire. She bit her tongue to keep from screaming as her hand withdrew with a hideous sucking sound and the corpse rolled slowly off her body. Wriggling free to one side of the tunnel she scrambled down into the standing pipe.

Tearing off her putrid clothes, she screwed her skirt and blouse into a ball and tossed it up into the overhead tunnel. Her shoes followed. Then she ducked down through the hatchway and ran out into the basement. It was the only way she could think of minimizing a trail of gore. Her eyes darted around, searching for a weapon in case he suddenly reappeared, but the floor was clear of tools and there were no convenient lengths of pipe to be found.

Across the room, the red entrance door stood wide. Beyond, the whine of the elevator heralded its imminent arrival. She pressed back between the pipes unarmed, thrust into the darkest corner she could find.

Clarke entered the basement.

In one red, contorted hand he held a padded handkerchief, in the other a clear screw-capped bottle. He walked towards the standing pipe, then stopped. Paula held her breath. A maggot dropped from her hair to her breast but she did not dare raise a hand to flick it away. It twisted obscenely back and forth before finally dropping to the floor.

The accountant pulled the top from the chloroform bottle, poured a little liquid on to the handkerchief, then approached the pipe. After a moment he ducked his body and vanished inside.

Paula launched herself across the basement to the panel which lay against the wall. She could hear the muttering echoes of his voice in the tunnel as she lifted the heavy plate and ran with it. The metal edges tore into her palms as she slammed it back into place and dropped the steel catch. There was a shout of anger followed by a reverberating bang as the accountant slammed himself against the inside of the pipe.

"Whore!" he bellowed, "you're dead, dead, do you hear me?"

He was still shouting and slamming his fist against the shaft as she ran from the basement and crashed the door shut behind her.

Heart thudding, she took the stairs. The night porter should be on the ground floor. She would tell him what had happened. No, he was about a hundred years old and virtually deaf, he'd never believe her. Or worse still, he would go down there and open the door.

It was impossible to think straight. She'd call the police from her office. There were some spare clothes in her bag, new jeans and a black T-shirt, thank God she'd forgotten to take her purchases home last night. She ran to the third floor washroom and put her head under a fierce cold tap, spraying icy water everywhere, rinsing the stinking fluids from her hair and arms.

Wadding up as many paper towels as she could, she strip-washed, then scraped back her wet hair. She spat into the sink basin until she had no saliva left, then gargled mouthful after mouthful of fresh cold water. Finally she opened the door of the washroom and forced herself to take deep, slow breaths. The accountant's horrible bellows were still rumbling through distant pipes into the bowels of the building, like the enraged howls of a trapped demon.

She limped out into the corridor. The typing pool was bright and friendly and deserted. Row after row of neat grey dustcovers protected the typewriters. The cleaners had emptied the wastebins and moved on to another part of the office block. At her desk she splashed an entire bottle of perfume over her body before pulling on the T-shirt. She cocked an ear. The bellowing abruptly stopped, and the building subsided into silence.

She lifted the receiver of her telephone and listened. The high-pitched continuous tone told her that the switchboard had closed down for the night. Some of the telephones had night-lines, but she had no idea which ones. She would wait until she was far away before calling the police. The T-shirt felt crisp and clean and fresh on her skin, the purchase tag still attached to the collar. The jeans lay folded in the bottom of the cardboard shopping bag. Reaching down, she pulled them out. She carefully unbuttoned the flies and unclipped the label from the back pocket, concentrating on every action so that it would allow her heartbeat to gradually return to normal.

She was on one leg and about to climb into the jeans when she heard a new sound, a chittering, a squeaking noise like a bat, or nails on steel. Slowly, she turned around.

It was coming from the air conditioner behind her. Letting the jeans fall to the floor, she leaned forward and peered through the grille into the ventilation shaft.

Beyond the gray plastic bars, two mad eyes stared at her from the darkness. Clarke's arms burst through the grille and grabbed her, lifting her feet off the ground in one powerful movement and dragging her screaming into the inky depths of the tunnel.

Eventually, her anguished cries faded down through the steel labyrinth and turned into guttural, sickly echoes of laughter.

Some weeks later Karen applied for a job with a local pharmaceutical firm.

"Now let's find out a little about you," said the kindly interviewer, leaning forward on his blotter. "Which aspect of this job particularly attracted you to our company?"

"The open windows," said Karen with a shiver.

LOST IN LEICESTER SQUARE

ALTHOUGH THE CLUB itself was old and respectable, the building which housed it had definitely seen better days. Gilt-edged architraves bordered the red plush walls of the smoking room, but the carpets showed dark patches of damp, and the warped floorboards beneath them caused the floors to slope. High-backed green leather armchairs still stood in clusters, the daily newspapers were still arranged on a small teak side table, but in the corner there was now—horror of horrors—an illuminated cigarette machine. Jacket and tie were still compulsory wear, of course, but the clientele these days was much younger and more—how did one put it without causing offense?—*cosmopolitan* than it had been before the war. The murmuring of male voices discussing the stock market was now punctuated with the raucous laughter of the wholesale trader. The quiet ticking of the silver Charlemagne hall clock was now often drowned by the bleeping of a radio pager. And while it was true to say that the windows of the smoking room were no longer cleaned so frequently, and that the pewter soda siphons were polished with insufficient attention, at least the same head barman of old still pottered behind the marble counter, still—mercifully—refusing to mix cocktails.

They always occupied the two best-placed armchairs in the room. In truth, they formed the perfect picture of respectable old age. Club ties, smart blazers, pinstriped trousers, chased silver cufflinks and collar studs, gin and tonics standing by in huge cut-glass tumblers, they were two elderly gentlemen who reminded most people of cricket club captains, retired and forever reminiscing.

"And I never hear anything of Cecil these days, either."

"My dear chap, didn't you know? Frightful thing, he went and married some American, Amelia somebody. Sort of person whose intimate conversation could be heard right across the street. Appalling woman.''

"Cecil must have liked her."

"Oh God, yes, doted on her. He sold off the Surrey home and moved into some poky little flat in Belgravia where all the furniture was rented.''

"Good Lord, didn't he mind?''

"Not a bit. Told me that part of the fun of rented furniture was knowing that one day you had to give it all back.''

"No, I meant about giving up Surrey.''

"Well, he'd long since stopped following the cricket. Said that once he'd seen Gary Sobers reach three hundred and sixty-five Not Out back in 1958 there wasn't much else worth watching.''

"Wasn't that the year young Hanif Mohammad had his legendary sixteen-hour innings?''

"Yes, but of course he was a nig-nog. It was a frightful shame about Surrey, but the place was far too big for Cecil to keep up alone.''

"I thought he had a housekeeper living there.''

"Mrs. Fountain? No, she went into hospital in 1973 to have her veins stripped and never came out.''

"Sorry to hear that. Care for another?''

Leather creaked, and cut-glass rang with the sound of fresh ice tumbling in. The afternoon sunlight streamed through the dust-streaked windows, and the two old gentlemen smiled to each other as they recalled the faces of long-dead friends.

His name was Chip Kimberly, he was seventeen years old, he came from Washington, and he was completely lost.

He stood in the center of Leicester Square looking from one side to the other, hoping to see some kind of signpost or wall plate that would indicate the direction of the nearest YMCA, but he found none. This was his first time away from home, and it showed. Sweat stained the seams of his college sweatshirt as he eased the nylon backpack from his shoulders and propped its aluminum frame against the green-painted railings which surrounded the dusty little park.

The paved walkways around the square were thronged with cinema-goers, tourists queuing for cheap theatre tickets, con men selling fake Rolexes from suitcases, drunks, crazies and tramps. Chip stood tall and ea7sed his aching back. He had begun his journey two weeks before in Paris, bidding farewell to his parents at the République Holiday Inn and vowing to meet up with them back in Washington in one month's time. He unfolded the map once more and searched it from corner to corner. There was supposed to be no language barrier for Americans in England. This was patently untrue. He found it just as hard to be understood here, among the hot dog stands and video arcades and all-night cab ranks, as in Paris. He looked across at the passing crowds, trying to pick out someone who looked as if they might know the area and be able to give him directions in simple English.

Finally, he found a friendly face. Collecting his backpack, he crossed the pavement to ask the way.

Moments later, Chip was congratulating himself on his great good fortune in finding someone so helpful as to volunteer to walk him to the YMCA. Back home, the young American prided himself on his ability to pick reliable friends, people in whom he could place trust. As he looked up at the starlings chattering in the tops of the trees, he noticed that it was already dusk. He turned to talk to his new-found friend, and quickly found himself describing his family, his journey, and the circumstances which had brought him to London.

Up ahead was an alleyway between two cinemas. Here, a drunk sat slumped on a step, a bottle of cheap sherry in shattered pieces between his legs. Urine formed a stagnant pool around his shoes. He was crying. Chip's freckly smile faltered. He slowly turned. His guide smiled back and beckoned onward. Night fell, and Chip was truly lost in Leicester Square.

"Is that the dossier?"

"Yes, sir."

"About bloody time. Well, don't just stand there, you gormless little nit."

Martin Butterworth handed Detective Chief Inspector Ian Hargreave the slim file and stepped back to the farthest edge of the carpet. He knew that this was the minimum safety area when dealing with Hargreave, who tended to fling his arms around and lash out at objects both animate and inanimate when angered or frustrated. Although Butterworth was only a detective constable, and as such had nothing really to do with this case, he was well aware that he would be blamed for the late arrival of the file, and planned to stay well out of the way if Hargreave hit the roof. Butterworth was twenty-three and learning fast.

Hargreave read the dossier from cover to cover, grunting a

little as he did so. He tweaked his peppery moustache, thinking. His eye skipped the irrelevant passages in the typed text and jumped on the noteworthy points, assembling them in an order which would make sense when he came to submit his own report. He suddenly turned his attention to the young constable.

"Butterworth, I'd like you to pay attention to what I am about to say."

Butterworth stood up straight and assumed a look of attentiveness.

"Just stand at ease, boy, you don't have to look as if you've been hypnotized. I am about to summarize the main points of this report to you, so listen carefully.

"Over the past four months, six people have disappeared in an area of London the size of a football pitch. I am referring to the region of Leicester Square. From the times that they were last seen, we can figure their disappearances to have occurred just after dusk.

"All of the missing persons are under twenty years of age. Three—that is, half—are female. All of them were visiting this country as tourists." Hargreave checked the dossier. "Four from the USA, one from Japan and one from Australia. What do you make of that?"

"Funny place to disappear, sir," ventured Butterworth.

"It's not difficult to vanish in the crowds of a London street, Butterworth, but to vanish without a trace! That's bloody strange."

Of course, Hargreave considered, these days Leicester Square was a hell-hole, a pedestrianized disaster area which had been redesigned to emulate the appearance of a European shopping precinct and had ended up looking like the wrong end of 42nd Street. The number of petty crimes taking place daily around the square was phenomenal. But this was nothing so petty . . .

It wasn't his job to find missing persons under normal circumstances, but this was beginning to look like the work of a serial killer, and Hargreave was under pressure to clear the matter up quickly. It didn't help that the father of one of the missing American kids—Kimberly, his name was—had turned out to be a powerful Washington Republican who possessed the ability to cause considerable trouble for the entire department. If only there were some bodies for the forensic lads to examine. But there was nothing to go on at all. No one had reported seeing anything remotely suspicious.

Hargreave tipped back in his chair and looked around the

room. Before him stood Butterworth, eager to please, desperate to be helpful. The boy was bright. It was probably only his physical appearance that was holding him back. He simply didn't look old enough to be on the force. With his baby-blue eyes and ruffled sandy hair he had the appearance of a seventeen-year-old schoolkid.

"Butterworth, you grubby little worm," smiled Hargreave, "I think I have found the perfect way for you to make up for your ridiculously juvenile appearance."

Butterworth blinked uncertainly. "Sir?"

"Do you own a backpack?" asked the detective inspector.

Over at the bar an American club guest was expressing his annoyance at the head barman's inability to mix a Tequila Sunrise. Two grey heads turned to watch for a moment, then, losing interest, turned back to the drinks which stood freshly poured in front of them.

"I blame air travel, myself."

"Well, you have to, old boy. That's the root of the trouble. And we're expected to be so *nice* to them, that's what I can't stomach."

"Yes, it's all tolerance these days."

"I don't understand it at all. We managed to get by without tolerance in the old days. Why, there was no such word in the language."

"Condom. Nobody ever used to say condom, either."

"Digital. New word."

"Pre-menstrual tension. Didn't exist."

"Lesbian. Something unheard of."

"That's because they were invented by the Labour Party in 1964. You know, I feel like telling these damned tourists to turn around and go home. Don't they realize that everything here has been seen to death? After the last one leaves, we could turn out the lights and all go to sleep for a while, let the country get its breath back."

"Mind you, they bring in the money."

"My dear chap, that's precisely the problem. They bring it in and where do they put it? In the hands of the working classes, the great unwashed. I mean, what do tourists spend their money on? Souvenirs, trinkets, gew-gaws. Cheap suits and bad theater."

"Andrew Lloyd-Webber."

"Exactly. And once they put money in the hands of those who are unused to handling it, what happens?"

"What?"

"Well, it all gets spent on rubbish. Washing machines and video nasties."

"How frightful."

"And they wonder why we have anarchy. Nobody does what they're told any more."

There was a sigh as an empty glass was set down on the table. The leather armchairs creaked once more. A cigar was lit.

"A dose of national service would work wonders. Look at the French, conscription never hurt them."

"Inasmuch as anything affects the French, you mean."

"Quite, quite. Appalling people, I agree. Even so . . ."

"Jolly decent cigar, this."

Smoke softly filled the air, wreaths of blue-gray vapor, rising slowly in the shrinking shafts of sunlight.

"Soon be dark."

"One for the road?"

"Don't mind if I do."

"And you're sure that it's one of the names on the list?"

"Quite sure, Hargreave. It's the Washington boy, Kimberly, all right. The dental check matches. They found a backpack in a trash bin near the body, and several of the items inside have his initials on them."

"Fully dressed, was he?"

"Yes, T-shirt and jeans."

"Anything in the pockets?"

"The motive wasn't robbery, if that's what you're wondering. He had money on him."

Hargreave tucked the receiver under his chin and tore a page of notes from his desk pad. "I assume they've already taken the body down to Charing Cross. Any idea who the forensic man will be? Finch?"

"Probably. Give him a call. But you may want to go over and take a look yourself."

"Why?" Hargreave hated visiting the morgue. For a man dealing frequently in the business of murder, he was surprisingly squeamish.

"There's apparently something odd about the state of the body."

"It figures," sighed Hargreave. "There are no straightforward murders any more."

On his way to the morgue he walked across Leicester Square and found himself staring into the faces of the hawkers, drunks and buskers. Over the past few days many of them had been interviewed, but few had anything of interest to reveal. Most were transients, petty criminals, junkies looking for easy pickings in an area which attracted a large number of naïve young visitors.

Hargreave had hoped to be confronted by the boy's body in the storage room of the morgue. At least there it was likely to be unopened, sealed away inside its stainless steel refrigerated chamber. Unfortunately for his stomach, however, the inspector was directed to the autopsy room next door, where Finch was talking enthusiastically with Willard, the coroner. Between them on the table lay a covered body which Hargreave correctly assumed to be that of Chip Kimberly.

"Hello, Hargreave, long time no see!" Willard greeted him gleefully. He knew full well why Hargreave so rarely put in an appearance here, and consequently revelled in grotesquely detailed descriptions of his findings. It was a private game that he and Finch liked to play with the more sensitive police officers.

"Interesting problem, I think you'll find," said Finch as he drew the rubber sheet from the body. Hargreave was nauseated to discover the cadaver in mid-autopsy, thin butter-yellow streaks of fat revealed by the V slit over the boy's stomach.

It was obvious, even to Hargreave, that this was not the usual state for a body to be in. The skin of the corpse was hard and dry, the interior appearing quite bloodless, as if it had been drained of all fluid.

"We know when the boy went missing," said Hargreave, silently praying for his stomach to stay calm, "but how long has he been dead?"

"That's the funny thing," said Finch. "The two time periods are almost identical, between seventy-five and eighty hours . . ."

"So he was killed almost immediately," interrupted Hargreave. "And yet the body turns up in a restaurant trash bin in Leicester Square, days later." He forced himself to examine the body. "Cause of death?"

"A very heavy blow, here"—Willard pointed above the boy's right eye—"to the frontal bone. It's completely shattered one of the two membranes forming the forehead. I should think he died instantly.''

"I don't understand," said Hargreave. "If the boy's been dead this long, how come there's no putrefaction?"

"Exactly what we were wondering," replied Finch, pulling the heavy rubber sheet back over the body. "We're relying on you to uncover the circumstances of death.''

"And right now," said Hargreave half to himself, "I'm relying on the nitwit Butterworth.''

The mime artist leapt and spun as he pretended to balance on a high wire, represented by a line of chalk on the pavement. He wobbled and fell, then bounced back up and presented a small child with a paper daisy. Butterworth wanted to punch his teeth down his throat. He had seen the same act thirty times so far today. Around him, the crowd of tourists applauded even as their pockets were being picked. The whole area depressed Butterworth, who was now on his third day of patrolling the square dressed as a ludicrously obvious American tourist. It seemed that no matter how many police were stationed in the area, you only had to stand still for two minutes to witness a dubious transaction of some sort taking place.

Another twenty minutes and it would start to get dark, and that, for Butterworth, was the witching hour, the time he had to convincingly fake looking lost, rattling his map in each corner of the square and staring up at the starling-covered ledges of the restaurants and cinemas. He hitched up his baggy plaid shorts, adjusted the huge orange nylon backpack once more, and hoped that this time something exciting would happen.

"And Mowbray, one never hears anything of him these days.''

"With good reason, my dear fellow. Surely you must have heard about him?''

"Not a peep since Calcutta, I assure you.''

"That's right, you used to hunt together, didn't you? He was married to that extraordinary woman, called herself an astrologer. Absolutely barking.''

"And plain.''

"Plain? Looked as if she'd been born under the sign of the pump.''

"I take it he left her.''

"Oh, absolutely, left her in India, came back here, got a job in the civil service and turned queer.''

"Never!"

"Worse than that, I'm afraid. Developed a penchant for young boys."

"Probably thought he was back in India. Young boys, eh? Poor old Mowbray."

"Tragic. Didn't come out of the closet so much as out of the toy cupboard."

"There are so few of the old crowd left now. I do miss them so."

"There's still Dimkins."

"You can't really count Dimkins. His mother was Welsh."

"That's a point. I was just thinking. When this place has gone, our breed will have vanished with it."

"You don't have to say it, old boy, I know. But at least these days the evenings provide some small recompense. A reminder of the thrills of yesteryear, albeit a rather pallid one."

"I suppose so. Come on then, finish your gin and we'll be off."

A glimpse of blazer, of snow-white cuff and deeply polished shoe showed as the elderly gentleman stirred from his armchair, and waited for his old army pal to finish his drink.

Hargreave paced back and forth behind the glass walls of his cluttered office. He crossed to the filing cabinet in the corner, unstuck the mug which stood on top and drained the cold tea from it. Then he returned to his desk and began to write down a list of questions. The restaurant behind which the boy's body was found had confirmed that their trash bins were emptied at the end of every evening. Kimberly's corpse had been dumped there long after his death. So where had it been kept in the meantime?

Hargreave licked his pencil and began a new paragraph. The body had been found in a totally dehydrated state. Why was there no blood in his veins? In fact, why would anyone only want to murder people from other countries? In order to make it harder to trace the bodies, perhaps? And speaking of which, where on earth were the other five cadavers?

Hargreave read back his notes, painfully aware that something was still missing from the puzzle.

At this moment, he received the answer to one of his questions.

"Another of the missing tourists, sir," said the voice on

the other end of the line. "Head bashed in, body perfectly preserved . . ."

"Don't tell me," said Hargreave. "Completely dehydrated."

"That's right, sir. Not a drop of blood in him."

After he had replaced the receiver Hargreave checked his notes again. Sundown. No blood. He pulled open the bottom drawer of his desk and removed a book from within. He flicked through the paperback edition of Bram Stoker's *Dracula* thoughtfully. No, the idea was too preposterous—and yet . . . He telephoned Finch at the morgue.

"I know this is going to sound crazy," he began, "but I'm up against a brick wall here. I want you to check something out for me."

"Fire away," said Finch genially. "What is it?"

"I'd like you to examine the throats of both bodies."

"Why, what exactly are you looking for?"

"Puncture marks," he replied. "Small, twin puncture marks."

Butterworth's feet hurt. The American track shoes he was wearing pinched his heels, and in the cooling evening air his knees, unused to being exposed to the elements, were starting to lock up. He loitered at the lower, darker end of Leicester Square, pretending to study his map for what seemed like the millionth time, but no one even came near him. Perhaps the murderer preferred not to approach in the gloom. Perhaps he stood under the yellow fluorescence of the nightclub signs at the top of the square, where the passing crowds would serve to confuse and obliterate any semblance of strange behavior.

Still clutching his map, Butterworth trudged slowly past the queues of early evening cinemagoers. He was covered in goose pimples. The thin American college T-shirt he was wearing allowed too much night air to his skin. The sky was quite dark now. He decided to give it another ten minutes before heading back to his station locker and donning a decent warm sweater.

Butterworth realized he had been standing absently staring at the map when a hand touched him on the shoulder, making him start.

"You look as if you need assistance," said a cultured voice.

Butterworth turned to face the stranger who had tapped him. "Gee, I sure do," he drawled in what he considered to be a reasonable American accent. "I'm trying to find the, er . . ."

Hargreave had given him a list of places that tourists were

most likely to head for. He racked his brains now for one of the names on the list.

"The British Mooseum," he announced finally. He had forgotten that by this time it would be closed.

"What a coincidence!" exclaimed the stranger. "I am by way of heading in precisely the same direction."

"Gee, that's swell, what a piece of luck!" said Butterworth, wondering if he was beginning to sound just a little too much like a character from a U.S. soap opera.

"Come, walk along with me and I'll show you a shortcut," said the stranger, making a sudden turn into one of the alleyways that branched away from the main square.

Butterworth hesitated. He was wearing a small walkie-talkie, but needed a chance to use it without arousing suspicion. The alleyway was underlit, and populated only by sleeping drunks. The smell of urine and stale food was everywhere. From here they branched into a second narrower alley, passing by the back of an old hotel where tramps sat slumped on the heated air vents. The stranger was a few steps ahead of him when he paused and turned with an eerie half smile. Butterworth suddenly realized how inexperienced he was at the game of staying alive.

Above Leicester Square, behind the dusty panes of the gentlemen's club which stood in a forgotten backstreet, were two empty leather armchairs. Between them stood a small rosewood table with a raised brass trim, and on this were two empty tumblers, side by side. A folded copy of the *Daily Telegraph* was tucked down one of the seats. A waiter moved in to clear the table and wipe the ashtray, then all was as it had been once more.

"But these days, everything's changed. I mean, you chaps from America—you come over here, staying as long as you like, spending however much you please, chucking your money about like water. Am I right? Of course I am, and it's not just you who gets the benefit from the loss of our empire but the rest of the world. These days we have the nips coming here, the fuzzy-wuzzies, the Fiendish Turk, even *Australians* for heaven's sake, but that's progress for you, I suppose. They keep building faster aircraft so that we can all go and visit each other, but nobody asks us if that's what we want to do."

Butterworth decided that his initial fears were unfounded. His guide was a harmless old gentleman of the old school, more right wing than Attila the Hun perhaps, but more intent on re-

membering the good old days than trying to wring the life from
his body. He relaxed as he listened to the old boy describing
hunting trips in India, and failed to notice the heavy darkness
of the street they were entering.

They passed the back of another old hotel, where tramps
stayed curled between vast bins filled with half-eaten meals.
Broad steel ventilator shafts belched stale air over them.

"Funny old world, isn't it?" said his elderly guide as they
passed the snoring tramps. "Our hotels are filled with overseas
visitors, while our own people are around the back sorting
through the food you couldn't manage to eat."

Butterworth didn't like this sudden personalization of the conversation, or the way it was heading. For that matter, he wasn't
entirely sure about the direction in which he himself was heading. They appeared to have doubled back behind Leicester
Square. They certainly weren't anywhere near the British Mu-
seum.

"Look, I don't think this is the right . . ." was all he managed to say before the old gentleman grabbed his arms with
surprising agility, and a second old gentleman, equally dapper,
stepped from the shadows armed with a long, club-like instrument.

The blow lifted Butterworth off his feet with a resounding
crack which sounded like Botham hitting a six and deposited
him on top of a crate of Chinese vegetables with his head split
clean in two. The first old gentleman watched the second as he
deftly wiped the blood from the end of the cricket bat and stood
it down.

"My dear fellow, that was a superb swing."

"I really think I'm developing my left arm, don't you?"

"You improve a little every time."

They surveyed the corpse for a moment, then unseated it from
the vegetable crate and began to drag it by its legs to the nearest
air shaft.

"Not that one, old boy. That's warm air. He'll go off. Over
to the cold vent, there's a good chap." He pointed at a battered
refrigeration shaft. "That way he'll dehydrate like beef jerky."

"We're going to have to throw out another body if we do that.
All these vents are full."

The two old gentlemen puffed and panted as they switched
one of the old bodies in the shafts for their latest victim. It had
dried out nicely, they noted before tossing it into a nearby res-

taurant bin. The operation over, they decided on a nice brisk walk in the cool night air before returning to the club.

"Ah, the pleasure of the hunt, the thrill of the chase," sighed the first old gentleman. "Then the closing in for the kill . . ."

"Not a patch on India, of course, still it's nice to keep one's hand in."

"Absolutely," agreed the first. "If you can't bag a tiger in Leicester Square, you can at least pot a tourist."

"And rid the country of a beastly pest at the same time," said the second. "I miss my elephant rifle, though."

"I agree, waiting till you see the whites of their eyes. Perhaps we should treat ourselves to one."

"Not a bad thought. I must say I've worked up quite a thirst, haven't you?"

"Last one to the club's a Trotsky."

Hefting the cricket bag between them, the old gentlemen strolled back to the club, once more to discuss times gone by. Behind them, the lights of Leicester Square glittered on, bright and strange, luring fresh faces to a cunning old city.

Despite all evidence to the contrary, poor Detective Chief Inspector Hargreave spent the next nine months trying to avenge Butterworth's death by hunting vampires, even after the murders had ceased (due to the demise of one of the participants).

Through a clerical slip-up he somehow failed to receive a note from the forensic boys informing him that a corpse hung in a dry, cool draught will lose its blood and mummify to give it the appearance of a vampire's victim. Sometimes the inspector sat morosely munching a lunchtime sandwich and staring at the black-edged photograph of Butterworth which hung on his office wall, wondering to himself what on earth could possibly have happened.

No one ever told him it had just been a Big Game.

SHADOW PLAY

THE FIRST THING you notice is that there are no trees. But look again carefully: there are. Sad, sickly things, sticking up out of the coarse concrete slabs as if they were weeds searching for soil in the cracks of a garden path. Their leafless branches are a dingy dead brown, their color sucked out by the endless gray stone acres in which they have been planted. They rattle in the icy wind which howls about the huddle of grim tower blocks collectively known as the Farmsmeade Estate. The estate was designed by middle-class architects to house the poor, who were supposed to be so grateful that they'd never notice the lousy workmanship, the construction shortcuts or the ill-considered layout of the place. The result was a multi-story concrete waste-land, where apartments were called "housing units" and a cluster of litter-covered benches surrounded by graffiti-ravaged shops became a "leisure area." By day, a grimy collection of statistics sealed in concrete, criss-crossed with crumbling walkways. By night, a silent city of ghosts.

Jay and Andy usually came over to Malcolm's house on a Saturday night. All three lived with their parents, but Malcolm's were best because they were always out. Besides, at seventeen Malcolm was the oldest, and had many friends on the estate. He had lived there ever since it was built, back when the phrase "High Tech" had meant something futuristic instead of something ugly and dated.

Malcolm often had girls around on a Saturday, and as his older brother worked in customs and excise there were always drugs available for chemical recreation. The three of them, plus who-ever else had been invited for the evening, would sit on the floor in Malcolm's bedroom listening to records, drinking Malcolm's dad's beer and smoking Malcolm's brother's hash, and Malcolm didn't mind because he enjoyed being popular and everyone did what he told them to.

God knows, there was nothing else to do on the estate on a Saturday night except visit one of the three grisly new pubs, each of which was equipped with a Yamaha organ, a fat singer and at least one set of their drunken parents. Of course, as Jay pointed out on the last evening they all met together, there was the Farmsmeade recreation centre, a freezing concrete hall the size of an aircraft hangar where the truly disturbed and untouchable kids went to play table tennis and attack each other in the toilets with flick knives. And outside on the street there was always the possibility of running into one of the local roller hockey gangs—provided you enjoyed being threatened with a crossbow. They were better off up here, thought Malcolm as he lit up a joint and passed it on to Jay.

"You've got damp coming in," said Andy, pointing to the corner of the ceiling.

"I know. The whole bloody block's got damp coming in. It's sinking, this is. They didn't put the foundations down deep enough."

"Sling us a beer."

Andy rolled a can over to Jay with his foot.

"Don't do that, fuckface, it'll spray when I open it." Jay broke the ringpull under his sweater. "Who else is coming over tonight?"

"I can't remember," said Malcolm. "Melanie, I think. Steve, and maybe Bryan."

"Bryan? Bryan Turner?" Jay was aghast. "He's fifteen. What d'you want to invite him over for?"

"He asked me, didn't he? What else could I say?"

"You could have said no."

Malcolm turned the record over and opened another can of beer, spraying froth on to the purple candlewick bedspread. He had left school over a year ago and was still looking for a job. He'd have liked to work with his brother in customs, but there were no vacancies. Jay and Andy were both about to leave school. Neither had a clue as to what they wanted to do. The school careers master had spent most of last term away, moonlighting. Little Bryan, on the other hand, was already making definite plans for the future, and he was only fifteen. He was the classic schoolkid nobody talked to. Bookish, bespectacled, shy and shunned, he never sat with the kids at the back of the class fooling around. He could usually be found in the library making notes for tomorrow's test. According to some of the guys in his class, Bryan's life at home was so hellish that for him studying provided a comforting retreat.

Malcolm still didn't know why he'd invited Bryan to the house tonight. Maybe he felt sorry for him. Maybe he thought that something the kid had brain-wise would rub off. Later, it was a question the police asked him over and over, and something he was never really able to answer.

At half past nine Bryan turned up, and so did Steve. Beers were passed around. Melanie, the lovely Melanie, sweetheart of the Lower Sixth, failed to put in an appearance, which caused Jay and Andy to complain about the lack of girls, and ask how on earth they could spend the rest of the evening. At first, Bryan was nervous in the company of what he considered to be the school's fast set, but a couple of beers soon loosened his tongue. He even shared a joint with them, and pretty soon everyone was laughing.

"Here, what time are your folks comin' back, then?" asked Steve, the monster of the group. He was six feet two inches tall and thought he was a new-wave hippie, sporting a headband and shoulder-length hair that he refused to wash for anyone.

"They're out for the night," grinned Malcolm. "She's over with the neighbor and he's fucking his girlfriend. We can do anything we want."

"Great," said Jay. "We got no money, no girls and nowhere to go."

"Remember when we used to play hide and seek on the estate?" asked Andy.

"How about a game now?"

"Nah, too cold. I vote we get ratfuck stoned and watch some videos."

"Good idea."

Which is what they did for a while, but even the fun in that wore off eventually. It had all seemed much funnier two weeks ago, when Malcolm's brother had got hold of some psychedelic drug and they had all taken it before settling down to watch the remake of *The Fly*.

Bryan seemed to be enjoying the rather monosyllabic—except when it was sexually oriented—conversation of the company, but never really relaxed his guard as they slumped around the TV passing dope to one another. Perhaps he was suspicious of the group's friendliness towards him. He need not have been for it was largely drug-induced, and though they felt no malice to-

wards the boy, they treated him in a somewhat condescending
and offhand manner. Bryan was sensitive enough to be aware
of their attitude, and bright enough to accept the situation without complaint. He shared their beers but after a while refused
the joint when it came around, telling Malcolm that he smoked
all the time when of course he had never smoked before tonight.
The violent coughing which followed his first inhalation of
smoke attested to that.

By midnight everyone was bored with the video, and Steve
and Andy took speed to keep themselves awake. It was then that
the idea of hide and seek once again took hold.

This time even Malcolm agreed to play. He turned off the TV,
and in the silence that followed laid out the rules of the game.

All those going to hide had three minutes in which to do so,
starting from the square outside the apartment building. Having
successfully hidden, they could then make their way back to
base. The object was to reach home without being caught.

"I don't think I'm going to come along with you," said Bryan
as he rose unsteadily from the floor. "I don't really know this
area . . ."

"What are you talking about, you've lived here for at least
two years," said Andy. "It'll be a laugh. There's never anyone
around this time of night. It's like a fucking graveyard out there."

"Hey, Bryan, c'mere, I wanna talk to you." Malcolm put
his arm around Bryan's shoulders and led him into the kitchen.
A minute later they re-emerged with Bryan suddenly ready to
join the others, who wondered what exactly Malcolm had said
to get him to come along. They trooped out of the block into
the cool night air and Malcolm held up his arms for silence,
making them all stop and listen. There was not a sound anywhere, not a car or a conversation to be heard, however distant.
It was one of the features of the estate. The concrete walls and
walkways deadened all noise in the town, giving the area an
artificial, lifeless feel, especially at night.

Malcolm's breath formed vaporous ghosts as he talked. Behind him rose the blue-gray walls of the recreation center, the
lower halves of which were spray-painted with obscenities. Bryan
lived on the other side of the estate, rarely venturing over here
to the oldest blocks, which were now cracking and sinking noticeably back into the marshland over which Farmsmeade had
been built. He felt woozy and light-headed, the cold air pricking
his eyes and numbing the ends of his fingers.

"Who's going to be the hunter first, then?" Malcolm was asking.

"I will," volunteered the monstrous Steve, who despite his appearance was soft-spoken and seemed gentle enough. "Get going, you lot, I've already started counting."

Bryan found himself running with the others across the square into the darker valleys formed by rows of apartment buildings. He saw Jay galloping away to his left and vanishing into a subway entrance, and caught a brief glimpse of Andy climbing the steps towards one of the overhead walkways. Then, quite suddenly he was alone and all was silence.

Ahead, the side of a block of maisonettes glowed palely in the lamp light of its small concrete courtyard. Bryan ran across this and into the darkness on the far side. A dog, sensing movement outside, barked from within someone's house, the sound echoing dimly down the alleyways of concrete. He had to concentrate on the names of the walkways if he was to find his way back. Essex Way, this one was called. He pulled his army jacket tighter across his chest and ran on.

Beyond the back gardens of the maisonettes was a wide, open piazza of stone, gleaming dully in the wan moonlight and surrounded by towering blocks of flats. These were linked to each other with pebbledashed concrete paths on stilts, the walkways of Farmsmeade. Bryan could not see an easy way to reach them, but knew that if he could, they would provide a perfect observation point over the rest of the estate. In the center of the piazza was a large, shallow lake, one of three across Farmsmeade, in which stood a mountainous and grotesque piece of statuary formed with sheets of steel. A continuous drumming sound emerged from it, hollow and lonely, as jets of dyed green water piddled feebly downwards from the top. Bryan felt sorry for the people who had to daily open their curtains on to the sight of it. At least his bedroom window at home just faced a wall.

Suddenly Bryan heard the sound of running feet, sneakers slapping cement, moving rapidly towards him. He took off again, heading in the direction he considered Malcolm's flat to be.

Along the edge of the piazza tall steel street lamps cast pools of ice-blue light on to stone. Dodging between these, Bryan ran the length of one side, then turned on to another. Pausing to look behind him he saw Steve closing in with wide effortless strides. Bryan skidded off away from the piazza, down to the mouth of a stairway leading below one of the apartment buildings. He clattered down the steps to the bottom, and found himself in an oblong concrete chamber half filled with cars, one of the estate's many underground car parks. Pressing himself flat against a wall at the nearest end of the chamber, he tried to prevent his breath from rasping, and strained for the sound of Steve's sneakers on the steps above.

Nothing. The graveyard silence had closed in again as quickly and surely as the fen grass which continued to crack and uproot the paving stones of the town above his head. Farmsmeade did a good job of keeping nature at bay. No fish would ever spawn in the poisoned waters of its lakes. Bryan listened for another minute, then moved out from the shadows. As he was moving back towards the stairwell he heard a cry, a strange mewling sound from the far end of the garage, like a baby in pain. He turned and listened again, and a moment later, there it was once more. Surely no one could have abandoned a baby down here. He walked slowly between the cars, bending his knees so that he could see some way underneath them. The sound was coming from the very end, where several small trucks were backed up into the darkness of the damp stone walls.

Suddenly out from behind the last vehicle shot a terrified fox cub, then another, and then a third. Bryan laughed with relief as the animals sped across the concrete ramp and vanished to the floor below. He had heard that foxes used to fill the marshes before the new town was built, but he had not expected to find them living in a car park. Was there any other secret life on the estate he didn't know about? He was pondering this as he left the stairwell on to the piazza and big Steve laid an enormous bony hand on his shoulder, and he very nearly had a heart attack.

"You're the first to be caught," said Steve. "You get to be the hunter next time."

Being the hunter rather than the hunted suited Bryan much more. At the start of the next game he waited for three minutes, then, shaking off a growing headache, ran off towards the first of the raised walkways to get a good view of the estate.

He found the entrance easily enough, and climbed the stairs to the first floor, which opened out into a wide balcony running alongside one of the apartment blocks. Standing on the walkway looking out over the southern side of the town, he thought he caught a glimpse of one of them, a small body vanishing around a corner. Andy's perhaps. He saw the shape again at the next corner, running quickly and silently. Then nothing. Bryan crossed backwards and forwards over the walkway, watching carefully all the time, but nothing disturbed the scene below. He was about to give up and head for one of the other walkways when he turned around and caught sight of the running figure again. It was small and hunched, a ghostly, luminous white.

Bryan was a fast runner, but the creature ran faster, rounding the next corner and disappearing into an alleyway at the back of the piazza. Bryan slowed down and caught his breath, standing against a wall with his hands on his knees, breathing hard. Just as he stood up, the creature reappeared from behind a tree and ran across the alleyway laughing. Bryan started after it once more. At the next corner he gained on it, and halfway down the length of the alley made a wild grab which connected.

It was not a creature. It was a small, elfin-faced boy wearing no shoes, no shirt, only shorts. His hair was almost translucently pale, his complexion that of an albino. He was icy to the touch.

"You caught me!" said the child gleefully. "Now catch the others!"

"You're not in our game," said Bryan. "Who are you?"

"I live on the estate with the rest."

"What rest? Aren't you cold?"

"Come with me," said the child, grabbing his arm. "I'll show you the others."

"I'm in the middle of a game," protested Bryan, reluctantly following the child towards one of the walkways.

"Oh, leave them, they're not interested in playing with you. They don't even like you."

"How do you know that?" Bryan said defensively. "I don't know you."

"Oh, yes you do," said the boy, giving him a mischievous look.

"I'm going back . . ." Bryan began to pull away.

"This will only take a minute. I want you to meet the others." The boy sounded much older than his years. He turned on to one of the walkways which led to the lake and stopped at the junction of this and another concrete path.

"Just there, see?" He pointed down the path to where it joined the building ahead, and an area of shadow was formed. Within the darkness was a cluster of moving pale shapes. Bryan and the boy moved slowly towards them.

One by one the shapes stepped from the shadows. They were all young children, boys and girls, none of them over the age of ten, all as pale as death, and all just wearing ragged shorts. The translucence of their skin gave them the collective appearance of undersea creatures. They looked shyly at him, some of them offering a nervous smile. The one who had led Bryan here was more brash, and spoke more loudly than the rest.

"Come on out, all of you! We have a visitor." Still more children appeared from the darkness. They reminded Bryan of Peter Pan's lost boys.

"Who are you?" he asked, amazed.

"We're children who live here in Farmsmeade, just like you," said one of them with a smile. He spoke gravely, and sounded strangely old-fashioned.

"I don't believe you. And you should all be indoors, in bed. It's freezing out here."

"We don't feel the cold," said another, a little girl of about seven. "This is where we live. We are the children of the dark."

"I don't know what you mean," said Bryan. "Don't you have parents?"

"Not any more," said a tiny boy with white hair. "We play up here at night. You should play with us."

"I'm already hanging out with some guys down on the piazza," Bryan pointed out, trying to sound adult. "They're older than any of you."

"You shouldn't play with them," said the tiny boy. "They're only out to make a fool of you."

"No, they're not!"

"But they are! Why do you think they invited you over? To make fun of you. Why can't you find any of them? Because they've gone home and left you standing around like an idiot."

"That's not true."

"You know it is true." The little girl gave him a huge smile. "Come and play with us, just for five minutes?"

"Oh, please! Please!" shouted all the others, reaching out to grab his arms. The shimmering shoal of children quickly surrounded him, touching and clutching at his jacket, each one trying to attract his attention, like pupils eager to answer a classroom question.

"I'll play with you for five minutes, no more, and on one condition," Bryan shouted back. "That you tell me who you really are."

Laughing, they agreed, and dragged him off along the walkway leading to the lake.

Jay and Andy stood stamping their feet in the alleyway beside Malcolm's apartment block, scanning the pathways around the recreation center for any sign of the others.

"Why don't we just go in and get warm?" said Jay. "It's borin' hanging around out here. I'm freezing." The effects of the joints and the alcohol in his body had been neutralized by the plunging temperature.

"Malcolm's got the front door key," Andy pointed out. "We'll have to wait for Bryan to catch him." He turned the collar of his jean jacket up and blew on his hands. "This was a really stupid idea."

"This place . . . it's like being dead. Be more fun in a morgue than here." Jay gazed above the gray canyons at the bare, white moon.

Beyond the recreation center boots echoed on concrete. The length of silence between each footfall indicated that it had to be Steve approaching. In another moment he appeared, closely followed by Malcolm.

"Any of you get caught?" he called.

"No," Jay shouted back. "Didn't you see Bryan?"

"I saw him a while ago," said Steve. "He must still be wandering around by the lake."

"Yeah, well the game's over cause we all got back before him. Let's wait inside," said Jay. "Open the door, for fuck's sake."

Malcolm unlocked the outer door to the block and let them in before returning to the step and staring off into the darkness. A look of worry creased his face as the others trooped up into the block, and the alleyways beyond returned to chilly silence.

"I can't get down there, it's too steep." Bryan looked at the almost sheer concrete slope which began just beyond the toes of his shoes.

"Of course you can. We do it all the time." The elfin boy turned to the others for confirmation.

"We do," said a thin young girl with cropped white-blonde hair. Despite the chill of the night air, her breath failed to condense before her.

"It's the quickest way to get to the walkway above the lake."

"I didn't know there was another walkway down there." Bryan looked dubiously down into the darkness. "Are you sure?"

"It's a service ramp. The maintenance men use it to get to the fountain. Come on, we'll make sure you don't fall."

"No, it's dangerous. I'm bigger than you, heavier."

"Then we'll help you."

"No, I think . . ."

"You promised." The elfin boy held out his hand. It was tiny, the fingers as cold as ice. Bryan was surprised by the child's powerful grip, then found himself supported on all sides by small cold hands. In a matter of moments they had descended the slope as a group, almost running down and coming to a stop by the low brick parapet at the bottom. Bryan looked over the edge. Fifteen or twenty feet down was the green water of the man-made lake. Behind him, the children were laughing and whispering amongst themselves.

"How do we play this game, then?" asked Bryan, impatient to be free of these strange, giggling creatures.

"First we pick a leader," said the tiny blonde girl. Despite her nakedness, she also seemed oblivious to the freezing atmosphere. "Then we follow him wherever he goes."

"Follow the leader is a baby's game," said Bryan. "Tell me who you are. Why haven't you got any warm clothes? Who looks after you?"

"It's not a baby's game the way we play it," said the elfin boy, ignoring his questions. "Let's pick a leader."

The group immediately huddled together and started whispering. They pushed forward the very young-looking girl, who flashed her broad, adult smile at Bryan and waltzed past him to take her place at the head of the children. She was obviously a favorite of the group. Unlike the others, she wore a white scarf wrapped around her head and shoulders.

"What's your name?" asked Bryan.

"It's Karen," said the girl. "I'm an expert at this game."

"Why's that?"

"Because," she said with a disarming grin, "I go where none of the others will dare to." And with that, she turned and skipped off along the ramp, leaving Bryan and the rest of the children to follow her.

"He's probably gone home," said Jay, settling back on the couch with a can of lager. "He can't still be out there wandering around."

"I don't know what you're so worried about," said Andy. "You won't see him from there, anyway."

Malcolm let the curtain fall back over the window. Frowning to himself, he paced across the tiny lounge and into the kitchen.

"What's the matter with him?" asked Steve in a low voice. "What's he so concerned about? He hardly knows the kid."

"Yeah, he doesn't even give a stuff about his real mates. Something's going on." Andy stood up and went into the kitchen. Malcolm was standing at the refrigerator, lost in thought.

"He'll have gone home by now, Malc. It's nearly three o'clock." Malcolm drained his beer can without reply. A thought suddenly crossed Andy's mind.

"What did you say to him?"

"What?" Malcolm lowered the beer can and looked at Andy.

"When he came in here, before we started the game. He wasn't going to play, he was going to go home. You called him in here, and when he came out he was happy to join us, couldn't wait. What did you say to him?"

"Nothing," said Malcolm slowly. "I didn't say anything."

"You're lying."

"Why don't you just fuck off home, Andy?" shouted Malcolm suddenly.

"Not until you tell me what went on in here," replied Andy, as the others started to come in from the lounge.

"We have to jump this bit," said Karen, as the ends of her white cotton scarf flapped around her neck in the wind. In front of them was a two-foot gap in the maintenance ramp where repair work was being carried out. Below, scaffolding poles jutted at dangerous angles.

Bryan stepped the distance easily, but some of the children had to jump. Had any of them missed, it could have been a fatal fall, on to the scaffolding or into the lake. The water below was supposed to be very shallow.

"I'm going to have to go back in a minute."

"Stay a little longer," said Karen. "We know all the bits of the estate where nobody ever goes. There are roadways and tunnels which no one ever uses because they aren't finished, and never will be." She turned and ran ahead into the darkness.

Out here on the concrete service ramp there were no more street lights. The catwalk passed beneath one of the broad walkways leading to the estate's main shopping area. The ramp itself looked half finished. Lengths of rusty wire poked from end sections of half-constructed cement walling. Several times Bryan had stumbled in the dark over pieces of brick lying across the causeway.

"Come on over here," called Karen. "Look." She was standing on a concrete path no wider than the length of a single brick. It extended from the ramp, which came to an abrupt end just ahead of them.

"You'll fall!" shouted Bryan in alarm. "Come off of there!"

"You silly, it's quite safe, look." She stamped her bare foot repeatedly on the stone. "It leads to another part of the ramp. If I can do it, you can."

"I weigh more than you. It might not take my weight."

"Of course it will, it's concrete. Come on over to the other side. I'll see you across safely."

Something about the way she said this struck a chord. Bryan stared at her in the softening darkness.

"Who are you?" he asked. Behind him, the other children waited patiently. "I'll come over if you tell me who you are."

"You did *what*?" shouted Andy incredulously. "You fucking idiot!"

"I thought it would be a laugh. I only gave him half."

"What's going on?" Steve stuck his head around the kitchen door. Malcolm looked pale and shaken.

"I got them from my brother. I wasn't to know."

Andy turned to face Steve and Jay, jerking his thumb back at Malcolm. "Bright boy here gave Bryan Mindjoy."

"Excuse my ignorance, but what the fuck is Mindjoy?" asked Steve.

"It's a drug, comes in little pink tablets," explained Jay. "It's a big thing in America."

"He didn't want to come along, so I gave him half a tablet to perk him up. It was supposed to be a joke. My brother got hold of a load. I thought it was like Ecstasy. You know, just a gentle high, feeling good, that sort of thing."

"What does it do, then?"

"It's a hallucinogen," said Jay. "It's like a cross between acid and speed. It gives you strong hallucinations, and a lot of energy. Works on your subconscious, too. Real dangerous stuff, man."

"How long do the effects last?"

"I dunno, three, maybe four hours."

"Come on, then," said Steve, already heading for the door. "We've got to find him."

"Do you have a coin?"

"What for?"

"You have to give me a coin. Then I'll tell you who I am."

Bryan felt in the pocket of his jeans and produced a tenpence piece, which he handed over to the girl. He was just wondering where she was going to put it, as she obviously had no pockets in the ragged cloth tied around her waist, when she placed it in her mouth and swallowed.

"You want to know about us?" she asked, slowly unwinding the scarf from around her head and neck. Bryan's eyes widened. Her throat had been slashed wide open in a jagged, bloodless arc. The flesh of her neck protruded from the wound, just dry red meat.

"These are the children of the dark." She gestured back at the group milling behind him. "All of them died in neglect and sorrow, here in this damned world of concrete and glass, where love wastes away and compassion is as cold as the corpse of a child . . ."

She reached for Bryan's hand and slowly led him out on to the concrete perch. "They are the unplanned-for. The unloved, the unnoticed, the unimportant. The Betrayed. At home, at school, nobody ever cared for them. Just as nobody cares for you. Despite what you think, it makes no difference whether you are dead or alive."

"No!" shouted Bryan. "That's not true!"

"You know in your heart it is true."

Behind him the children shuffled forward.

"He's got to be somewhere around here," shouted Andy, out of breath from the long run around the lake. "You go that way and I'll circle back to the rec centre."

"I'll see you round the other side," Jay shouted back as he dashed off across the piazza. Above them, Bryan stood alone on the cracking stone ledge, at the end of a forgotten path.

"But who are you?" asked Bryan once more, as he walked further out over the lake with his guide.

"I told you," said the girl. "I am Karen." There was something odd about the way she pronounced her name.

"Spell it," said Bryan, as realization dawned.

"C-H-A-R-O-N," said the girl, slowly smiling as she retreated into the darkness. "Come and join us in Hell."

He felt the concrete crumble beneath his feet, and heard the splash as the first chunk hit the water beneath him. As he slipped and fell, his last thought was that he could probably survive the fall to the lake. Either way, he felt in safe hands as he hit the rusting metal blades of the fountain.

The razor-sharp daggers of the estate's single concession to humanity succeeded in piercing and bursting his heart, his blood coursing across the sculpted steel to finally mingle with the garish green water of the man-made lake.

DECEIVING THE LIZARDS

W ITH THE TEMPERATURE touching a hundred degrees, Cory barely had the energy to relieve his boredom by torturing the wildlife. Beyond the dunes where he sat cross-legged in the sand, cars and trucks growled through the distant rush-hour streets of Larnaca.

Stacks of builders' breeze blocks and fencing staves lined the tufted hillocks, the wind humming between them as the boy bent over a small hand-dug pit, preoccupied with his lonely game. Today, Cory was well protected from the scorching sunlight by an enormous long-sleeved Dodgers sweatshirt. Janice had insisted upon him wearing it, knowing the kind of trouble she would get into if she returned the boy with a sunburned back.

It was almost worth taking off the shirt and getting burned, thought Cory, just to drop her in the shit. Below the rolled turn-ups of his shorts his chubby knees were already beginning to stain with angry red blotches. When they returned home to Philadelphia he would make sure that any remaining marks came to the attention of his father, and with any luck he would dock Janice's salary, just as he had done when she brought Cory back from the boating lake soaked to the skin last spring.

As Cory waited for lizards he tried to concentrate his hatred of Janice enough to make her fall down sick wherever she was this minute, but he had tried this before and it had never worked, and he eventually turned his attention back to the trap.

The upturned lid of the biscuit tin was now painful to the touch. The wire pegging its sides rose and closed overhead in a scalding dome. Cory turned to the scrumptious assortment of dead flies and rotting fish he had laid out at the top of the hill and sat back on his heels. He did not have to wait very long. This one was a beauty. A large emerald sand-lizard with shim-

110

mering back scales and yellow globed eyes sat watching him just a few feet away. After a few minutes it ran closer, its body twisting this way and that, legs shooting out on either side as it crossed the hot sand. This would be the third one today. He was already running out of ways to make them die. Frying seemed to be the most fun, watching them skitter about in the wire cage as their footpads stuck to the searing metal floor. The lizard moved closer to the food pile as Cory crouched above it ready to pounce. Yesterday he had slowly constricted one by tying string around its stomach and tightening until it noisily popped. Another he had dissected alive—very messy, that had been. Cory outstretched his hands above the lizard, scarcely daring to breathe. It had stopped at the edge of the food, and was licking its lips with a thin black tongue, ready to dart into the shade and feast . . .

"Cory! There you are! I've been looking all over for you! What on earth are you doing!"

The lizard dashed away to the safety of the long grass as the ground beneath it vibrated with the approach of a human. Cory looked up in fury.

"Cory! What are you making? Can't you do it by the pool?" Janice was patting a neatly folded handkerchief across her forehead as she stared down at him.

Quickly he drew the jar filled with the remains of sun-dried lizards in behind his back where the enemy could not spot them. Without her spectacles Janice was hopeless.

"Why do you always have to ruin everything?" he shouted. "I was trying to catch a lizard for a pet an' you scared it off. Least I would have had a friend to play with then." Cory pouted furiously and thrust his stumpy hands deep into his pockets, playing the friendless schoolboy.

"I don't think you should touch the lizards, Cory. They're probably riddled with foreign diseases."

Cory could tell that going for pathos would not work. It was wasted on her, like everything else. How typical it was of Janice to think that lizards could harm you! In her world, everything, in some mysterious way, was harmful to children. Steps were for tumbling down and cracking your head open, seas were for being sucked out into after not letting your lunch go down, food was full of germs and streets were for becoming lost in. Janice was so prim and sniffy. Janice was English.

"Come here, you've got dirt on your face." She leaned over,

licking the peak of her handkerchief and dabbing it against his face until he managed to squirm from her grasp.

"Really, Cory, you're not making things any easier for me, you know. Come on, let's go back to the hotel. You know how your father feels about you wandering off."

"My father lets me do whatever I like. It's only you who doesn't let me do anything," Cory called back as he ran off across the dunes.

Janice pushed the handkerchief back into the pocket of her floral cotton skirt and shrugged. She wished they had never come here. Cory was impossible enough back in Philadelphia, but here, away from the—albeit minimal—control of his father, he was behaving like an animal. In a way, she supposed she felt sorry for him. Raised by his wealthy industrialist father, a man who spent his rare hours at the house either on the telephone or behind a computer, he had been allowed anything his heart desired. Perhaps if he had known the love and attention of a mother he would have grown up differently. Instead, at the age of nine, he had now been spoiled and indulged to the limit, something Janice had tried in vain to correct. She watched as he slowed to a walk and turned back along the shoreline, kicking at clumps of grass with the toe of his shoe until he had broken their rooted hold on the sand.

What would happen if she turned and walked away, she wondered, leaving the boy to his own devices in this disconcertingly foreign city? The thought was an idle one, of course, yet how she wished she could do just that. Three nannies before her had resigned without even being prepared to work out their notice. The boy, everyone agreed, was a monster—but who was to blame? And besides, the money was excellent, and she enjoyed living in America to a point. With no secretarial skills and no natural talents, what could she possibly do back in England?

After Cory had grown bored with his sulk, he fell silently in alongside her as they returned to the hotel for lunch in the coolness of their suite.

As the balcony had fallen into shadow, they decided to eat outside, high above the noise of the traffic. The hotel faced out on to the beach road which bordered the city, a smart white building built for the tourist trade but oddly deserted much of the day. From here it was a ten-minute walk to the markets and café, but as Cory screamed when taken into town, making passers-by stop in the street and stare at Janice as if she were a child batterer, they stayed mostly at the hotel.

Janice watched as her young charge pulled pieces of meat from his hamburger and flicked them over the balcony.

"What is wrong with it this time?" she asked wearily.

"It's raw, that's what. This isn't a Big Mac. It stinks, like this place. I want to go home." Cory threw his fork into the corner of the balcony, kicking back in his chair.

"Cory, you pick up your fork this *instant*, you hear me? I've had enough of you today."

"You do it. You're the nanny. That's what my father employed you to do."

"Indeed he did not employ me to run around after you clearing up. Now do as you're told!"

"Why haven't you got a boyfriend?" Cory switched to his favorite tease. "All my other nannies had boyfriends. You haven't cause you're plain and fat, that's what my father says."

"That's enough!" Janice's voice wavered as she slammed the flat of her palm on the table. Cory sat back with a reproachful look.

"I'm sorry, Janice. I'm just lonely. There's nobody here my age to play with. Only Marcus comes and plays with me. He's going to take me out early on his day off." Cory rolled big, sad eyes at her, pulling his face down into a comical frown.

"That's all right, Cory," Janice sighed as she collected up their plates and placed them on the tray. "I know you don't mean any harm. Now stay still and I'll see if we have ice cream for dessert."

She was such a pushover. Even though there were still several weeks to run before his tenth birthday, Cory decided to go easy on her until she had coughed up a decent present.

In the cool blueness of the room, Janice blew her nose on a fresh handkerchief. The boy was too young to be deliberately cruel to her. She had to keep in mind that Cory was a special case. Given his upbringing, there was no other way for him to be. She would do her best to see that this holiday was a memorable one for him. That was the least that she could do.

At sunset, Janice lay face down on her bed, writing letters to her friends in England.

Dear Susan,

As you can see I am in Cypress. I am here with Cory for two weeks' paid holiday while his father is in the Middle East on business (Very big sales deal!) The weather is very hot, but makes a change from Philadelphia. My skin does not react well to the sun, but Cory is already as brown as a berry. As expected, his behavior, especially with me, leaves much to be desired. I am now halfway through my contract, with nine months in Philadelphia still to run, but after this time I am seriously thinking of moving home to England. At the moment I am saving all my money for . . .

Beyond the balcony doors the sinking sun had seared the sky with crimson. Janice stepped outside and rested her freckled arms along the cool white ledge before her, surveying the edge of the city below. From the room next door she could hear the electronic pinging of Cory's video game. In the distance a café band was playing, the sound of guitars ebbing into the gulleys of surrounding office blocks. After Cory was asleep she would bathe and dress before slipping downstairs to the bar, where she would sit looking out to sea, sipping a frost-cold gin and tonic and savoring the peacefulness of being alone. Cory rarely showed any sign of wanting to be with her, but would scream if she tried to slip away by herself. He awoke early and, refusing to eat in the hotel restaurant, would insist that the hours of early morning be made entertaining for him. It was no use trying to sleep if Cory was awake. The air was turning cool. She returned to the bedroom and unfolded a cardigan from her case, calling into Cory's bedroom as she did so.

"I'm going downstairs to post a letter, Cory. All right?"

"Bring me a Coke."

"You could try saying please."

No answer. The electronic game began to ping once more. Janice stared at the wall between them with irritation.

Downstairs the wind whistled mournfully beneath the glass doors of the hotel entrance. Although a road lay between the hotel and the beach, the marbled foyer floor was coated with a thin layer of sand. In enormous electric-blue nylon armchairs sat a sad-looking Indian couple. The thin mother jiggled a crying baby distractedly on her knees. Janice crossed to the hotel doors and pushed them apart, to stand looking out at the dusty pink and white city. Mopeds raced crazily past ancient trucks loaded perilously with melons, hay and rusty drums of oil. On the pavement stood groups of sailors in smart, strange uniforms, with the names of their ships written on their white caps. Janos, the man who rented bicycles to the hotel patrons, was packing up his stand for the evening. Although she had walked only briefly through the city streets with Cory at her side, she felt ill at ease about the place, as if there was trouble to be found in the shadowed alleyways and street cafés filled with laughing soldiers.

To be sure, Cyprus had beautiful beaches, but here in town there was a sense of angry restlessness, as if the Turks might come at any time and fight for the other half of the island. The airport had been the scene of hijacks recently, and the ever-present militia, even when they doffed their caps and smiled, made her nervously cast her eyes downward as she and Cory headed over to the beach in the mornings.

Janice let the glass door close, and instantly the evening wind began to moan beneath it once more in descant to the crying Indian baby. She posted her letter at the reception desk and bought Cory a warm can of Coke in the hotel shop before returning to the foot of the stairs. Across the hall the waiters joked with each other as they prepared the tables for the evening meal. All of them were tall and dark, with shiny black hair curling over the frayed collars of their uniforms. The day she and Cory had arrived, the waiters had been playing volleyball on the beach, performing spectacular gymnastics for the benefit of the female guests, their hard brown bodies turning in the sun as middle-aged ladies covertly watched from behind their paperbacks. Janice could imagine their chests and thighs, darkly scented with sun-oil, beneath their tight tuxedos. One of them turned and caught her watching, and brazenly stared back with an impish smile. Janice quickly turned away and climbed the stairs, hurrying in revulsion past a dead green lizard sprawled across a white step, back to the suite where Cory waited impatiently for his drink.

That evening, the two of them sat on the balcony playing *Mille Bornes* until dinner arrived. Janice rose to collect the trolley before finishing her hand, instantly prompting a fit of temper from the child who sat scuffing his shoes against the balcony wall.

"But you want your dinner, don't you?" Janice steered the trolley over the lounge carpet.

"Not if it's that shitty meat again."

"Cory! I've told you about swearing before!"

"Shitty. Shitty. Shitty."

Janice ignored the boy and began cutting up his steak, knowing that he would eventually eat it. She longed to eat downstairs, where the waiters would bustle around them, laughing and teasing as they served up the meal, but Cory simply screamed if she tried to get him down to the dining room.

"Who were you talking to today at the pool?" She had seen the boy playing with one of the waiters earlier and, in a rare moment, laughing.

"Marcus. He's the only guy worth talking to in this dump."

Why any waiter would befriend the child when there were other, nice people about she had no idea. Janice wished the waiters would cluster around her, showing off, as they did with the other girls at the pool. At nineteen, it was true that she was overweight, and plain enough to be ignored by the slim young men who stretched out on the sand. Removing her glasses helped improve her looks, but also rendered her virtually blind. Tonight she would once again go to the bar and sit looking out to the beachside cafés strung with white lights, where sunburnt tourists sat drinking retsina at tiny raffia-topped tables and smiling waitresses served huge glass bowls of oily salad. The atmosphere on the long, flat roof where she sat with her drink only served to emphasize her loneliness, for the tables were filled with young German couples in white cotton holiday clothes, whispering and cuddling before they headed out to the city's nightclubs. A week and a half of such evenings stretched before Janice like a prison sentence . . .

"Are you coming down to the beach today, Marcus?"

"No, today I have to work. Your lady friend will take you, I am sure."

Marcus removed the cloth from the breakfast trolley and turned to Janice with a smile. She flicked her eyes down at her shoes as the waiter removed the plates from the tray and set them down.

"*Her*? She's not my friend, she's just a nanny," announced Cory.

The waiter punched him lightly on the shoulder. "Hey, you shouldn't be so rude. She's a pretty lady. You be nice, or you be in trouble with Marcus, AOK?"

He flashed her a white smile and stood down her coffee cup. For a moment her eyes met his. Marcus, she suddenly realized, was the same waiter who had grinned so impudently at her last night. He stood there, one eyebrow raised at her, bouncing the empty tray on the palm of his hand. The muscles of his chest tightened his shirt. She looked down to her breakfast. When she looked up he had gone, quietly leaving the room with his tray tucked under one arm.

"He thought you were pretty. He must be blind." Cory made a face and dug into his egg.

"Not everyone's as rude as you, you know."

Janice sat back in her chair. Marcus had thought she was pretty.

The day was a pleasant one, hot without being unbearable. In the afternoon she and a reluctant Cory walked through the streets of Larnaca, watching the fruit sellers arguing with the sailors, and the construction workers hammering into the foundations of skeletal office blocks with their drills.

That evening, after Cory was asleep, Janice ventured down to the bar. As all of the outside tables were taken she perched on a high cane stool, sipping her gin and trying to look nonchalant, as if perhaps waiting for a friend to join her for dinner. Beyond the glass wall the restaurant emptied out. The barman refilled her glass. The night deepened.

"You are on your own tonight?"

Janice turned on her stool to find Marcus standing alongside her at the bar. He had changed out of his uniform and now wore a white T-shirt tucked into faded blue jeans. The darkness of his arms seemed to make the T-shirt glow.

"Oh, yes. Please, have a seat." Marcus slid his beer glass along the counter top and sat down.

"So, you are here for two weeks, looking after the little boy?" Marcus stretched his powerful arms flat along the bar.

"That's right." Janice toyed with the edge of her coaster, searching for something to talk about.

"You do not go out in the evenings? I have seen you here at the bar, two nights."

Janice smiled wanly. "I don't know anyone here. And Cory is alone in his room. He doesn't like me to leave him."

"I would feel the same if I was him," said Marcus earnestly. "But I do not like to see a lady drinking by herself, all alone. If you can get away tomorrow, I will take you out for a meal. Then you will know someone, yes?"

Janice swallowed drily and stared hard into her glass. Then she straightened her back and turned to face him. "Yes," she heard herself saying. "I would like that very much."

Marcus raised his glass. "A toast. To my new friend." Their glasses clicked.

Janice and Cory spent the next day at the beach once more.

Janice had allowed Cory to remove his sweatshirt, and relative harmony prevailed until she refused him a second ice cream before his lunch. After this Cory sulked until teatime, wandering off into the dunes with his magnifying glass, on the lookout for lizards. He managed to dispatch four to their reptilean heaven before the onset of evening, and returned in a happier frame of mind to play cards with Janice on the balcony.

Impatient for the night, Janice played with a new urgency which Cory seemed to sense. He threw another tantrum at bedtime and refused to get into his pajamas. Finally, Janice realized that she would have to leave him in order to meet Marcus on time at the bar.

"If you won't get into bed, I'll leave you here and go out, and you can do what you like. I'm sick of your behavior, Cory, and I'm going to tell your father how naughty you've been when I see him."

"Yeah? Well, I'm going to tell him about you too, you old witch."

Cory was still jumping up and down on his bed as Janice slammed the door behind her and returned to her bedroom. Before her reflection she changed clothes several times, finally settling for a baggy cotton dress which made her look a little older and a little slimmer. She arrived at the bar to find Marcus in what was obviously his best suit. Together with a totally unsuitable tie it fitted very badly, but made his appearance all the more endearing.

They ate at a small open-air café tucked away from the crowded beachside streets. Their talk was light-hearted and peppered with misunderstandings, usually on Marcus's part. Janice told him about Philadelphia, and of her desire to eventually return to England. Marcus, too, wished to see England, where so many of his family had lived since the Turkish invasion. Soon it was midnight, and at the bottom of the stairway in the hotel, as the wind moaned sadly beneath the foyer doors, Marcus kissed her gently on the cheek, letting his face linger close enough to hers for her to feel the warmth radiating from his body. With a promise to meet the next evening, she crept up to her room, passing the petrifying lizard on the stairs, and quietly let herself in, pausing before Cory's door to make sure that he was asleep. Hearing nothing, she went to bed, and slept without stirring until nearly nine the next morning.

"Cory, would you like to eat downstairs today?" Janice knocked again on the boy's door. No sound came from within.

"Come on, lazybones." Janice pushed open the door and found the room empty, the bed unslept in, with its counterpane neatly folded down.

"Cory? Oh God . . ." She quickly pulled on jeans and a sweater, and ran out into the corridor.

A few guests were making their way down to breakfast. At the far end of the corridor the maids were already starting to change sheets in the rooms. Neither of the Cypriot women with their bundle-filled arms had seen the boy, or indeed even recalled his appearance. Cory had spent so much time in his room that few of the staff had come into contact with him. At the reception desk a temporary member of staff helped departing guests to sort out their bills. She had not seen Janice before, let alone Cory. In the breakfast room Marcus stood with the other waiters at the kitchen hatch, waiting for orders to be filled. His face darkened briefly when he saw Janice crossing the room towards him. Perhaps, she wondered, he thought that she was about to embarrass him by mentioning last night.

"Excuse me," she beckoned to Marcus. "Have you seen Cory, the little boy? He's not in his room."

"Have you looked by the pool? Perhaps he is having an early swim."

"His bed hasn't been slept in."

"Perhaps he made it before going out."

"He'd never do that. I don't know what could have happened . . ."

"Calm down." Marcus laid a soothing hand on her shoulder. "Let me ask the others." He turned to a small group of waiters behind him.

"Hey, Tony! The little boy, the one who comes to the pool with this lady. You seen him?"

They talked amongst themselves in Greek for a minute, then Marcus turned back to Janice and shrugged.

"Try the pool. Or the beach, he may have gone there."

Janice ran barefoot along the sand with her sandals in one hand. In the distance, the boys were raking the beach and starting to lay out chairs. Nobody was by the pool yet, and nobody else was on the beach. She slowed to a walk, trying to catch her breath. He would never have gone into town alone, surely.

"Are you sure you haven't seen a little boy? This high, rather fat?"

The bicycle man shook his head slowly, then continued setting the cycles out on their stands. "You should call the police.

They know what to do. If you want to go and look for him on a bicycle, I give you special rate.''

"Thank you, no." Janice ran back inside the hotel.

In the foyer the sad Indian couple with the crying baby were sitting on the couch as if they had never moved. Janice considered calling the police. She knew how angry Cory's father would be if it turned out the boy was simply teaching Janice a lesson by playing truant. The press were always more eager to report about his personal life than his business dealings. It was then that the first flicker of real fear touched the pit of Janice's stomach. She ran to the reception desk and rang the bell.

"Do you know, is there any mail for me?"

"Your room number?" The uninterested young girl crossed to the bank of pigeon holes.

"Room 2177. Hunt, Janice Hunt."

"Yes, you have a letter."

Janice felt a rising queasiness as she tore open the brown paper envelope, knowing what she would find inside. The son of an important US businessman, a diplomat for his country, dealing in the sale of arms . . .

> YOU WILL NOT GO TO POLICE
> YOU WILL NOT SPEAK TO ANYONE
> THE BOY IS SAFE FOR NOW
> YOU WILL ARRANGE FOR THE SUM OF £250,000
> TO BE DELIVERED TO YOUR ROOM AT NOON ON THURSDAY
> LEAVE ROOM EMPTY FOR ONE HOUR
> BOY WILL BE RETURNED UNHARMED
> YOU WILL BE CALLED WITH PROOF THAT BOY IS ALIVE
> YOU MUST TELL *NO ONE*
> AMERICAN CAPITALISM *WILL* PAY FOR ITS CRIMES

Janice's fingers tightened on the letter as she fought to stifle the rising bile in her throat. If she continued to stand here in the foyer someone would come and ask her what was wrong. She ran to her room and locked the door behind her, then picked up a telephone directory and scribbled out the code for America.

"Hello? Mr. Beckman's secretary, please."

"Speaking."

"Jerry? It's me, Janice. Where can I get in touch with Mr. Beckman?"

"Oh, hi Janice. Hey, give me a second to check . . . How's Cory?"

"Oh, he's fine . . ." Janice's grip on the receiver tightened.

"Janice, he's in Beirut at the moment."

"Can you give me the number?"

"I can give it to you, but you'll never get through." Janice wrote down the number.

"If I can't get him on the Beirut number, where will he be next?"

"He's taking a private plane to Dubai tomorrow. I can get you his arrival time if it's urgent. You know he won't like being disturbed."

"It is urgent, Jerry. Let me give you my number here, and you can call me as soon as you have his arrival time and where he's staying."

"Is there something wrong? Is there something the matter with Cory?"

Janice held the receiver away from her ear for a second and thought for a moment. "No, uh, Cory's fine. But I have to get in touch with his father urgently."

"OK. Listen, I'll call you at seven p.m. your time, and give you his itinerary details. You should be able to get him easy enough, but try the Beirut number first."

"Thanks a lot, Jerry. Speak to you at seven."

Janice replaced the receiver and collapsed on the bed. She needed to think. There was no question in her mind of going to the police. But she needed to talk to someone without leaving the hotel and possibly missing the phone call. She tried the Beirut number half a dozen times and gave up, then called the hotel switchboard to make sure that they would page her if a call came while she was out of the room.

At lunchtime she wavered outside the doors of the restaurant, watching Marcus as he slid smoothly between the tables with his luncheon tray. She realized now that the socially lethal combination of her shyness and Cory's rudeness had left her with only a Cypriot waiter as a confidant.

Later, sitting on Cory's neatly folded bed, she resolved to talk to Marcus after dinner. She felt surprisingly calm now, as if Cory's kidnapping were somehow strengthening her. At seven o'clock precisely, the telephone rang. Janice let it ring twice before answering.

"Jerry."

"Hi, Janice. Did you have any luck?"

"I couldn't even get hold of the Beirut operator."

"Yeah, it's like that most of the time. Listen, you'll be able to catch the boss, but you're gonna have to be accurate about calling on time. He's checking out factory sites, so he's travelling around. I'll give you the number in Dubai. You'll be able to get him there tomorrow evening between, uh, hold on, I'm working out the time difference . . ."

Janice listened to the line pinging and rustling across thousands of miles.

"OK, you still there?"

"Yes."

"Call between three and four p.m. your time tomorrow. He's scheduled to attend a conference then, but if for any reason you miss him, there's just one other time you'll be able to reach him, and that's at the Doha Intercontinental on Tuesday evening between ten and eleven p.m. your time. After that, he's in the air."

"Jerry . . . I have to tell you . . ." The words froze on Janice's lips. She had been told to speak to no one else. Suppose they were in the hotel, listening in on the conversation?

"Janice? You still there?"

"It's nothing. Give me the numbers."

After the call Janice went to Cory's room and stood at the door looking in. How did the kidnappers enter without a pass key? Could they have obtained one from the cleaners? Perhaps these old Cypriot women who trundled their disinfectant trolleys along the corridors had seen who abducted her young charge. Somehow, Janice doubted it. Whoever had taken the child had done so because they knew exactly who his father was. The whole thing would have had to be carefully planned. It was possible that the kidnappers had gained the child's trust and persuaded him to open the door . . .

Downstairs, in the pigeon hole labelled ROOM 2177, behind the deserted reception desk, there were two envelopes. Janice raised the counter flap, ran in behind the desk and removed them. In the corner of the bar, with a gin-filled glass, she tore open a corner of the first with trembling fingers.

Inside, there was a slip of paper, reading simply:

Dear Janice,
I have to go tonight and work a shift for a friend of mine at another hotel. I am sorry. Can we meet tomorrow evening after I finish?

Your friend,
Marcus

In the other envelope there was a single sheet of paper:

WE ARE WATCHING YOU ALL THE TIME
SPEAK TO NO ONE
THE BOY IS WELL

Enclosed was a lock of Cory's hair. It appeared to be authentic. Carefully, searching the room for watchful eyes, Janice folded the two notes and dropped them into her handbag. She reached for her drink. There was nothing she could do now but wait.

Later that evening a large party of Germans checked out of the hotel, leaving the reception area bare and silent. Janice found herself staring into the face of each passing guest and wondering if this face was checking her in return. Later, lying upstairs on her bed, staring at the ceiling, she tried to gauge her feelings towards Cory. The hours passed as if in a dream, a dream with two fixed points in time. One was the approaching hour of her call to Cory's father. The other was the hour of her meeting with Marcus. To fill the time, Janice painted her nails and set her hair as she listened to Cypriot girls chanting above the strange dirge-like music of the local radio station.

After dark she walked among the street cafés, hoping that somewhere here she would catch a glimpse of Marcus on his way to work. As the unfamiliar star formations began to appear in the inky sky, she realized that, for the first time in her life, she was truly alone. There was no one to influence or change the decisions she had to make. It was a disturbing, yet exhilarating feeling.

In bed that night she savored the cool freedom of the sheets, knowing that her loneliness was soon to end. Her dreams were crowded with images of Cory, and of glittering green lizards scuttling across the hot sand. Eventually these scenes were replaced by the sight of Marcus, shirtless and smiling, his slick brown body stealing the sun and turning all to darkness.

"Beckman. B-E-C-K-M-A-N. He's attending a meeting in one of your conference rooms at this moment."

"Please hold." The line went dead again. Janice looked at her watch. It read ten minutes before four in the afternoon. The staff of the Dubai hotel Cory's father was supposedly visiting had failed to locate him anywhere.

"Hello please? Miss?"

"I'm still here."

"I am afraid Mr. Beckman left a short while ago. He was not a registered guest, so we could not find him."

"Did he leave an address where he could be contacted?"

"He was not a registered guest."

"I *know* that," said Janice angrily.

"I am sorry, I cannot help you."

She slammed down the receiver and sat back on the bed. This left only tomorrow, Tuesday evening between ten and eleven, two days before Cory was marked to die if the money was not forthcoming. Perhaps she should go to the police after she had spoken to Cory's father. And tonight she resolved to tell Marcus everything. It would bring them closer together.

Half an hour before the evening meal was due to end, Janice was dressed and ready to meet Marcus. She decided to head down to the bar early. Looking at herself in the mirror, she hoped that he would find the new white cotton dress attractive. After all, there wasn't much else about her that he could possibly go for. She possessed what her mother described as an "interesting" look, which basically meant that no amount of make-up could make her face appear any thinner. Guiltily chiding herself for worrying about her appearance when Cory could be sitting tied to a chair in a basement somewhere, she walked down the draughty white stairs leading to the lounge, passing the now calcified lizard as it lay undisturbed and unnoticed by all, it seemed, except her.

At the bar she ordered a gin and tonic, and turned her stool so that she could watch the waiters striding through the restaurant with trays as they cleared away the dinner plates. She unclipped her handbag and felt around inside for her lipstick, touching instead the two folded notes she had placed in there earlier. Withdrawing them, she looked idly from one to the other.

They were written on identical pieces of paper.

Same cut, same size, same smell even. The room dipped before her eyes. Not Marcus. She needed to think. How could it have been Marcus? She was with him the night Cory had vanished. But she had not gone into the boy's room when she returned. Marcus could have enticed the boy out after she had fallen asleep . . . which would mean that he didn't really care for her at all. That he was just using her, keeping her quiet, watching her every move.

He had befriended the boy at the pool. Cory was always telling strangers about his father, and how rich he was. Marcus had courted her, charmed the child, and when both her and the boy's defenses were at their lowest he had acted. So where could Cory be? In the hotel, in one of the empty rooms Marcus would be bound to have access to?

Janice drained her drink and stood the glass down on the counter. Everything pointed to the waiter. And yet there was something that didn't fit . . . something wrong.

"You are early!"

Janice jumped at his touch, turning to see the now-familiar T-shirt and faded Levis which belonged to the smiling young waiter.

"You startled me."

"You are not afraid of my touch, I hope?" Marcus grinned at her impishly and sat down on the next bar stool. "You found the little boy?"

Janice could feel her skin prickle hotly. She tried to effect a casual smile. "Yes, thanks. He was at the beach after all."

"But I have not seen him today."

I bet you have, thought Janice. "He has sunburn. He wants to go home."

"And if he goes home, will you go with him?"

"No . . . I may put him on a flight tomorrow and stay on for a few days by myself." How easy it was to lie now. Nearby, the fat bartender watched them as he dried a glass. Could he hear what she was saying?

"What is the matter?"

"Nothing. Let's go and eat."

Janice rose from her stool and snapped her handbag shut. If he was watching her, she would sure as hell watch him.

As they walked into town, silently side by side, Janice's uneasiness grew, but as yet she could not pinpoint the cause. She watched the young man from the corner of her eyes as he concentrated on the pavement ahead. Occasionally he would look up and give a friendly nod to one of the waitresses working in the beach cafés. Eventually they stopped at a small open-roofed taverna and took their place at a table. In the course of the meal Janice astonished herself with the calculation of her charm, laughing and teasing, presenting the perfect picture of a silly, seduced girl. It was as they sat toying with their empty coffee cups at the end of the evening that her thoughts finally came into focus and the source of her uneasiness became apparent.

AMERICAN CAPITALISM WILL PAY FOR ITS CRIMES

How could this slow-witted waiter with the ambling gait and the cheeky smile have written that?

WE ARE WATCHING YOU ALL THE TIME

The man sitting opposite her fitted poorly the image of a sophisticated international terrorist with the resources to organize any sort of surveillance.

There could be only one answer.

Marcus was a con man, a dim and handsome waiter who had stumbled upon a relatively simple way of making a lot of money. Cory had said that Marcus had offered to take him away "early one morning." The boy had told him about his father, and Marcus had spirited him away, probably to relatives, while putting his plan into action. His one mistake had been to write out the two notes from the same pad. And now he was sitting here, being charming and biding his time until Janice arranged his financial escape from a world of waiting on tourist tables. Cory probably was not even aware of being "kidnapped." Pleased to be free of his nanny, he'd be having a whale of a time with Marcus's nephews somewhere. There was a way of checking.

"Excuse me for a moment. I have to go to the bathroom."

"Of course."

Marcus politely stood as she left the table and headed for the telephone at the back of the restaurant. She dialed the hotel.

"Hello, could I speak to the night porter, please."

"Hold on one moment."

"Night porter."

"Hello, this is room 2177. What time do you finish in the morning?"

"At seven o'clock, miss."

"You didn't happen to see a young boy, nine years old, rather fat, leave the hotel early in the morning two days ago? It's very important." There was a short silence on the other end of the line.

"Yes, I think I saw him. With a man, a tall man?"

"A young man, yes? One of the waiters?"

"I think so, yes."

"Thanks very much."

She returned to the table with renewed confidence, and smiled warmly at Marcus while she let him pay the bill.

As they walked arm in arm along the seafront, where the drunken sailors sat singing and playing the fool, Marcus hung his head sheepishly and turned to her.

"Janice, I have a confession to make."

She caught her breath. "Oh?"

"I am becoming very fond of you, here," he said, indicating a region somewhere under his arm. "In my heart."

"That's very nice, Marcus," she said, smiling viciously in the gloom. "And I am becoming very fond of *you*." Her tone was that of an efficient nurse about to administer an injection.

"That is good, very good." And with that he swung his face to hers and kissed her with a film-star ferocity that made both of them very nearly fall over a low wall into the sand.

At the door of her suite he attempted to wriggle his hand inside her dress as he kissed her. She returned his probing tongue, then slapped him smartly on the wrist.

"Really, Marcus. If you'd like to wait until tomorrow night, I can guarantee we'll have fun."

"I would like that," he said, going for her neck. She pulled him away.

"Good. Then I'll see you at the bar tomorrow, if not before. Good night, Marcus."

"Good . . ."

She had slipped inside and shut the door.

A few minutes later, breathing fresh, cool air from the sea as she leaned on her balcony, Janice thought things through a little further.

Tomorrow evening she would call Cory's father and secure the money for the brat's release. Money cabled to hotel. Money put in room. Room left for an hour. Cory returned. Big drama in the Beckman household, resulting in either her continuation as the monkey's keeper and a commendation for staying so calm in a crisis, or the sack for leaving him alone in the first place. Either way, good old reliable Janice did not exactly come out on top. And after it was over, Marcus would dump her and vanish, having no further need for her. She smiled coldly down at the empty streets.

The tough kidnapper and the starstruck virgin. Well, never again.

Janice poured herself a very stiff gin.

Tuesday evening arrived in a blaze of crimson, then settled to a black and starry sky. At seven Janice bathed and perfumed and dressed for dinner. In the restaurant she seated herself in Marcus's section, so that he served her meal. Afterward, they met at their regular corner in the bar and talked in the warmly intimate way she had seen so many tourists behave. He suggested going out for a drink. She suggested going up to her room. Somewhat taken aback, he awkwardly agreed, and they climbed the stairs in a silence stretched tight with sexual tension. There were gins in the room. There were shoes on the balcony. And very soon, much to Marcus's surprise, there were clothes all over the carpet and a couple in the bed.

The luminous hands of the bedside clock read 10:00 p.m. when they began their lovemaking and 11:00 p.m., appropriately enough, at the climax of their passion.

As they clung sweatily to each other in the comfort of the dark, Janice softly spoke.

"Thank you, Marcus, that was lovely. But it's after eleven and I can no longer get hold of Cory's father, or the money. So this is what I want you to do. I want you to return the boy tomorrow morning, in return for my silence about this matter. And I think we'll be having a lovely time like this on a regular basis, don't you?"

The light clicked on. Marcus sat up in bed with shock in his eyes.

"What do you mean? You said your little boy was in bed with sunburn. Is he not?"

The look of simple puzzlement on the waiter's face drained Janice's amusement and replaced it with a slow but steadily mounting look of horror.

At noon on Thursday the two Turks burst angrily into the back room of the crumbling villa and shouted in Cory's terrified face for the very last time.

As they slit his throat, and the Dodgers sweatshirt flooded crimson, the lizards crouching like verdured dragons on the window ledge watched impassively on.

JUMBO PORTIONS

" **'E**RE, THIS CHICKEN don't half taste funny."
       Sharon squinted through mascara-caked lashes at
the thing on the end of her fork. It was orange and lumpy and
battered, and it was dripping grease on to Sharon's copy of *Girl
About Town*.

"I told you we should have had a bloody tandoori." Tracy
looked up from her crossword puzzle and waggled the sup-
purating chicken chunk between her thumb and forefinger. "No
wonder you never see a bloody cat in the West End."

"There was a big queue at McDonald's. I don't like to wait.
Anyway, their chips are crap. Is your chicken funny?"

"It depends on what you mean by funny," said Tracy. "If
you mean 'Am I amused by it?' the answer is no. If you mean
'Does it taste like a long-dead mackerel?' I'd be forced to answer
yes." Tracy propped her half-gnawed chicken leg against her
typewriter and wiped her hands on a Supermoist Lemon Tow-
elette. She and Sharon spent their days typing out invoices for
discount furniture in the dingy little room which overlooked
Oxford Street. The work was slow, repetitive and undemanding.
But then so were Sharon and Tracy, although their hearts were
in the right place and we should think none the worse of them
for merely being ordinary.

Their lunchtimes were usually spent in the office with a meal
in a polystyrene box purchased from one of the many takeaway
food outlets in the area. The pattern varied on Fridays, when
instead of eating, they went with the downstairs mailboys to a
nearby wine bar and got drunk.

"Of course, you *know* about takeaway chicken, don't you?"
asked Sharon as she continued to stare in fascination at the object on the end of her fork.

129

"What do you mean?" Tracy's Birmingham accent was as spikily pronounced as Sharon's heavy cockney.

"Well, they're all battery grown, you now, like in them little wire cages, millions of 'em. And they never see the light, so they never grow feathers. And there's no room to move, so they lose the power of their legs. They just sit there, all white and hairless, screaming at each other. And they're trained to eat from these chutes that pump fishmeal into them until they're full to bursting. That's why it tastes fishy."

"Oh, bloody fab." Tracy emptied the oily remains of her fried chicken carton into the wastepaper basket with a grimace.

"Only this tastes . . ." Sharon groped for the word. "Funny."

"Why don't you take it back and complain?" Tracy wiped her hands on her seat and proceeded to tear open a Toffee Crisp.

"I think I will. In fact, I think I'll go right now." Sharon shook the dripping lump free from the end of her fork and let it fall back into the box, which was leaking grease on to her desk. Carefully wrapping the carton in a plastic carrier bag, she rose from her chair. "They're supposed to give you sporks with the food, anyway."

"You what?"

"You know, sporks, them white plastic spoons with jagged points on the end. That's what they're called."

"Oh." Tracy returned her attention to a magazine article on unreliable smear tests. "If you're goin' past the sandwich shop, bring us back a sardine and tomato."

Sharon pushed open the door of the fried chicken takeaway outlet and dumped her carrier bag on the counter. The little Indian at the back of the store lowered his chip basket into a tank of boiling fat and waddled up to the service bay.

"Yes pliz?"

"Your chicken tastes funny."

"What you mean?" The little Indian wiped a lock of lank hair from his eyes and peered into the plastic bag as Sharon withdrew a half-eaten piece of breast.

"You taste it." She proffered the piece.

The Indian made a face. "Urgh," he said. "No thank you. Is horrible."

"Don't give me Is Horrible, you expect other people to eat it." Sharon dropped the breast back into the box with a look of disgust.

"Is not my fault I don' eat chicken. Nobody else complain."

"That's cause they're probably not alive afterwards." She shook the carrier bag. "I want my money back."

"You wait here." The Indian waddled off and disappeared behind several plastic sacks full of defrosting chips. A few moments later he returned with a sweaty young man in a vest which revealed the navel of his beer-swelled stomach.

"Wassamatter with the chicken?" he asked belligerently. Perspiration, if such a delicate term could be used, dripped from his pale, chubby face.

"She say it taste funny."

"Funny?" The podgy young man thrust his hand into Sharon's carrier bag and withdrew a chicken leg. He took a large bite, chewed for a few moments, and with the delicacy of a veteran wine taster spat the lump of chewed meat into the palm of his hand.

"The batter's off." He turned to the Indian, who in turn looked at Sharon with embarrassment.

"You 'aven't been using the batter in the bowl above the frozen yoghurts?" The Indian nodded nervously. The fat young man rolled his eyes heavenward. "No wonder. I could have told you that was off. You should have chucked it out before the weekend."

"Well, it's unhygienic," sniffed Sharon as she unstuck her hands from the glistening counter. "That meat could be curdled. You should stick a warning on the side of the box— 'Danger: Might Be Off.' "

"Look, you can 'ave a refund if you're gonna be funny."

"It ain't me that's funny, it's your chicken, mate."

The Indian dropped three pound coins and four grease-slippery tenpence pieces into Sharon's outstretched palm. Tossing her spray-glazed curls at the duo, Sharon clumped out of the takeaway and off along Charing Cross Road to find a Tandoori.

The young man stared after the closing door and tutted. "These people come in here expecting the earth." He turned to the Indian, who was gingerly removing Sharon's abandoned plastic bag from the counter. "It's all very well for them, all they got to do is eat the stuff, they don't have to sell it. They don't understand the problems you get with poultry."

"Thass right," said the Indian. "Me, I like a nice piece of fish."

"Well then, have a piece of chicken." The fat young man laughed. Then his face grew serious. "She had a nice bum on her, though," he said.

* * *

"How's your Tone these days?" asked Tracy as she stood at the photocopying machine collecting the printed advertisements for Dralon Boudoir Stools which were popping out of one end. "Is he still out of work?"

"No," said Sharon, "he's got a job on a van, deliverin'."

"Nice," said Tracy. "Deliverin' what?"

"I dunno."

"Oh." Tracy collected her copies and carefully squared their corners. "Still, nice though. Workin' an' that. I wish my Damon could find a bloody job."

"How long's he been out of work now?" Sharon folded a piece of gum between her glossy crimson lips and began snapping it into shape.

"Six bloody months."

"You should tell him. It's no good being trained up in wicker repair if there isn't the call for it."

"Yeah I know, but—well, you've met him—there's his problem to consider."

"What problem?"

"He can't apply himself." Tracy stuck a ruler up her skirt and scratched the top of her tights. "This heat's giving me a terrible rash."

"Can't apply himself? What, you mean he's stupid?"

"Basically, yeah. I'm gonna have to put something on this." Together they clumped away from the photocopying machine. "Let's get some lunch in."

"Good idea," agreed Sharon. "All I 'ad for breakfast was Fruit Crunch."

"What's that, health cereal?"

"I suppose so. It turned the milk red."

Sharon dashed through the rain along Oxford Street, heading for the nearest hamburger bar. When she arrived outside she was surprised to see plastic cladding draping the front of the building and a CLOSED FOR RENOVATION sign slung across the entrance. The rain was spoiling her spiky blonde coiffure, and would be bound to start leaking into her boots in a minute. Darting between the taxis, she found herself at the bottom of Tottenham Court Road, where shoppers hurried between broken paving slabs and flooded drains. Here in a no-man's-land of stereo component stores populated by listless Tunisian salesmen, there was only one takeaway within sprinting distance.

The little Indian recognized Sharon the moment he laid eyes on her. She stood at the counter shaking the rain from her hair like a spaniel, the only customer.

"Today we have good chicken, Miss. You want try?"

"It had better be good or I'll bring it back."

The Indian tonged hot battered chicken into a carton, added a variety of sachets and passed it to her. Sharon tucked the box under her arm and headed back out into the rain. The fat young man stuck his head out from behind the rotisserie.

"Her again? Glutton for punishment. I bet she brings it back. She'll find something wrong, you'll see. I know the type. Complain about finding hairs in their soup. Real moaners."

"She won't bring it back," said the Indian. "Bring it back up, perhaps. I don't know how you people can eat such rubbish. Kebabs. Fish and chips. Fried chicken . . ."

"Tandoori takeaways," added the fat young man. "Your lot's got quite a bit to answer for as well."

The Indian gave him a cool look and returned to his fat fryer.

"Now, this isn't so bad," said Tracy with her mouth full of chicken. She sucked a huge gulp of Diet Coke and carried on chewing. Her ancient desk was littered with magazines, spilt correcting fluid and polystyrene coffee cups with cigarette ends floating in them. There was little work to do today. "It's sort of"—she sought to articulate an impressionistic response—"you know . . . less fishy."

"Yeah, more, er . . ." Sharon stared at the gnarled lump of battered meat with a single bleached bone protruding from the end of it. "More burgery."

"Yeah, there is an aftertaste of burger, isn't there? Quite nice, actually." Tracy peered into her chicken box as if half expecting something to leap out of it. "I wonder why it tastes like that?"

Sharon tore the skin from a chicken leg and held it up to the light, examining it as she pondered the problem. "It's probably just from storage."

"What do you mean?"

"Well, the chickens, after they've been slaughtered—'cause they're killed in vast numbers at a time 'cause it's easy killing them, the chickens being very weak and unable to walk and nude from not growin' any feathers—well, after they're chopped up into the appropriate parts like breast an' wing, they get stored in huge fridges, then they get moved to smaller fridges which probably have hamburgers on some of their shelves, an' the

hamburgers drip meat juices on to the chicken, probably.''
Sharon sucked the chicken skin into her mouth, smearing her
lipstick as she did so. ''It's all just meat, nothing to worry
about.''

''So what happens to the heads an' feet an' stuff?'' asked
Tracy with a sickly look on her face. ''You never see deep fried
chicken feet.''

''There's no call for them—in white countries,'' Sharon replied darkly. ''They get ground up an' made into other chicken-
flavored products. Like when packet soup says 'chicken extract'
on the side. It's the ground-up bits no one else wants to have
anything to do with. Beaks and things.''

''You're putting me right off,'' said Tracy, blanching beneath
her make-up. ''I think I'll stick to sausage sandwiches in future.''

''You're no better off there. Cow lips and eyeballs, all
squashed up in skins, that's sausages for you.''

While Tracy visited the toilet, Sharon turned back to her deep-
fried thigh and read an article on cervical cancer in *Wow* magazine.

''Hang on, it's slipping.'' Tony shouldered the fruit machine
upright and together they lowered it from the ramp of the truck.
Standing it down on the pavement with a thud, he leaned on the
Formica top and wiped his brow. ''How many more we got
today, Steve? I'm knackered.''

Steve consulted his notebook. ''Just one more. We should be
through by six.''

''We'd better be. I'm meeting my Sharon outside Tottenham
Court Road tube station at six.'' Tony smoothed down his flat-
top and hitched up his white socks. There was no mirror available but he presumed he still looked terrific.

''That'll be handy for you,'' said Steve. ''We're delivering
just around the corner from there, to a Mr. Patel.''

Tony checked that the rolled sleeves of his tight white T-shirt
were still in place and prepared to shoulder the machine once
more. He looked good when he was lifting things. His muscles
bulged.

''Okay, let's get this one inside.''

After installing the machine, bolting it to the floor of the
Chinese takeaway and leaving the bemused manager with a set
of instruction booklets showing him how to operate the Missis-

sippi Gambler 2000 Electronic Blackjack game, Steve and Tony climbed back into the van.

Tony checked his appearance in the rear-view mirror and quickly slid a comb over his immaculately styled square hair. He squeezed a spot on his neck, then straightened the golden Taurus horoscope symbol Sharon had given him to wear as an earring.

"Where you off to tonight?" asked Steve as he started the engine.

"We're goin' up that new cocktail bar in Camden, opposite the market. We went there last week but we didn't stay long cause someone got knifed. Then we'll go for a kebab at the Chinese place next door."

"I've been there," said Steve. "They do really good curries. Real bum-burners."

"Yeah, there's nothing like a good curry, is there? Mind that old dear."

Steve shot the van over a zebra crossing and narrowly missed an elderly lady who was struggling with the wheels of her shopping basket.

"You gonna marry Sharon, then?"

"Nah. She wants to but I can't at the moment."

"Why not?"

Tony studied his reflection in the window. "I've got a kid. From this girl I used to be at school with. Sharon doesn't know. I keep meanin' to tell her. Watch out for that bloke on the bike."

"Well, you'd better pop her a postcard. It's quite important, something like that." Steve swung the van past a cyclist, who was forced to pull into the curb.

"I was gonna tell her before. The trouble is, I'm still seein' the mother."

"You randy sod," laughed Steve. "Go it, my son." The van turned into the one-way system at Tottenham Court Road, scattering pedestrians in every direction.

"Talking of food," said Tony, "you ever had frogs' legs? They're great. They taste like chicken."

"I'm never sure about French stuff. I mean, they eat horses, don't they? An' that's barbaric, to my mind." Steve cut into the next traffic lane and considerably surprised the driver of an invalid carriage.

"Me, I like all them exotic things," said Tony. "Snails, they're like whelks." He thought for a moment. "Whelks in garlic."

"I couldn't eat snails," admitted Steve. "I mean, you see

'em in the garden leaving slimy trails, don't you? An' when they're cooked, they look like something you'd find up a horse's nose.'' He pulled a face and beat a Ford Marina to a parking space outside the fried chicken takeaway which Sharon had patronized only yesterday.

"How can you have it here when you ain't got no power point to connect it up with?" Steve stood up and wiped his dusty hands on the knees of his jeans. The little Indian shrugged.

"You will have to speak to Mr. Duncan. I will get him for you."

"Thank you, Mr. Patel." Steve turned to Tony. "We ain't gonna get this machine fixed up tonight. They haven't got a proper junction box for it."

Tony looked over at the dormant fruit machine and scratched his head. "I could put in a bit of overtime late tomorrow an' sort it out," he offered. Just then, the Indian reappeared with the fat young man in the grease-stained shirt.

"I'm Duncan, the manager," he said. "Is there a problem?"

Steve explained the hold-up, and offered Tony's services the following evening. Duncan blew his nose on a paper serviette and agreed that tomorrow would be fine.

"Anyway," said Steve, "it's all fixed up and ready to go. Tony here will patch in your electrics. What time do you close?"

"At eleven p.m.," said Mr. Patel, "but you can come earlier. We're not very busy, early evening."

"That's no good," said Tony. "I've got to turn off your electrics, and that means turning off your fryer. I'll get here just before you shut."

"We'll be off, then," said Steve. "You got a chicken leg for us to be going on with?"

"There's a baby here that's been born with its head on backwards," said Tracy, setting her hamburger down on a folded copy of *The Sun* and reading the headline. She carefully dabbed bun crumbs from her lipstick. "The doctors are blaming it on faulty spermicide. What does your hamburger taste like?"

Sharon considered the question for a moment. "I dunno," she conceded. "You can't describe it really."

"You know what mine tastes like?"

"What?"

"Well, if you tore up an empty cereal packet, like into tiny,

tiny pieces, and then mashed it up with Bisto for about two hours, then let it set . . .''

"Yes?"

"Well, that's what it tastes like."

"That's cause cows, when they're slaughtered, these great hammers . . .''

"Don't bloody start that again," said Tracy. "Why's your Tone workin' late?''

"He's puttin' in a bit of overtime," said Sharon. "At one of the places where he's deliverin.' ''

"You don't think he's seein' someone else, do you?" asked Tracy.

"No," said Sharon. "He's not that bright. Can I have your ketchup sachet?''

The last customer had just left the fried chicken takeaway when Tony arrived. The night was warm, and the greasy heat in the store was almost unbearable. It clung heavily to his clothing as he unpacked equipment from his toolbox. Behind the counter Mr. Patel was cleaning down the shelves of the rotisserie. Further out at the back, Duncan was resealing sacks of frozen chips. The fruit machine sat dark in the corner. Mr. Patel paused in his labors and poured himself a cup of instant tomato soup. He slurped it thickly, leaving a fluorescent red circle around his mouth. Tony sorted out his tools and carried them across to the fruit machine.

"So," he said genially, talking to the wall as he worked, "how long you been here, then?''

"Two years," answered Mr. Patel as he finished his soup and prepared to wash the floor in the back of the shop. "It was doner kebab place but Greek boys got closed down by the health peoples.''

"Why was that?"

"They had a really disgustin' problem with the toilet drainage system," called Duncan. "Blowback. You don' wanna hear about it.''

"Blowback?" Tony grimaced and went about his work.

Presently, he looked up from the tangled mass of cable on the floor and called to Mr. Patel.

"Excuse me, do you happen to know where this lead goes?''

"Sorry." Mr. Patel shrugged and continued mopping the tiles.

"What appliances have you got wired up there? How many wall sockets? Hang on, I'll come back and have a look."

Tony raised the red Formica counter flap and let himself through to the back of the store, where Duncan was wringing a grey cloth into a bucket of filthy water.

"Mind you don't slip on the floor."

Tony traced the cable he was looking for, and sat back on his haunches to strip it.

"This wiring's a real old mess," he pointed out. "I wouldn't let anyone from the council see it if I were you. Here, I've been meaning to ask you something. What do you do with all the chicken that don't get sold? Do you take it home, like?"

"Urgh, indeed we do not," said Mr. Patel earnestly. "Chicken cooked in this manner is no good for you."

"Funny that," said Tony, "you not liking chicken and workin' here."

"It's because he works here that he became a vegetarian," chided Duncan. "Ain't that right, Patsy?"

"I do not like you calling me that," said the little Indian as he angrily tossed the remaining soapy water in his bucket across the tiles.

"Me," began Tony, "I love a good curry, but that's . . ."

He never finished the sentence, because as he spoke he moved forward towards the exposed box of electrical circuitry, slipped on the tidal wash of soapy water from Mr. Patel's bucket and fell face first into the junction box.

There was a loud bang, and a spectacular array of sparks fizzed in a halo around Tony's electrified head. His body jerked erect as the blast of electrical current from the mains supply tore through him, then he was suddenly thrown backward with his arms flailing, like a scarecrow in a hurricane. He hit the edge of the deep fat fryer with his pelvis and fought for a moment to retain his balance, both hands flying first to his blackened face, then clawing the air as he somersaulted backwards over the rim and into the fryer with an oily splash.

Duncan and Mr. Patel looked on in horror, their jaws dropped and their eyes bulging at the scene taking place before them. The fryer was built to hold three pans of chips. It was far too small to contain a human being. Unfortunately however, Tony had fallen head first, and as he fell had raised his knees so that he had entered the fat in a crouched position. Consequently, when the boiling waves subsided, all that could be seen of Tony was the soles of his track shoes.

For a moment the only sounds in the little takeaway were the crackle of electricity and the gentle bubbling of boiling fat as it popped and plopped around Tony's cooking body. Finally, Duncan spoke.

"Why didn't you turn the bloody fryer off?"

Mr. Patel suddenly became aware of the extreme likelihood that Duncan would try to pin the blame on him. He began to sweat profusely.

"I was not expecting anyone to fall into it," he said lamely. "Anyway, you are the manager, and you are not supposed to let anyone else back here for reasons of hygiene. It says so in the company manual."

Successfully countered, Duncan stood with his arms at his sides thoughtfully staring into the fryer while the device was turned off.

"Do you think he's dead?" asked Mr. Patel timidly.

Duncan exploded into life. "Dead? Of course he's bloody dead!"

"How can we get him out of there?"

"We'll have to wait until the fat cools down."

Already, a delicious smell of cooking meat was filling the room. Duncan peered into the fryer once more. "Oh Christ, he's starting to crust up."

Mr. Patel wrung his hands fearfully. "Whatever will we do?" he asked the ceiling.

"They'll take away our license if they find out, that's for sure."

"But we cannot just leave him in there cooking!"

"What time do the dustmen come by?" asked Duncan, shaking Mr. Patel by the shoulders.

"A little after midnight, I think. It varies. Sometimes they do not appear until seven in the morning."

"Let's pray this isn't one of those times," said the sweating young man. "What we'll do—when you've finished jumping up and down panicking—is first of all turn the fryer back on . . ."

"What? This is craziness!" the little Indian screamed.

"Listen to me," said Duncan. "We'll cook the corpse until it's unrecognizable. Then we'll drain off the fat, remove the body and put it into one of those heavy-duty hundred-weight bags that the chips come in. We'll leave it with the other rubbish out on the pavement. If anyone opens it and looks inside, all they'll see is a jumble of burnt meat and batter."

"And this will work?" asked Mr. Patel.

"For both our sakes," said Duncan as he switched the fryer back on, "it had better bloody work."

After the fat had been boiling for more than an hour, the air in the takeaway store was filled with the powerful aroma of overcooked meat. If he had not known exactly what was cooking, Mr. Patel might have found the smell quite delicious. Instead, he could scarcely keep from regurgitating his lunchtime samosas. Duncan appeared from around the corner dragging a heavy plastic sack.

"Smells good, don't it?" he said, lifting his porcine nose in the air and sniffing. "Almost seems a pity to waste it. 'Ere." He nudged the distinctly queasy-looking Mr. Patel. "I bet we could make a fair bit of dosh if we changed the name of the store to Sweeney Todd's."

Mr. Patel gave him a look of utter incomprehension.

When the fryer had been turned off and drained, Duncan beckoned Mr. Patel to come and take a look. Reluctantly, he came over and squinted into the grease-coated stainless steel basin. Inside, standing on his head and his kneecaps, was an unrecognizable Tony. If he had not been dead when he tumbled in, he would certainly have been battered to death by now.

"You get around one side of him," said Duncan. "Put your oven gloves on. I'll get around the other side and we'll lift him out together and stand him on the floor."

"I cannot do this," moaned Mr. Patel. "We are committing a sin."

"Yeah, well." Duncan tried to console his partner. "It's a good job you ain't a Catholic. This wouldn't sound too good in the confessional."

Mr. Patel gave a pained look and donned his floral oven gloves. Then he gingerly lowered his hands over the side of the fryer. Together they lifted the body out inch by inch. They had almost got it clear of the basin when there was a cracking noise, and it broke in half. Although Duncan swore angrily, this desiccation of the body made its removal much easier, as all the fluids had been dried out and the corpse could now be broken into several pieces, mixed with the day's batter scrapings and tipped into a number of different bags. Mr. Patel agreed to help, but kept his eyes screwed up tight throughout the operation, especially when Duncan cracked off Tony's deep-fried fingers and dropped them into a separate bag.

"You got all the loose pieces of batter up your end, Patsy?"

"I think so, yes."

"Good, then give me a hand with these sacks and we'll get 'em out before the dustcart comes by."

After the sacks were secured and placed outside the two men returned to the back of the store and wiped up the puddles of grease which had formed all over the floor. As Mr. Patel was mopping up the last pool, Duncan came by with the air freshner.

"Mmmm, lavender, that's better," he said, spraying everywhere. "You'd better put that cheesecake back in the cold cabinet or it'll go off."

Once they had finished clearing up, Duncan and Mr. Patel turned off the shop lights and sat outside in Duncan's car until they had seen the dustcart load and crush the sacks containing the hapless Tony to a pulp. Then, after promising to open the store as usual in the morning, they went home to their beds. For Mr. Patel, at least, it was a sleepless night.

Sharon and Tracy sat at their usual places in the dingy office with their lunch spread out before them. Sharon was processing a requisition form for Buffalo Suede Reclining Chairs, and Tracy was waiting for her nails to dry before starting into her box of fried chicken. She held up two cans of fizzy drink.

"Which one d'you want, Shar? Orange?" She pointed from one to the other. "Or yellow?"

"What's the yellow?" asked Sharon as she opened her carton and removed the napkins, sachets and spork.

Tracy examined the printing on the can. " 'Tropical Fruit Mix,' it says. Could be anything. 'Produce Of More Than One Country. Made From Concentrate. Contains Saccharin.' "

"Causes cancer in laboratory rats, does saccharine," said Sharon as she pulled out a chicken leg and bit into it.

"Well, we're not laboratory rats, are we?" said Tracy.

"Oh, give me the orange."

"Did you see your Tone last night?" asked Tracy, passing over the soft-drink can.

"No. He was supposed to come round but he never showed up. Men."

"Is he normally reliable, then?"

"Not really, no."

"No, well they're not, are they?"

Silence fell in the office while Tracy opened her chicken box and started on a wing. She looked over at Sharon.

"Blimey, you polished off that leg in record time."

"I was hungry," she said through a mouthful of meat. "Friday tomorrow. You gonna come up to the wine bar?"

"Yeah, but I don't much like that house wine they have. It comes out of purple plastic barrels. It doesn't seem to have travelled well."

"I should think it's travelled very well if it's in plastic barrels. It's probably been all over the place."

"That's a point."

Silence fell once more. Sharon set down her denuded chicken bone and delved into her box for another piece. Tracy drank her Tropical Fruit Mix and studied the portion of cheesecake sitting on her desk. She leaned forward and sniffed it.

"I *thought* that's where it was coming from," she said. "This cheesecake smells of lavender."

"Probably a new flavor." Sharon chewed on slowly. "Now this chicken really *does* taste funny."

"Oh Shar, you always say that. You're too bloody fussy, that's your problem."

"No, it really does." She carefully examined the piece in her hand. "And anyway, what piece of a chicken makes this shape?" She held it up to let Tracy have a look. The battered piece was small and semi-circular, and rather flat.

"I dunno," said Tracy, puzzled. "It's shaped like someone's ear."

"Chicken's don't have ears." Sharon peered at it more closely. Set in the bottom of the fried portion, something glittered. She carefully picked away at the batter.

Underneath, pinned through the meat, was a small golden Taurus horoscope symbol.

Sharon's subsequent scream was so loud that shoppers in Oxford Street stopped dead when they heard it, and even Mr. Patel, in the middle of serving a customer, looked up and wondered.

SAFE AS HOUSES

"**A**ND TWO AND three and four and stretch. Keep those legs high, ladies, keep pumping, and now push, and push, and push, and push again. Feel the muscles in your legs stretching, stretch, and stretch, and stretch, and . . ."

Disco music pounded from the portable TV as, onscreen, the muscular blond instructor twisted his body to the left, then the right. Behind him in the studio danced thirty adoring women in pastel tracksuits, leotards and leg warmers. As he crouched into another workout position, the muscles in his arms bulged in time to the music, and his tousled hair bounced rhythmically above his neon-blue eyes.

To Winifred, it looked suspiciously like sex.

Flashing a brilliant smile at the camera he shouted a command at the jiggling women, who obediently rolled over on to their backs and began cycling their legs in the air, with varying degrees of success. The instructor jumped up and walked among them, straightening the odd leg and patting a bottom or two, shamelessly flirting with them all. He was presumably gay. The music doubled in its tempo and the women squealed with the extra effort.

"I . . . don't . . . know . . . why . . . you . . . make . . . me . . . do . . . this!" gasped Winifred from the tiled kitchen floor where she lay on her back with her legs in the air. Behind her, dressed in a powder-blue jogging suit, her husband was running on the spot.

"Because it keeps you trim, Winifred," he shouted back without taking his eyes from the TV screen. "It's for your own good. No wife of mine is going to get out of shape just because she's in her fifties."

"Fifty, Morris, I'm just fifty." Copying the actions of the women on the television, Winifred reluctantly rose to her feet and began to swing her arms high above her head. Her husband was already starting to perform the next exercise.

"Remember how you used to be, forever baking those giant cakes and complaining about your weight? You can't tell me you were happy with yourself."

"Believe me, Morris . . . I was happy. Now can I . . . can I stop?" Winifred's breath was coming in ragged gasps.

"Okay then, take five." Morris stopped jogging and wiped his forehead with the towel which hung around his neck. "But I want you to remember to do your exercises this afternoon. To make up for yesterday."

"Yesterday! But I—"

"You missed yesterday, didn't you?"

"I did not, Morris! I swear to God I—how did you find out?"

"I checked your sweatbands. They were unused." Morris gave her a smug smile. Behind him, the television was showing a commercial for a vitamin supplement, created "for the healthy way you live today."

"I wanted to do just a little baking this afternoon." Winifred gave the unused cooker a longing look.

"How many times do I have to tell you, Winifred? Sugar is a killer. Why do you think I won't allow you to use the oven? Because cooking food . . ."

"Destroys all the nutrients, I know."

"Right. That's why we only eat organically grown raw vegetables, to get protein and plenty of fiber."

Winifred slumped over the kitchen counter trying to get her breath back while Morris headed for the shower. She hated having to work out every day. Apart from anything else, it was so undignified. Last week she had been lying on the floor with her legs in the air when the postman looked through the window. She still held fond memories of the days before Morris had embarked on his health kick. She used to cook all the time then. Upside-down cake, summer pudding, baked alaska, key lime pie, crème brûlée, pancakes with lemon and syrup and lashings of cream . . . She admitted to herself that she was a little on the plump side, but she was fifty years old for Christ's sake, not a girl of nineteen. When she had pointed this out to Morris, he had launched into his usual speech, untucking his Adidas shirt and slapping his hard little stomach.

"Look at that, Winifred," he would say. "Not an ounce of fat. Not an inch to be pinched. A man's body is a temple. I'm fifty-four and fitter than any young lout."

Of course, the mention of young louts would really set him off, and he would then switch into his "This Country's Going to the Dogs" routine. Winifred could never see what all the fuss was about. She rather liked young people, especially since she had no children of her own. They possessed so much energy, and seemed so receptive to new ideas. Her husband's were positively worn thin from retreading.

When she had married Morris, four long years ago, he had seemed the ideal husband for her, stable, sensible and strong—quite a change from the previous man in her life. It was a second marriage for both of them, and Winifred had lately begun to wonder if Morris's first wife hadn't died from sheer exhaustion.

"I tell you, Winifred," called Morris from the bathroom, "if we all let our waistlines go to hell there'll be no one but ourselves to blame when the wrong elements walk into Parliament and seize power."

Waiting in the doorway until she could hear his voice vanish beneath the sound of running water, she tiptoed over to the refrigerator, opened it and felt around the back, behind the vegetable crisper, for the piece of cheesecake she had hidden there. Locating it, she raised the slice to her mouth, about to savor the first delicious bite, when there was a movement behind her. Whirling, the cheesecake guiltily tucked at her back, she found herself facing Morris, who was wrapped in a bath towel and watching her angrily.

"You disappoint me, Winifred," he sighed. "I can't trust you for a moment. You're only hurting yourself, you know. Is it any wonder you look like you do? We had better double this afternoon's quota of sit-ups to compensate for all those extra calories."

"But I didn't eat it yet, Morris . . ."

"The thought, Winifred, is father to the deed. Double sit-ups. Now give me the cake." Ashamed, she handed him the paper plate, which he tipped smartly over the waste disposal unit.

"Junk food has already undermined the constitution of the country. It's not going to have the same effect in my house, do you understand?"

Morris dropped the empty plate into the pedal bin below the sink. A vein pulsed at the side of his neck. There could not have been a worse moment for the cat to stroll into the kitchen. Morris saw it and released a theatrical gasp.

"How many times have I told you that this creature is not

allowed to roam freely about the house! The germs, Winifred! Are you aware how many species of flea there are in a cat's fur? If you can't . . . keep it locked in the garage, you know what will happen . . ."

"It will have to be put down," Winifred recited.

"That is correct." The little man headed back to the bath-room, waddling absurdly along the passage in his towel and plastic bathing cap. Suddenly remembering, he turned to his wife.

"And Winifred, I don't want you going out today. Hinkley is coming to fit some new locks."

"But Morris, I made arrangements for the guild this after-noon. We can't possibly need any more locks."

"Yes we can, Winifred. There are two windows in the attic which have only simple burglar catches. A child could break them open. You'll just have to cancel your meeting. I have to be at my golf lesson by noon. Stay here and let Hinkley in—and make sure he does a better job than last time."

"What are we protecting?" asked Winifred, throwing up her hands in exasperation. "What's a thief going to find worth steal-ing in this house?"

A familiar wheedling tone crept into his voice. "Now, you know I'm only doing it for you. I have to protect my old girl."

"I'm not an old girl."

After her husband had gone she poured herself a cup of caffeine-free coffee and slumped into a chair. Winifred had lived in South London all her life. Morris was from Cardiff, but had come to the capital when the clothing company for whom he worked had relocated. He loathed the city and perpetually com-plained about it, endlessly comparing it to his home town. The few friends he had made here were solitary businessmen who spent their time skulking around the local golf course before setting the country to rights over drinks in the clubhouse.

Business was going well for Morris, so they had recently moved from their modest terraced house in Wandsworth to a larger, more isolated property in Dulwich Village, bordering a small but attractive park. To their friends this move was seen as a natural progression to a better lifestyle, but Winifred knew the real reason for the change of address. Morris was mortally afraid of being burgled. Last year, he pointed out to her, the statistics for breaking and entering in the Wandsworth area had leapt. People were moving out of the built-up areas and heading for select parts of the suburbs. In town, he said, the mugging rate was rising fast, more cars were being stolen, and decent womenfolk were no longer safe in their own beds.

Typically, Morris blamed it entirely on the kids, and although he would not admit it across a bridge table, the black kids. Of this he had no proof beyond what he saw on the nine o'clock news, and even then he selected facts to fit his own narrow view of life. Winifred stared into her cooling, insipid coffee. She wished she had the strength to leave him. She was familiar with all his bullying tactics, and ultimately knew that she would succumb to them. It wasn't just the little things she hated, like being switched to foul Lo-Cal wine at dinner because "it's better for your figure," it was losing old friends and being told that they did not matter because "we have each other," when it was patently obvious to Winifred that this was the one thing they did not have.

"Cottonwood, come here you little creep, getting your mistress into trouble again." She reached under the table and scooped up the cat, carrying it towards the back door of the kitchen. Morris hated all animals, and especially Cottonwood, because it had belonged to Winifred's first husband. He had taken to feigning an asthma attack whenever the creature appeared. There was very little that Morris seemed to approve of these days. Winifred wondered how long it would be before Morris ceased to approve of her.

"That should hold it, Mrs. Kirby," said the locksmith, standing back and surveying his work. He looked around at the other attic windows, then dropped his voice to a lower register. "I know it's none of my business, but how come you have so many locks? We've put double security locks and bolts on every damned door and window in the house. And if you don't mind my saying so, I think the new wire-glass you have in all your downstairs frames spoils the view."

"I'm afraid I have to agree with you, Mr. Hinkley." Winifred brushed a straying gray lock of hair behind her ear. "As you know, my husband is very security minded. He says it's the only way a man can be sure of protecting his valuables these days." In saying this, Winifred was not entirely sure that she was included on the inventory.

"That's fine by me," said Mr. Hinkley. "I can do with the business. But he should get a good alarm system if he's that worried. I could put in photoelectric cells, pressure pads, stuff like that. Course, there's no real way of keeping a thief out if he's determined to get in."

Winifred smiled to herself. Perhaps there were thieves who dealt exclusively in direct-outlet furniture, threadbare rugs and keep-fit equipment, but she somehow doubted it. No, there was nothing Morris owned which was remotely worth stealing. He could afford to buy nice things. He simply failed to see the point of such expenditure. The house was depressingly barren of home comforts. Morris did not approve of paintings. "Art is produced by fools who need money for fools who wish to be deprived of it," he would say. Winifred's efforts in creating a homely atmosphere in the downstairs lounge had been destroyed when Morris had built his own exercise equipment right in the middle of the floor.

"Everything a man needs to keep his body healthy," he'd told her proudly, unveiling the steel monstrosity which now stood permanently bolted to the stripped pine floorboards. "It'll save me a fortune in gym subscriptions."

"The floor, it's ruined," Winifred had complained. "It's so ugly. Couldn't you have built it somewhere else, in the garage?"

"Don't be absurd, Winifred, the damp would ruin it. Besides, what do we ever use this room for?"

"We could use it for entertaining . . ."

"By entertaining," she remembered him saying, "you mean listening to your friends' loony-left views while they sit around drinking my wine. Not in my house."

"You're right," Winifred had said bitterly. "Let's *turn* the lounge into a gymnasium. What else do we need it for?"

"You'll see. This way, the rooms gets put to some proper use."

"Mrs. Kirby?" Mr. Hinkley touched Winifred's shoulder lightly, causing her to start. His face smiled down, broad and friendly. "I'll be off now. Tell your husband to give me a call if he wants to talk business on an alarm system."

"I'll do that, Mr. Hinkley, and thank you."

"My pleasure, Ma'am."

Winifred watched his retreating back and wished that he could stay, if only for a few more minutes. The house was so large, and few of her old friends ever stopped by these days—Morris had made sure that they were not welcome.

She stood at the barred front window and watched as Mr. Hinkley's van pulled away down the drive. Cottonwood's tail brushed against her legs. She looked down at the Siamese cat and smiled.

"Cottonwood, you keep coming in here and he's going to wring your neck one day." She beckoned the purring cat. "Come on, let's see if there's any tuna fish in the cupboard."

Morris pulled the weight bar over his head one final time, and locked it back up on the stand. A superior piece of equipment, even if he said so himself, and built for a fraction of the cost of a shop-purchased machine. The long, leather-topped bench press ended in two steel columns, across which rested a weight-laden barbell. Connecting the barbell to the columns was an added feature not found on shop models—Morris's own invention—a curving steel arm notched with teeth, at the top of which was a ratchet. This allowed the barbell to be raised and lowered on a fixed path, to ensure that each repetition was identically performed. The device resembled a home-made version of Nautilus equipment. Morris sat up on the bench and wiped his forehead.

"Are you nearly ready?" called his wife.

"I have to shower yet. My health comes first."

Winifred entered the lounge. She wore a long blue gown which accentuated her height and neatly reduced her bulk. With her hair piled up, she appeared strikingly attractive.

"You look nice, Winifred. But makeup doesn't become you. It makes you look cheap. I think you'd better go and take it off, don't you?"

Damn, thought Winifred, I nearly got away with it this time. I only put on a little blusher and lipstick. In the bedroom she stripped off her makeup while Morris showered and emerged to recomb his wig in the dressing table mirror.

As she emerged from the car she smoothed down her dress and looked nervously up at the house ahead. They accepted dinner invitations so rarely, she prayed that it would not show in her conversation.

"We'll have to invite them back after tonight," she told her husband as he attached the anti-theft device to his steering wheel.

"I don't see why we have to."

"Morris, it's what people do."

He was still looking perplexed about this as she rang the doorbell.

The evening was not a success. Over dinner, one of Morris's golfing friends mentioned the city's rising crime rate and sparked an argument.

"I tell you, Larry," said Morris, waving his fork in the face of his colleague, "the only real way you can protect yourself these days is to get hold of a gun. The city used to be a clean place, safe to walk the streets. You could leave your door open. Try doing that now, with the trash that's walking around out there."

Winifred sat in silent shame while her husband outlined his plans for putting the country back on the right road. The other wives looked across the table at her in secret sympathy.

When they returned home, they discovered that they had been burgled.

"I don't believe it!" Morris kept saying as he paced across the broken glass on the bedroom floor. A drainpipe had been scaled, and a lock on a side window had been forced. A small amount of jewelery was missing, nothing more. Morris harangued the police for two hours, turning, Winifred noted with some amusement, a peculiar shade of maroon as he did so. She asked Morris why he was making himself so upset when it was she who had suffered the loss. For a moment she thought Morris was going to self-detonate.

The next day Mr. Hinkley was called back in and asked to come up with a foolproof alarm system for the big gray house at the edge of the park. He talked quietly with Morris for half an hour, walking from window to window, lifting corners of the carpet and pointing to the tops of doors, then he wrote a figure on his pad and held it up for Morris to read. The little man's pupils contracted when he saw the amount. Nevertheless, he nodded his head and the deal was struck.

"How could you have used my money, Morris?" asked Winifred later.

"It's a joint account," replied her husband.

"You knew what I was saving up for. We never had a honeymoon. You promised we would eventually, and now you waste it all on silly devices."

"How can I make you understand?" shouted Morris, advancing on her, his gray sideburns thrusting ridiculously from beneath the sides of his auburn wig. "This is not money tossed away on some frivolous trip to Europe, this is an investment in something worthwhile!"

"What is worthwhile about an alarm system designed to protect a house in which even *burglars* can't find anything worth stealing?" screamed Winifred.

"This system gives us security!" Morris bellowed back.

"Don't you realize that someone could break in here one night and kill us while we slept? Do you want to go to bed at night worrying about rape?"

"I don't care! Morris, I'm sick of having to worry about the bad things that can happen! I want some fun for once, just once in my life!" she sobbed, her head dropping to her hands. "You always promised that we would take a holiday . . . you did promise."

"How can you be so ungrateful? You know I'm only doing this for you!"

"That," said Winifred coldly, "is the one thing you are not doing. All you ever think about is yourself."

Morris raised his flattened palm to strike her.

"Go ahead," she dared. "There's no difference between you and the louts you imagine on the streets."

His hand fell hard across her mouth.

The next day a defiant Winifred went to a burger joint with her old friend Alma, a big loud redhead who wore a sweatshirt, jeans and sneakers wherever she went and who never stopped talking for longer than thirty seconds.

"So this fella's trying to break into my car," she was saying between bites of cheeseburger, "in the driveway, no less . . ."

"Wait, what time was this?" asked Winifred.

"Two in the morning."

"And he got away?"

"Sure, I wouldn't go near him. I mean, what if he had a knife? But I managed to scare him off."

"What with?"

"A Junior Slugger baseball bat and an omelette pan. I woke the entire neighborhood."

Winifred collapsed in a fit of laughter. When she had recovered her breath she looked up at Alma, who always appeared to be having fun even when everyone knew that she couldn't be.

"We should do this more often," she said. "Morris doesn't like me going out. He's just so—different—these days. So intolerant."

"You shouldn't have let him use your money, Win, that's for sure." Alma hefted the cheeseburger in her hand, then looked at Winifred's diet salad. "Hey, this burger weighs more than my first child, you should have had one."

"I couldn't. Morris would know."

"How could he?"

"He weighs me." Winifred lowered her eyes to her plate, embarrassed.

"You have *got* to be kidding me."

"No, every Saturday, before we go jogging. And—he hit me."

Alma was so shocked she stopped eating. "I don't believe I'm hearing this. That's it, Win, you're taking a holiday. God, if Fred did that to me I'd break his jaw. Go to Europe. I'll loan you the money."

"I couldn't."

"You could and you will."

Winifred thought it over for a moment, then came to a decision. "I'll pay you back as soon as I can, Al," she said.

"Whatever, just send a postcard." Alma picked up the burger once more.

"Al . . ." Winifred was touched by her friend's kindness.

"I know, I'm a regular Mother Theresa." She turned in the direction of the waitress and shouted, "Hey, could we get another drink over here?"

That evening Winifred packed her case while Morris watched on.

"I'm warning you, Winifred," he threatened, "if you make this trip you needn't bother coming back."

Winifred crossed to the wardrobe, removed a stack of blouses and folded them deftly into her suitcase.

"Go to Europe and as far as I'm concerned you can stay there, with all the rest of the damned Eurotrash."

Winifred turned on her husband. There was no love for him left in her eyes. "I am not giving up the chance to get out of this house, even if it is only for two weeks. I've worked long and hard for a vacation. I need a rest from you. And don't worry— I'm not using your money." She slammed the lid of the case shut. "If you want to come along, fine. If not, stay here with your locks and alarms and be miserable."

"Winifred." His voice softened to a whisper. "I've never seen you like this. You're talking like a silly child."

"Am I?" She gave a cold laugh. "What would you know about children? I can't believe you were ever young." She pulled her case from the bed and started awkwardly down the stairs with it.

As the time drew near for her taxi to arrive, Morris changed his angry tone to a wheedling plea.

"I'll be lonely if you go," he said sadly. "Stay and keep me company."

"You won't be alone, Morris. There are your pals at the golf club, your friends at work and your weights. There's scarcely enough room for me as it is." She rose and hoisted up her case as the cab pulled into the driveway.

"Goodbye," she said without looking back. "I'll send you a postcard."

"All right, go, and see if I care!" Morris's mood abruptly changed. "Go off and act like some stupid adolescent. You're pathetic, Winifred! You can't look after yourself. You'll probably get mugged before you even leave the airport!"

Winifred slammed the front door defiantly, but she was crying for the end of her marriage.

"And this one is a pressure-sensitive pad. It fits under the carpet, here. The slightest touch sets it off." Mr. Hinkley knelt down below the window ledge. "We put one of these below each of the downstairs windows." He rose to his feet and, taking Morris's arm, led him over to a small white plastic box installed on the wall.

"There are two basic systems here." He tapped the box lightly. "A perimeter system, and an internal system."

"What does that mean in plain English?" asked Morris. He was still in his dressing gown. Hinkley had annoyed him by arriving early to fit the alarms. His men had been hammering and drilling for the past three hours, and now Mr. Hinkley wanted to explain what it was exactly that Morris had purchased.

"It's a piece of cake, Mr. Kirby. You set the perimeter system by pressing this little button. That secures the windows and doors. If any of them are opened from the outside, the circuit is broken and the alarm goes off. Now, this other little button operates the internal system. If there's an intruder, he'd be trapped by the wired floorpads, which also trigger the alarm. Both systems ring at security headquarters, who in turn ring the police station, so in the event of a break-in the police would be here in, say three or four minutes."

"And how do I activate all of this?" Morris drew his dressing gown tighter and peered at the flashing LEDs on the control box.

"Couldn't be simpler, Mr. Kirby. Two switches, two systems, that's it. The timer can be set to activate the perimeter system when you go to bed, and you can turn on both systems manually or automatically whenever you leave the house.''

''Wait a minute,'' said Morris. ''Why don't I activate both systems when I go to bed?''

''Well,'' Hinkley explained, ''suppose you want to get up in the middle of the night. It would be easy to walk on one of the pressure-pads and set off the alarm by mistake. You don't want that to happen too often. The police don't take too kindly to it. Now this isn't hooked through to the station yet, but it will be from tomorrow, so be careful.''

''Thank you, Hinkley, you've been most helpful. A man's home is his castle, don't you agree? This should keep out the riff-raff.''

''I guess so, Mr. Kirby.''

''If I had my way, I'd wire the place up with a million volts and fry the bastards.''

''That man,'' said Mr. Hinkley to his assistants as they left the house and headed across the park with their toolcases, ''is getting a little paranoid. But what do I care, he wants his property secured, we secure it, right?'' He turned to look back at the sad, dark house standing behind the marasmic elms on the north side of the park. ''I'd certainly hate to be caught breaking in there.''

Morris was enjoying his freedom. Just two days after his wife had left for the continent, he was arranging to play cards with ''the boys,'' organizing golfing tournaments and planning expeditions to a variety of drinking haunts. He half hoped Winifred would like Europe so much that she would decide to stay there. Perhaps the plane would crash, or she'd fall into a Venetian canal. He had forgotten just how much fun it was being single, although ''being single'' simply meant to Morris being as rude as you like to people without having to worry about ever seeing them again.

He hurriedly changed into his gym kit. If he was quick, he'd be able to do a full workout and still arrive at the clubhouse on time. He began with a few warming-up exercises that set his pulse racing. These he followed with a quick-fire course of bent-leg sit-ups, squats, crunches, dumbell swings, curls and flies. Finally, panting hard and heavy, he threw himself back on the leather bench and prepared to raise the heavily weighted barbell from its perch. Beyond his sneakered feet, the setting sun threw golden squares across the polished floorboards of the lounge.

The beauty of the approaching evening was, however, wasted on Morris, who was busy wiping the sweat from his eyes as he increased the size of the weights on his barbells. This last exercise would pump up his muscles enough to impress Stephanie, the attractive waitress he had been eyeing at the clubhouse, of that he was sure.

Morris drew a deep breath and raised the barbell from its columns. The steel tooth of the ratchet had been turned away from its corresponding notches in the curved metal arm, so that it could not catch or jam the weight bar. Morris adjusted his grip and guided the bar down smoothly over his chest, then slowly back up until his arms were once more outstretched. Feeling that he was lying too far up on the bench, he slid his body down a little and raised the barbell once more in a pull-over. He could feel his pectorals, intercostals and serratus muscles hardening with each pull. Lowering it until the bar almost touched his throat, he pushed out and up again to a full arm extension. The bar was moving smoothly now as he used his chest muscles to pull it back up to its original position. Three repetitions finished, seventeen to go. Why did he waste himself, he wondered, on such an eager-to-please little homemaker like Winifred when with a body like his he could have anyone he wanted? He pulled on the bar, raising it high above his head, then down over his throat. Outside, small birds had begun to sing in the trees, heralding the onset of night.

Ten reps down, ten to go. The trouble with his job in the clothing trade was that it did not attract the right women. He needed a uniform. If only he'd been a policeman, as he'd always wanted to be, he'd like to have seen kids break into his house then. It was a pity that he'd been too short to qualify for the force in those days.

Fifteen repetitions done, five to go. Kids, he thought, what did the kids of today know about how to treat women? What did they know about mastery and control? Women had to be kept in their place, or else they tried to take over . . .

It was unfortunate that Morris was thinking this during his twentieth and final repetition of the exercise, because just as he made an extra exertion to pull on the bar, his wig came unstuck at the front and swung backwards like a flung open trap door, still attached at the nape of his neck. The sudden cold air, and a certain amount of vanity—even though there was no one around to see him—caused Morris to lose concentration for a split second. His grip on the bar faltered, the bench wobbled, and the metal ratchet swung down on the serrated arm attached to the barbell, preventing Morris from raising it back up to its steel resting posts. He grunted with the strain of holding the weight as his wig divorced itself from his head and dropped to the floor like a flattened rabbit. The veins began to stand out on Morris's neck. He shoved the bar up with all his might, but could not raise it above the point where the metal ratchet was wedged in place.

Slowly the weighted bar grew heavier. Morris's eyes searched wildly as the strength in his arms faded and the bar sank back on its arc, curving slowly down to his exposed throat, the ratchet clicking as it did so. As the muscles in his arms gave out completely, the ticking increased. To Morris, the bar before his eyes seemed to be moving in slow motion. He knew that it would crush his throat in another moment. Four weights totalling fifty pounds hung on either end. He screwed his eyes shut and prepared for the worst.

Suddenly, there was silence.

The ratchet had ceased its clicking. The bar had stopped two inches above his throat. Why? Turning his head very, very slowly, he searched but could see nothing impeding the path of the bar, nothing blocking the ratchet. He was terrified of moving his arms in case the extra support they were giving to the bar was enough to cause it to drop when removed. He could only assume that the bolt connecting the steel arm to the column had become over-tightened and would not allow the bar to move any lower. His hands were beginning to cramp up. He gingerly started to remove their grip. Immediately, the ratchet clicked and the bar dropped half an inch nearer before sticking. When he swallowed, Morris could feel the hairs on the skin covering his Adam's apple brush cold steel. He felt like some gigantic insect specimen, pinned to a board, slowly losing its life.

Just one more click of the ratchet and the steel bar would be brought into contact with his throat. Morris gulped hard. The back of his tracksuit was slick with icy sweat. He could not slide sideways along the bar and off the bench, because at either side the twin steel columns built to support the barbell were touching his shoulders. In addition, the whole device was bolted to the floor. Morris had not wanted the bench to slide about and mark the boards while he was exercising. As far as he could see, there was no other way out from beneath the bar. There he lay, flat on his back, feet squarely placed on the floor at the end of the bench with the barbell across his throat, prevented from crushing it simply because the joint of the arm on which it swung lacked oil. He needed something to prop under the bar, something strong. A poker. He twisted his head so that he could see the fireplace. The poker stood in its bronze scuttle just a few feet away, but the distance could have been one of miles for all the good it could do him.

As the shadows lengthened across the room Morris began to realize the seriousness of his predicament. He was alone in the house. There was no one expected to call. His wife was away for two weeks. And at any moment, with the passing of a heavy truck, the bar might drop a further fatal inch. Morris turned his head in panic and tried to slide out from beneath the bar, but his chin blocked the way. He began to cry. The room grew darker. The birds had now stopped singing.

In the corner there was a pinging sound, and a red light popped on. Of course! The alarm was set to turn itself on at five thirty p.m. But which alarm had he set? The light glowed softly on the left side of the control box. The interior alarm! He was saved! All he would have to do would be to throw or kick something on to one of the three large rugs around the room in order to set off pressure-sensitive pads beneath them, and ring an alarm in the local police station.

Gingerly, he looked around. There was nothing within reach, nothing at all. The nearest piece of furniture was a table, several feet away. Wait, what about his shoes? Carefully, he pushed the toe of one sneaker against the heel of the other until he was dangling the left shoe from his big toe. Aiming slowly and carefully at the rug by the lounge door, he kicked hard. The shoe fell short by a mere inch—the same distance that stood between his throat and the bar.

Fighting back stinging tears, Morris struggled to remove the remaining track shoe, pushing against his heel until the nails split and dig into flesh. The shoe came free. He aimed much more slowly this time, ignoring the thumping in his chest, then kicked. The shoe landed on the rug. He closed his eyes in thankfulness.

Nothing happened.

The shoe had hit the rug, but not the pad beneath it, which was a little smaller in area. That was that. He had nothing else to throw. Without thinking, he dropped his head hard back on to the bench and caused the ratchet to click down again. The bar dropped to his throat and hovered there, stuck, the cold metal just touching his skin. He hardly dared to breathe, an involuntary whimper rising in his throat.

Just then there was a movement, or rather he sensed a movement, in the corner of the room. This was followed by a noise—a small scraping sound. Flicking his eyes to the left, as far as they would move, he saw the door of the lounge move open a few inches, then close. Looking down, he saw Cottonwood the cat staring at him distrustfully.

"Thank God!" he sobbed at the ceiling. "Here, kitty. Come on, walk on to the rug, there's a good goddamned cat." He had completely forgotten about the animal he had banished to the garage, and had even forgotten to feed her. Now she had come in search of food. In order to get to the kitchen where Winifred daily prepared her bowl, the creature had to pass across the floor of the lounge—a tortuous route indeed if she were to avoid all of the pressurized mats. He whispered prayers at the animal now, coaxing her onward with the tips of his fingers. The cat flicked her tail disdainfully and strolled off around the room, skillfully missing the lounge door rug by inches.

She slowly passed behind Morris's head, out of his vision, a foot wide of the second mat. Finding little on this side of the room to interest her, Cottonwood strolled back to the lounge door rug, stopped a little to one side of it, then gracefully seated herself on the bare floorboards. In truth, she was feeling full and rather sleepy. Her mistress, fearful that she would return to find the animal dead from starvation, had left a plentiful supply of cat food in the garage, and Cottonwood had severely overindulged herself. Drowsy, her eyes began to close.

"Wake up, you stupid bloody cat!" shouted Morris fearfully. "Get up! Come to Daddy, please please please, and I'll give you all the food you want, you dumb son-of-a-bitch cat!" His neck ached from trying to keep the animal in his line of vision.

Cottonwood stretched and yawned, then slowly rose to her feet. She began to move towards the rug, then stopped just at the edge of it. She seemed to be staring at something. Twisting his head agonizingly, Morris followed the cat's line of vision. On the other side of the pressure-sensitive mat stood a small mahogany table, and on the table rested a small vase. Above this hung a mobile of filigreed glass fish, tinkling and turning slowly in the fading light. As she had been so many times before, Cottonwood was transfixed into a kind of cat-stupor by the ornaments. Normally Morris shooed her from the room before she could attempt to reach these twirling crystalline morsels. Now, it seemed, there was no one to stop her.

"Attagirl!" rasped Morris, his teeth clenched above the suspension bar. "Go for the fish!"

Cottonwood continued to stare stupidly at the mobile, not moving a hair as her eyes followed every turn of the fish, their glowing dorsals holding the blood-red rays of the setting sun. Very slowly she walked around the rug, never once touching it, and jumped gracefully up on to the chair. She could not have performed the operation better if someone had trained her to specifically avoid stepping on rugs. Morris grimaced.

Cottonwood climbed from the chair to the table and rose on her hind legs, paws clawing the air below the mobile, but she could not quite reach.

"Go on, you contrary bloody furball," shouted Morris hoarsely. "Jump!"

As the mobile turned and tickered, Cottonwood jumped.

She missed the mobile completely, but managed to knock the vase from the table as she fell back. And the vase smashed squarely into the middle of the mat with an almighty crack.

The circuits of the pressure-sensitive alarm were instantly activated, and a piercing siren began to blast, ripping through the house and into the night. At the headquarters of the security company a light flashed, and an urgent call was made to the local police station. Not far away, a snoozing police constable sat bolt upright.

"Hallelujah!" bellowed Morris, careful not to move as he said it, naturally. The siren wailed out. The cat, suddenly startled out of its skin, screamed and performed a spectacular leap from the table. On to the end of the barbell.

The ratchet racketed, and Morris's scrawny old neck was snapped in two like an autumn branch.

The police arrived in due course, but they had the most terrible trouble getting in. Naturally, they notified Winifred, who was forced to cut short her holiday in Europe for the funeral and the reading of the will.

"Come on, ladies, I know you can do this. Lift those legs, and one and two and three and four, now the arms . . ."

Cottonwood lay curled in her basket, oblivious of the nearby TV screen, where the instructor was busy whipping his acolytes into a frenzy of burning calories. Winifred was bent over the oven, peering through the door at the rising dough. Humming to herself, she rose and took another sip of her gin. In a few minutes she would go and change into her party dress. On the counters around her, trays of succulent canapés were waiting to be taken through to the newly decorated lounge. The kitchen windows were wide open, a breeze flapping the curtains. Nearby, colorful napkins were prevented from being blown away by one of Morris's barbell weights.

The warm air carried the smell of baking bread out into the garden, where Morris's bench press lay overgrown with crimson roses.

THE MASTER BUILDER

"**T**HE PLACE I went to see on west Forty-fourth?"

"Mmm—I'm lighting a cigarette—go on."

"It turned out to be a miniature attic with a small circular window and a sloping ceiling. The kind of room you couldn't even lock a small child up in. Although of course you could lock a small child up in almost anything."

"You're not going to be single all your life, Laurie, then you might feel different about having children."

"I doubt it. My favorite story is still the one about the princes in the tower."

"Tell me the rest. There's obviously more, otherwise you wouldn't be dragging this out for so long."

"OK . . ."

"I mean, of course you're not going to find another place in midtown Manhattan for God's sake. You should have made Jerry move out."

"Alison, it was *his* apartment!"

"Then you guys should have stayed together. It was worth it just for the location."

"Shut up, Allie, and let me finish. So, this was the fifth apartment I'd checked out since noon, and it was raining, and naturally there was as much chance of finding a cab as there was locating the ark of the covenant, and I find myself in Herald Square so I jump the PATH train . . ."

"Oh my God, you're moving to New Jersey."

"Well, Hoboken. It's . . ."

"I know, I know, only ten minutes from town and half the rent. But you know what they say, once you move off the island you never get back on. Still, I guess it's kind of *semi*-fashionable to live there now. Go on."

"OK, so Hoboken. Well, I was walking along a street somewhere off Washington, right down by the river, and I saw a For Sale notice in this window.''

"Wait, you're gonna *buy*?"

"I figure, why pay rent all your life? The point is, I put in a bid and it's been accepted."

"Can you afford it?"

Laurie laughed. "No, of course not. It's on the second floor, above a Korean deli, and it needs a hell of a lot of work, but it has a View. I mean, there's the river straight ahead, then the lights of the city are spread out before you."

"Sounds perfect. What's the catch?"

"No catch, at least I don't think so. I want you to come out and see it with me before I start alterations. You're so good with design ideas, and you know I've no sense of color coordination."

On the other end of the line, Alison sighed. "Yeah, I guess I owe it to your future boyfriends to make sure that your apartment doesn't end up looking like you won it on *Wheel of Fortune*. Name a date and we'll go check it out."

"How about Saturday?"

"Fine by me."

The September wind which blew across from the Hudson felt humid and unhealthy. It swirled around the old ferry buildings and down into the entrance of the subway as Alison rebuttoned her coat and left the station. She checked the address on the slip of paper and headed up along Third Street, past a clutch of smart new restaurants which characterized Hoboken's reborn status as a desirable neighborhood. She quickly located the delicatessen near the corner and looked up at the windows above. The building itself appeared to be rather nondescript, its gray brickwork fascia blending with the slight architectural variations on either side. She looked back down in time to see her friend striding along the pavement toward her. As always, Laurie looked immaculate. Glossy dark hair brushed her shoulders as she turned her head and smiled. The expensively simple black suit she wore emphasized her tiny waist. She had a figure that only a dedicated career woman could afford to keep.

"I'm not late, am I?" Laurie hiked up her coat sleeve and checked her watch, revealing a slender white wrist.

"No, I was early. Looks like you'll have all the stores you need right here." Alison gestured along the street.

"Hey, don't knock it." Laurie stepped into the doorway beside the deli and searched her purse for keys. "I mean, have you seen the Stylish Modes Beauty Parlor two doors along? How could I ever think of getting my hair done anywhere else?" She unlocked the outer door and beckoned Alison inside.

"It still smells a little funky in here," she said, wrinkling her nose. "The old lady who had the place kept cats."

A second door admitted them to a gloomy narrow hallway and a flight of gray-carpeted stairs. Laurie gestured dismissively at the bare walls as they ascended.

"At the moment this is just so—*hallway*. Don't look at it."

"I guess you could brighten it up by bolting some prints to the wall."

"Allie, this is *not* Manhattan, it's a much safer neighborhood." She had to fit three separate keys to the door locks before they could enter the apartment.

"Oh, sure," said Alison, studying the burglar bolts as she passed them.

The room before them was presumably intended to be a lounge/diner. The faded purple carpets released a pungent and unmistakably feline odor. Stained brown wallpaper revealed the shapes of long-removed paintings and light fixtures. Against the farthest wall a broken-backed sofa slumped, its corduroy covering worn smooth with use.

The two women moved into the adjoining room, turning around as they did so. The cramped kitchen alcove consisted of a mustard-yellow counter and a number of cheaply finished wooden cupboards. Mouse droppings lay scattered on most of the work surfaces.

"Admittedly the place doesn't look like it's been cleaned since the fifties," said Laurie, gingerly running a manicured finger along the top of a shelf.

"Hygiene Hell," agreed Alison, moving gingerly between the fittings, careful not to touch anything. "If you're serious about this, all I can say is that you must have more design vision than I gave you credit for."

"I have more than vision," said Laurie, "I have a View." She tugged on a dirty gray curtain draped across the far doorway, and there it was. A huge, spectacular room with double windows and an unspoiled view of the Hudson and the city beyond.

Any objections Alison could have raised about her friend's planned purchase were felled at a stroke. Watery sunlight streaked the sides of the distant skyscrapers which filled the room's horizons like a living fresco. Barges could be glimpsed passing between the shoreside buildings, their horns sounding in forlorn cadence against the cries of wheeling gulls.

"Can you believe the previous owner had actually boarded over the windows?" said Laurie, pointing to a stack of planks standing in a corner.

"Why would anyone do that?" asked Alison, moving to the glass.

"I don't know. I guess she must have been a little crazy. I believe she was very old."

"So when did she move out?"

"She didn't. She died. The apartment went to her nephew, but he lives in the Midwest and just wants to sell it."

Laurie turned from the window and led the way to a far door across the room. Beyond lay a short flight of steps leading to the first of two bedrooms. Alison took a step inside and halted. The room was dark and musty with the smell of stale blankets. Here, the windows were still nailed shut with sheets of hardboard. Laurie reached across and switched on the overhead light, a single naked bulb which illuminated the sagging bed, an unravelled wicker chair and an ancient, badly painted dresser.

"I think you're going to find yourself with a lot of structural alterations on your hands," said Alison. "Even the walls you keep will all need replastering. You'll never be able to live here while it's being fixed up." She tried to avoid looking at the bed, its bare mattress stained dark, perhaps with the secretions of the old woman's dying body. She looked over at Laurie, who seemed to be reading her mind.

"She didn't die here. She was in the hospital for a long time. The bathroom's through the corridor in the far corner."

The cheap modern tub with the cracked floor seemed almost wilfully misplaced in the large bathroom. A much older china handbasin stood against a partially tiled wall. Most of the plumbing seemed to have been connected in plain sight, with pipes jutting from every corner.

"It's going to cost a fortune to do it properly, you know that."

"Look at the outlay in terms of long-term investment," said Laurie. "I'll never get another chance like this."

"Maybe you're right. There's plenty of scope for renovation, I'll say that. And the property can only go up in value."

Laurie led the way back to the main lounge, passing another much smaller bedroom. "You think that's too small for a guest room?" she asked. "Maybe it should be knocked through."

"I don't know . . . you don't want to reduce the number of rooms too much. Suppose you decide that you want someone to live with you."

"Oh no," said Laurie firmly. "I'm not living with anyone ever again. And I'm never going to get married, you know that."

"Yeah, you say so now, but maybe in a year or two . . ."

"In a year or two we could all be dead." Laurie gestured at the walls, anxious to change the subject. "So, could it work? What do you think?"

"What I think is the apartment's wonderful. But you're going to need a real professional to come in and handle the renovation from start to finish."

"How do I find someone to do that?"

Alison smiled. "I know a master builder," she said.

Laurie Fischer worked for a large publishing house on East 50th Street. She had been employed there as a commissioning editor for nearly four years, and in that time had lived up to her reputation as a formidably bullish negotiator. Three years before, on her twenty-seventh birthday and against her better judgement, she had moved into an apartment with an advertising executive named Jerry, but her relationship with him—never once referred to by either party as a romance—had all too quickly degenerated into a series of uncomfortable powerplays.

On the surface, things had seemed perfect. If the idea of co-habiting with such a man had been presented to Laurie in the form of a business deal, she would have jumped at it.

Jerry had an inquiring mind, great plans for the future, perfect teeth and a house in the Hamptons. Unfortunately, he also had an ego the size of his real-estate holdings and a lump of rock where his heart should have been. He was a grown man of thirty-four who wanted to live with a beautiful, independent woman and still be allowed to play the field. When the strains on the relationship started to affect Laurie's work, she moved out. The final parting was recriminatory and messy.

Now she was single again, still the subject of longing glances from colleagues and friends, still the woman whose private life remained a delicious mystery to all but a few.

Alison had known her for more years than she cared to admit. The two of them had gone to high school together, had shared most secrets. The only remaining unchartered territory of their friendship was that part concerning sex. Even at school, Laurie had never dated. Her academic success had been qualified by her lack of popularity with other students, most of whom had felt threatened by such a noticeably superior combination of beauty and brains. Boys had quickly christened her "The Icicle," and she gave them no cause to reconsider the propriety of the sobriquet.

In Alison's opinion her friend was a biological time bomb waiting to explode. Surely nobody could hold back on so much for so long. Years earlier, she had forced friendship on her glacial classmate when everyone else at school had given up trying to do so, and she had never been sorry for making the effort. Laurie, once you got to know her, was an extraordinarily kind person, a generous friend, irascible and acid-tongued at times to be sure, but always true. And although Alison considered herself to be much the less attractive of the pair, she had never felt her personality eclipsed by Laurie. After all, hadn't she been the one with all the dates, and wasn't she now still enjoying a long-term romance, albeit with a married man, while Laurie dressed for success and worked late most nights?

Alison reminded herself to call Laurie and give her the telephone number of the builder. She had never met the man personally, but friends were unable to praise him highly enough. Last year he had apparently transformed an apartment belonging to an opera singer at the Met into an award-winning *Homes & Gardens* photospread, yet his fees remained low and his daily rate was considered—by New York standards at least—to be very reasonable. But then, of course, there were other reasons for the glowing testimonials of his clients . . . Smiling to herself, Alison picked up the telephone and dialed.

After half an hour of sitting in the empty apartment with a sketchpad, Laurie gave up. She rose and smoothed out the legs of her jeans, laying the pad on a pile of screwed-up paper balls. Alison had been right. Her design sense just wasn't up to the task which faced her. The deal on the property had gone through quickly enough, and the deposit had now been paid. The escrow had been handled with almost supernatural efficiency, and she saw no reason why the completion date should not be kept. What bothered her more was that she would have to continue staying with friends until the work on the apartment was completed, and who knew just how long that would take?

She looked around the room. The day's dying sunlight glanced from the river on to the walls of the lounge in soft golden hues, investing the apartment with a hint of the grandeurs to come.

Checking the ancient Bakelite telephone to see if the line was still connected, she dialed the number Alison had given her that morning, and asked to speak to the master builder.

He answered the phone himself, in a voice which was deep and slow, and gave the impression that he was weighing and judging each word before committing it to use. The job provided marvellous scope for creativity, Laurie explained, but would have to be finished this side of Christmas. Could he possibly come and take a look at the property before the weekend? He reckoned he could. She gave him the address and fixed a time for the meeting. After she had hung up, she wrote the number of Mr. Ray Bellano in her Filofax under "Service: Builder."

"You gonna do this properly, you gotta take it back to scratch and start again." He ran a broad hand across the lounge wall, knocked on it with his knuckle, picked at a loose edge of wallpaper which lifted away from the plaster with alarming ease. "This here is a support wall. Reckon you could replace it with a couple of central pillars, but for what? It's a big apartment. Taking out the walls'll make the den look out of proportion to the rest of the place. Now you can do that if you want, but you're gonna be sorry you did."

In the half hour since Laurie had opened the door to the builder he had torn down every idea she had presented. A simple yes or no didn't seem to suffice with him; there was always an adverse comment to be made. The man was downright rude.

"Sure, I can do that if you want me to, Miss, but it'll look real ugly. We can put a window in through there, but I'm telling you it'll look kind of stupid." *We* can put a window in, as if he and Laurie were buying the apartment together. She stepped back against the far wall with her arms folded across her chest and watched as he lumbered between the rooms, digging into the plaster with the end of a metal ruler, stooping to prise up a broken section of floorboard. He was well over six feet tall, broad-chested and ugly-handsome, clad in boots and dirty jeans, dark hair curling up from the neck of his sweatshirt. When he passed her, he trailed a smell of Brylcreem and sweat.

"Come in here a minute." He was calling to her from the main bedroom, as familiar as if they were newlyweds. Well, she would quickly put a stop to this.

"Mr. Bellano," she began in her coldest business-voice, "let's get one thing straight around here." She walked to the doorway and waited for him to stand and look at her.

"Please, call me Ray," he said, turning slowly and rising to his full height. "All my good friends do. And as it looks like this job is gonna take some time to get right, I figure we're gonna become good friends."

Then he smiled, a dangerous white smile that squared his jaw and ran from one side to the other of his bristle-shaded face. Laurie stopped in her tracks, suddenly aware that she was alone in the apartment with a complete stranger.

"I suppose you're right," she said in a careful, clear voice. "Although as I'll be staying with friends in Manhattan until the work is completed, I don't suppose we will be meeting very often." She gestured at the bedroom walls. "I'd like you to submit plans within ten working days, together with a quote for your time, building materials and so forth."

"Now wait just a minute," said the builder, raising a broad palm. "I haven't said I'll take the job yet."

"Why, are you fully booked up?"

"No, I just don't know if I want to do it."

He wandered from the room, leaving Laurie to fume at the man's arrogance. Who the hell did he think he was? Okay, so he'd made a good job of some hot-shot opera singer's apartment, but that didn't make him Andy Warhol. If he was so great, how come his prices were so low? She stormed after him and was about to deliver a frank sermon on male arrogance when he strode out of the bathroom, almost bumping into her, and said, "I'll do it." And that was the end of that.

Or rather, the beginning.

Because two weeks later Ray Bellano delivered his plans and his estimate, and another argument developed between them. The master builder had ignored her instructions, and had designed the apartment entirely to his own specifications. Only the finest materials were to be used, but this would force the final bill to the very limit of her financial allowance.

"I cannot let you do this," said Laurie as she studied the plans in her office. "Why do the walls have to be so thick? And why use hardwoods when you could use pine? This is going to clean me out, Ray, and I still have to buy furniture once it's finished."

"Look, Ms. Fischer," said Ray, "I'm sure you're great at your job—whatever it is you do—but I guess you're gonna have to trust me a little bit. I'll tell you what I want you to do. Take down this number. I want you to call one of my previous clients and ask them about me. Check it out. Then call me back and approve the fee.''

After he had rung off, Laurie decided to call his bluff. She telephoned the number he had given her and asked to speak to Mrs. Irene Bloom.

''Ray Bellano? The man's simply a genius. He changed my life. He rebuilt my duplex with a selection of the oddest materials, things I would never have dreamed of using, but it worked! Inlaid redwoods and fumed ash in the kitchen! After that I commissioned him to completely rebuild my other properties. If you'd like to see some pictures of his work I could get them over to you . . .''

''That won't be necessary, thanks,'' replied Laurie.

After she had rung off, she sat by her office window and watched the teeming life in the city streets far below. It looked hot down there. Sometimes, working alone in the air-conditioned silence of her office, she felt completely cut off from the outside world. Perhaps it was just an aftereffect of leaving Jerry, but she was beginning to question the point of working so hard and sharing so little with other people. The couple she was staying with were being terrific to her, cooking almost every night and filling her spare evenings with easy conversation. Still, she knew that there would be a limit to Peter's and Fran's hospitality. At dinner she made the seating numbers odd. She was a single that others were forever trying to pair up. She knew that, despite all protestations to the contrary, there would be sighs of relief on both sides when she eventually moved into her own apartment. Without further hesitation Laurie called the master builder and gave him the order to start work immediately.

A week later she pushed open the door of the Hoboken apartment and stepped into a nightmarish explosion of brick and plaster debris. A dull thudding shook the room as she lifted her high-heeled shoes across the planks which covered gaping holes in the floor. The reverberations were coming from the bathroom, where, cocooned within a storm of plaster dust, the builder stood swinging a sledge-hammer at a network of twisted pipes. Coughing, Laurie stepped back and watched from a safe distance as he lifted the hammer above his head and slammed it down into the plumbing again and again. Finally he saw her and approached, wiping rivers of sweat from his forehead and flicking it to the floor. He was stripped to the waist, and wore only his faded Levis and cowboy boots. Although it was unintentional, Laurie could not help noticing the powerfully defined pectoral muscles of his chest and the thick line of darkly curled hair which trailed across a hard tanned stomach into his jeans.

"I wouldn't advise you to come in here, Miss," he cautioned. "These walls ain't too safe at the moment."

Laurie avoided his gaze and concentrated on brushing a smudge of plaster dust from her suit. "You don't seem to have anyone helping you, Mr. Bellano," she said stiffly. "I felt sure that you'd employ a team. You can't possibly handle the job yourself."

"I think you'll find that I'm more than capable of handlin' this alone, Ma'am," he replied, a smile playing on his lips.

Did she imagine it, or was there a hint of sexual suggestion in his voice? Could it be that she was acting the uptight New Yorker with this amiable Midwesterner whose gaze was as direct and unflinching as his attitude? Not caring to analyze her feelings any further, she left the chaotic apartment with a promise to return in a week's time. He was to call her office if he needed to pay cash for any builders' deliveries. The complexity of her current work schedule made it necessary for her to ask him to limit his calls to emergencies and requests for money. She was sure he understood.

When she returned to the office she found herself in the middle of a crisis. Her secretary had been frantically trying to contact her. Where the hell had she been? Laurie was suddenly aware that she had slipped away to the apartment without telling anyone where she was going. The motive for this course of action still proved elusive to her as she headed back to Peter's and Fran's at the end of the day.

"It's really not too soon to start thinking about dating again, you know," said Fran as she ladled linguini on to her plate. "You don't need to be told what a terrific catch you'd make someone."

"God, Fran, you make me sound like a teenaged kid." Laurie started to carefully wrap pasta around her fork. "Dating is not a fun activity for a thirty-year-old woman, believe me. You had the taste and good grace to marry Peter when you were twenty-six. I'm past that point and moving into the Twilight Zone as far as males are concerned."

"I think you're just being cynical," said Peter, who had the annoying mealtime habit of holding his wife's hand under the table as he ate.

"It's not just cynicism. After a while you get to know all the types and their variations. The divorced guys who are either looking for reincarnations of their ex-wives, or want to tell you about their plans for getting back custody of the kids. The ones who admit that they only beat up on their girlfriends when they step out of line or make eyes at someone in a restaurant. The late-starters, the Peter Pan Syndromers, the holistic health nuts, grown men who still go to discos, for Christ's sake . . ." She fell silent, toying with her pasta, embarrassed.

"Do you know when the apartment will be completed?" asked Peter in an attempt to change the conversation which looked exactly like an attempt to change the conversation. "This side of Christmas, right?"

"This side of Thanksgiving, hopefully," said Laurie. "I have to get furniture in before Christmas, but it's going very slowly at the moment."

"You know," said Fran carefully, "if you were staying on the premises you could keep a much more watchful eye on the work, and maybe speed things up."

Laurie realized then that her friends were anxious for her to name a departure date. She finished her meal in forced good humor and retired to bed early.

When she arrived at the office the next morning, the first thing she did was speak to Mr. Bellano.

"I guess I could finish one of the bedrooms in the next week or so," he said in that infuriatingly half-asleep voice of his. "You wouldn't disturb me by moving in."

That's nice to know, thought Laurie, angrily closing a file disk on her P.C. Jeez, I'd hate to inconvenience you. She shoved the silky black hair from her eyes and stared hard at the computer screen, not seeing the pale green paragraphs which unrolled before her.

That evening Laurie Fischer visited a newly opened night-spot called the Slum Club with a young, supposedly hot new novelist from Los Angeles, who went by the unlikely name of Dig. She picked her way home through the garment district at three thirty the next morning with little more than some business cards and a hangover to remember the evening by, although she was sure that nothing very interesting had happened.

The following Saturday afternoon she moved into the Hoboken apartment. As Ray had promised, the bedroom was at least habitable. The room had been cleared of planks, bricks and plasterboard, and the door closed as far as a door without a lock and handle could. The light in the room was a soft yellow, the color and smell of light pine, the walls awaiting fresh paint or clean bright wallpaper. She lay on the mattress and gazed up at the ceiling as the afternoon sun fell below the water and threw slivers of light across the ceiling.

She listened to Ray working—quietly, for once—in the next room. It sounded as if he was planing wood. She could hear the metal edge dragging lightly and then lifting as he inspected his work, running his fingers across the grain, checking the finish. The man was a fifties caricature. He probably took women to bed by throwing them over his shoulder. She wondered where he lived, who his friends were. She had forgotten that there were men like him, straight-arrow guys who worked with their hands and didn't spend their time smart-talking women around in circles. How had Alison come to meet him? The slow back-and-forth of the plane on the wood gradually lulled her into light, warm sleep.

She awoke to find the room half in darkness and the builder's backlit silhouette filling the bedroom doorway. He was standing very still and looking on, plane in hand, still stripped to the waist. She raised her hand to her forehead, shielding the remaining light from her eyes. He was watching her with a contented half smile.

"What is it?" She raised herself on one elbow and smiled back.

"You called out. I think you was dreaming."

"Really? What did I say?" Laurie was intrigued.

The builder looked down at his boots, embarrassed. "Oh, nothin' much."

"Come on, what did I say?"

"You called my name."

"I wonder why I did that."

Suddenly he walked to the bed and dropped down on to her, his broad, fleshy lips fitting over hers in a powerful kiss which forced her head back into the pillows. His right hand found her forearm and pinned it beside her head as he used his free hand to tear open the front of her shirt. She twisted in protest, raising her leg to find it met by his powerful thighs as he lowered himself on top of her, the heavy base of his erect penis pressing a denim-clad column into her crotch. With her free hand she tried to prevent his hairy chest from pushing down on to her breasts, but found her fingers digging into his back and sliding down into the waistband of his tattered jeans. In a single swift movement he tore open her thin silk brassiere, cupping her right breast with his broad, warm fingers, tweaking the small nipple between thumb and forefinger. Lowering his head, he ran his tongue into her cleavage, leaving a broad band of saliva between her breasts, continuing down to her flat, pale stomach. Feeling no resistance now, he freed her arm and used both hands to lift her buttocks and rip open the seam at the back of her skirt, pulling it to one side and allowing it to slide from the bed. The wide palm of his hand covered her pubic area as his fingers probed inside her pants, forcing them down around her thighs. His eyes, darkly glittering, caught hers and held them as he fumbled with the opening of his jeans, freeing himself from within. She felt his hands exploring her, forcing her open as his pelvis pressed down and the head of his organ slowly entered her. She cried out, the builder's thick shaft following the rhythm of her ragged breath as inch by inch its entire length was enclosed by her shuddering body. The weight of his torso eased as he partly withdrew, holding himself aloft for a moment before pressing down hard into her, retreating and plunging again and again, the muscles in his dark arms lifting and broadening with each stroke until she felt their powerful mutual climax reach flashpoint within her and flood out in streaming neural pulses, causing her to scream now in involuntary spasms of pain and gratification.

"It was weird."

"Weird? *Weird?* The greatest sexual experience of your life, and all you can say is it was weird?"

"That's right." Laurie thought for a moment, her elbows on the table, the coffee cup poised between her hands. The restaurant was almost empty, but she still spoke softly. "Dangerous."

Alison lit a slim gold cigarette and gestured impatiently with it. "Explain what you mean."

"There was no tenderness. It was sex on the most basic level. No small talk, no protection, just a fast hard . . . fuck. Afterwards, he just sat on the end of the bed refusing to even catch my eye. I was lying there with my clothes in shreds around me, feeling like I'd been in a serious car crash, and he wasn't even out of breath. He rose and walked to the mirror, flicked his hair into place, shoved the comb into the pocket of his jeans, then went straight back to work."

"You're kidding. What did you do?"

"I guess I went a little crazy, called him a few names. He just looked up from his carpentry and smiled, so I left the apartment, took a walk around and tried to cool off. I felt so ashamed.''

"Have you seen him since?''

"Sure. The next day he turned up at the apartment, on time as usual, and began work as if nothing had happened.''

"So what are you going to do now?''

"I'm not sure. Obviously, the situation can't be allowed to repeat itself.''

"But you need him.''

"To finish the job, I guess I do.''

Alison studied the end of her cigarette, a slim smile slowly forming on her face.

Two days later, despite Laurie's promises and protestations, it happened again. Through the master builder she allowed herself to enter a world of sexual experience that she had never before encountered. She tried to understand her willingness to take part in the increasingly furious bouts of lovemaking which left her bruised and exhausted, but she knew that the explanation for her behavior lay with first understanding her enigmatic partner. Ray Bellano rarely spoke, was barely civil to her, but made love with a passion and intensity that shocked Laurie to her core. Each performance became a display of power more violent than the last, but afterwards he always dressed and left the apartment at once, returning home to who knew where. She managed to establish that he was single, and that he originally came from a town in Southern Texas. Beyond this, she knew nothing.

That week, colleagues at work began to pass comments. She had started arriving at the office less than immaculately dressed. Her hair was often out of place, her blouse not quite so well pressed. She seemed a little wilder now, a little less composed. Her attention seemed harder to hold. She explained the reason for the change to no one. Perhaps, though, some of them guessed when she was forced to use make-up to cover the bite marks which now blossomed like overripe fruit on her throat. And the apartment started to take shape.

Electrical circuits were laid, pipes were plumbed, walls were erected, then skimmed and painted. The kitchen was to become a bedroom, the bedroom a bathroom. Imported Italian tiles were to be juxtaposed with inlaid parquet blocks. And in the debris of the apartment, in the shavings and wood chips and wiring and plaster and brick dust lay Laurie, with the builder towering above, dripping sweat on to her upturned face as he thrust rhythmically into her, as powerful as a glistening piece of oiled machinery.

One rainy Sunday afternoon late in October, as she sat on the floor of the bare guest room watching the rain sweep in from the river and spatter against the windows, she asked him why he made love to her so fiercely.

He thought for a moment, his fingers tracing the delicate red scratches that embroidered her back. As he rose to pull on his white cotton boxer shorts, he told her that he thought it was because he wanted to possess her. It was the closest she ever got to an explanation.

Laurie decided that it was time to discuss her situation with someone she could trust. With a high-collared jacket of stiff gray linen covering the smarting welts on her shoulder blades, she left the office and went to lunch with Alison.

As she picked her way through her spinach salad she told her old schoolfriend about the strange relationship she now found herself involved in.

"What I fail to understand," she concluded, "is why I'm doing this. It just isn't like me."

"Sex is a great release," said Alison. "Sounds to me like you're getting your ashes hauled without having to worry about any responsibility. If you were a man, you wouldn't think twice."

"Well I'm not, and I am." Laurie pushed the half-eaten salad aside.

"Laurie, I have a confession to make," said Alison slowly. "I kind of expected this to happen."

Laurie frowned. "You 'kind of expected' what to happen?"

"Well, let me explain. A few months back there was a woman at the office whose apartment had been rebuilt by Bellano, and she kept going on about his brilliant craftsmanship. But I got the feeling that she meant something else entirely. It transpired that among her female friends he was very popular for . . . giving great decor." Alison ground out the cigarette, coloring with embarrassment. "Let's say that the guy has a reputation for being more than just a terrific builder."

Laurie sat in dumbstruck silence for a moment. Then she rose to her feet, unclipped her handbag and threw some money on to the table. "You booked me a stud?" she asked, her voice taut. "I looked that desperate to you?"

"But I didn't mean any . . ."

"I'm sure you probably thought you were doing the right

thing, but believe me it wasn't, Allie. It really wasn't.''
She turned on her heel and left the restaurant.

That evening Laurie worked late. At nine thirty, seated on the
PATH train going home, she considered her options. One, she
could dismiss Ray from the job and hire someone else. But
would she be able to find someone who could take over from
his plans? Two, she could confront him and settle the matter out
in the open. Then she would face the risk of him walking out,
leaving the place unfinished. Three, she could act as if nothing
was wrong and let him complete his work in peace. But what
would happen when he made a move to continue their liaison?
Carrying on with someone who had turned out to be little more
than a male prostitute was unthinkable.

As Laurie alighted from the train she knew that the affair was
over.

When she arrived back at the apartment she found the builder
still there. Ray Bellano was sitting in the middle of the lounge
floor surrounded by blueprints, panels of plasterboard and sawn-
off lengths of plank. The room smelled of shaved wood and
fresh paint.

''I'm glad you're back,'' he began slowly, climbing to his feet
and dusting down his jeans. ''I need to talk to you about the re-
siting of the kitchen.'' His unruly black hair was greased neatly
back as if, in anticipation of her anger, he was now anxious to
make a good impression. ''You look real good.'' He gestured
at her suit. ''Kind of severe, though.''

''Listen, Ray,'' she said coolly, ''I have to know something.
What happened between us the day before yesterday, was that
all part of the service? When you decorate a place, do you usually get to sleep with the mistress of the house? Was I supposed
to be thrown in as part of the deal?''

''I don't know what you mean.'' He took a step towards her,
but she backed away behind the low wooden counter he had
built along one side of the room.

''No,'' she agreed, ''I don't suppose you do. I'm talking about
sexual liberties.''

''Hey, I don't take liberties. You wanted it.'' He suddenly
moved around to the other side of the counter and reached out
his hand, grabbing the hem of her skirt and pulling her towards
him.

''Let me go,'' she said firmly, disentangling herself and moving away. The last thing she wanted to do was provoke him into
leaving the apartment, but at the same time it was important to

establish the new boundary lines between them. "You've been employed to do a job of work, and it doesn't involve giving the kind of service you're used to providing. Just leave out that side of it from now on, and we'll get along fine."

Ray stared down at his boots, as if he had been caught betraying a trust. "You just made a mistake," he said finally. "I really need you. But if that's the way you want it, you got it." He returned to work without another word.

After that she tried to spend as little time in the apartment as possible. Chance meetings with Ray merely invoked injured looks and uncomfortable silences. She left him money to purchase the materials he needed, and passed long evenings working late at the office. At the beginning of November she took a two-week vacation to visit her parents in Florida.

When she returned she found the apartment finished and a set of neatly labelled keys on the new kitchen counter, along with a final handwritten bill for labor. There was no sign of the builder. He had left her no personal message of any kind. She wrote a check for the bill and forwarded it to an address in Queens. Then, as a peacemaking gesture, she invited Alison over to inspect the property and come up with a few furnishing ideas.

"It's unbelievable," Alison marvelled as she passed from room to room. "I'd never have known it was the same apartment."

Even without furniture the transformation was nothing short of miraculous. Every lintel and surround gleamed with proud detail. Alison sat on a packing crate staring about her as Laurie made coffee in a kitchen of gray slate and black marble surfaces.

"I'm sorry for what happened between us," said Alison as she stirred her coffee. "It was all my fault."

Beyond the windows, a flotilla of tugboats heralded the arrival of a large South American freighter. Laurie came over and stood beside her friend, watching the pale sunlight sparkle against the bows of the ship as it progressed up the river.

"Forget it," she said. "It was nobody's fault. I chose to let it happen." She fell silent for a moment. "Help me pick out a dining table instead."

"A dining table?" said Alison, equally eager to change the subject. "What do you need a dining table for? You don't cook."

"No, but I eat. And I may learn to cook."

"I'll believe that when I see it."

"You know, I'm going to love living here," Laurie said, sitting down on the broad window ledge. "It feels right."

On that frosty autumn evening of dying sunlight, Laurie had no idea that her troubles were just starting.

By the first week of December most of Laurie's new furniture had been installed, and the first bad blizzard of the winter had thundered into the Manhattan streets.

In her Hoboken apartment Laurie sat in her soft blue lounge overlooking the river, curled in her mother's old patchwork blanket watching a rented video movie and eating peanut-butter sandwiches. The film had almost reached the end of its running time when the picture suddenly faded and died. Laurie irritably jabbed at the remote unit, but nothing happened. The screen remained blank. The video machine refused to play or rewind.

"Godammit." She unwrapped the blanket from her body and walked over to the set, but there was nothing she could do to restart the tape or remove it from the machine. A minute later, the film started up by itself. By now, though, Laurie had grown tired of watching television, and prepared for bed.

After she had rinsed her cup and plate, she walked into the gleaming bathroom and ran the shower. Immersing herself in the cone of steaming water, she replayed the events of the day. The publishing house was looking at ways of cutting back on personnel, and after Laurie's recent failure to secure the rights to Dig's hotly sought-after new novel, she knew that it was time to strengthen her position in the company by putting in some extra hours.

She was just considering the best way of doing this when the shower jets slowed to a trickle, then ceased altogether. The sound of roaring water fell away to a single echoing drip as she started to shiver and reached over the frosted cubicle door for a towel.

But instead of cotton brushing her hand, something cold and slippery seized it. Yelping with fear she pulled free and jumped back against the tiled wall. She could feel her heart pounding as she slowly pushed open the glass door. The towel lay neatly folded across the heated rail, just where she had left it.

"I tell you, that's the last time I watch a horror movie by myself," she told Alison over the telephone at work the next day. "I could have sworn there was something there."

"Don't tell me." There was a pause as Alison lit her customary cigarette. "I can't even watch the eleven o'clock news without getting goose bumps."

"You mean the mugging reports?"

"No, George Bush. Too scary. Speaking of which, did you see the news last night?"

"No, I went straight to bed and slept with the lights on. Why?"

"I guess if you're nervous I shouldn't tell you. It's in all the papers this morning."

"I don't have time to read the papers. Tell me."

"Okay. Hold on." Laurie smiled, knowing that Alison was making herself comfortable on the other end of the line. "You remember all that trouble at Rockaway beach last July when those AIDS-infected syringes washed up on the sand?"

"Didn't they find a pair of legs as well?"

"That's right, and a bunch of dead laboratory rats and a human stomach lining. Well, it's started again. Only this time they don't think it's medical waste."

"What do you mean?"

"Some woman just got washed up on the shore at Rockaway last night, or rather parts of her. She'd been taken to pieces with a bone saw."

"Allie, I haven't had my lunch yet. Why are you telling me this? You know I live alone, you know how I get!"

"Sorry." Alison did not sound very sorry at all. "I thought you'd be interested. Maybe there's a book in it."

"No thanks. We already did a children's guide called *Things to Look for on America's Coastline*."

"I'd buy you a drink after work . . ."

"But you know I'm working late. And I am. I'll have to take a raincheck. The weekend, maybe."

"Okay."

Laurie worked until nine, then went home and reheated some lasagna. As she ate it she studied the freezing silver river which glowed dimly beyond her window. The apartment was so warm that the snowflakes melted the second they touched the pane. She undressed in the bedroom and emerged in a loosely tied kimono before heading for the television and turning it on. The screen showed a policeman being interviewed by a CNN reporter on a bleak, snow-swept beach. Behind him on the sand a pair of fat white female legs protruded from one end of a tethered tarpaulin.

"Fears are growing that another consignment of laboratory

waste is being washed up on New York's beaches," said the announcer. "Last summer's outbreak saw the closure of many beaches and plunging attendance figures at nearly all of the major resorts. But with the thermometer staying at around the zero mark, that's one problem New York may avoid. This is . . ." The picture suddenly dwindled to a point of light.

"Damn it to hell!" Laurie searched for the remote unit, but it was nowhere to be found. "This is ridiculous . . ." She pulled out the sofa cushions and stacked them on the floor, running her hand around the back of the seat. After a fruitless search she rocked back on her heels, perplexed. "It has to be here somewhere," she said to herself. "Things don't just vanish."

Finally, she gave up looking and went to bed.

That was the first time she heard the rat.

At least, it sounded like a rat. Its movements were small and sharp, and could only be heard if she kept very still and held her breath. There, behind the familiar sounds of the old building, beneath the creaking of the floorboards and the clicking of the cooling waterpipes, was another noise, like nails tickering across wood. Laurie sat up and reached for the bedside lamp switch. She clicked it on, half expecting to see a rabid laboratory rat crouching on the counterpane ready to pounce, but there was nothing unfamiliar to be found in the room. The sound continued, so faintly now that she began to wonder if it only existed in her imagination. Laurie did not sleep well that night.

"There's nothing wrong with the set."

To prove his point, the TV repairman switched it on and off several times in rapid succession. "Or the video. It has to be your supply source."

"What do you mean?" Laurie gave the television a dubious look.

"The electrical system. You've just moved in?"

"What has that got to do with it?" she asked, sharpness in her voice.

"These buildings have old wiring. Half the time it's dangerous and you don't even know it."

"I've just had new wiring installed."

"There could be a fault in that, something overloading. Are you running any other appliances while the TV is on? The iron, maybe."

"I don't do the ironing while I watch TV," she said coldly. "I'm from New York, not Ohio."

"Well, I think it's your circuitry," said the repairman, closing his tool kit and heading for the door. "Get your electrician back in to take a look."

The next evening, an hour before Peter and Fran came by the apartment with Chinese food, the bedroom lights started to misbehave. Laurie was just changing into her jeans when the room was plunged into darkness. Swearing to herself, she checked the bulb and the fuses but found nothing wrong. Ten minutes later, the lights worked again. It was a very puzzled Laurie who opened the door to her old friends that night.

"So, how are you enjoying the place?" Peter asked through a mouthful of noodles. "It really looks great."

"There are one or two teething problems."

"What kind of problems?"

"Oh, lights, plumbing." She tried to make it sound casual. "And I think there's a rat."

"You're being melodramatic," said Fran, passing a cardboard box filled with bean sprouts across the table. "Every building has mice and roaches."

"I guess so. This sounds bigger. I hear it almost every night."

"You want me to take a look?" Peter offered, but he didn't seem too enthusiastic about the idea.

"No, it'll sort itself out. It's OK." She picked at the bean sprouts, wishing she was as confident as she sounded.

The next morning Laurie was seated at the kitchen counter dropping pieces of grapefruit into the blender when the Channel Eleven local news report began. Her mind was half on the preparation of breakfast, half on the day's planned meetings as the image on the screen changed. Lettering stripped across a beach scene: ROCKAWAY BEACH VICTIM NAMED.

"Police today identified the body of the murdered woman found on Rockaway Beach as Mrs. Irene Bloom, a forty-two-year-old CPA who went missing from her Upper West Side apartment last Thursday . . ."

At first Laurie failed to register the name. It wasn't until she looked up at the picture that her blood ran cold. The grapefruit knife slipped in her fingers, gashing the back of her hand. Blood welled in the wound and dripped heavily on to the marble counter as she continued to stare at the network's photograph of Mrs. Irene Bloom.

She was standing proudly in an apartment that appeared to be an exact duplicate of Laurie's own.

"It was the woman I spoke to, the woman he recommended I call to check his credentials. And her apartment is exactly the same as mine! He decorated it in an identical style, don't you see what that means?"

"This is stupid, Laurie, you know that? It's just a coincidence. You want to go to the police? You want to walk in there and say, 'Excuse me, officer, but I shared the same interior decorator as the murdered woman?' "

"You know damned well that we shared more than just the decoration."

Alison sighed. She hadn't minded changing her route to work so that she could meet a near-hysterical Laurie in the coffee shop on East 50th, but she was bothered by the sight of a good friend seemingly falling to pieces.

"Every painter has a style," she said, trying to sound as calm and rational as possible. "The apartments he designs are bound to be similar to some extent. You're working too hard, you know that? You should get out more."

"Maybe you're right." Laurie seemed to back down suddenly. "My imagination's been a little overactive of late."

"If you're so worried, I'll set your mind at rest. After all, it was me who put you in touch with this guy in the first place. I'll call him. Do you have his number?"

"I thought you had it. You gave it to me."

"That was just a temporary line. He was moving to somewhere in Queens."

Laurie thought for a moment. "That's right," she said, remembering. "I posted his check on." She began to rummage in her handbag. "I think I threw the piece of paper away."

"It doesn't matter. We know his name. I'll find out where he lives and give him a call. And you've got to promise me that you'll start taking things a little easier." Alison held out her hand and they shook. Laurie's fingers were freezing.

"Do we have a deal?"

"A deal."

Exactly two weeks before Christmas Laurie's ex-boyfriend turned up at her office. He had been meaning to see her for a while now, he said, just to bury the hatchet. Coincidentally, he had just broken up with his girlfriend Carol. Laurie was surprised but hardly flattered. Still, in the spirit of Christmas she went for a drink with him and actually managed to have a good time. At the end of the evening he tried to kiss her and she pulled gently but firmly away. She did, however, give him her new home telephone number, which was certainly more than she meant to do. Jerry was a louse, but a charming one, and she figured that he deserved something for at least possessing one good quality.

The following Saturday there was another strange occurrence in the apartment. Laurie had arrived home from work and was playing back her messages—one from Jerry suggesting dinner—when there was a thud and a bang in the room next door. Clicking off the answering machine, she moved back against the wall and listened. For a minute or so there was silence. Then a weight shifted and a floorboard creaked, not from the apartment above or the one below but right next door, the weight falling against the wall with a sudden heart-stopping thump. Laurie moved across the lounge to her work-desk and picked up the Indian letter opener of sharpened brass which lay on the desktop blotter. Slowly she crept towards the archway into the dining room. Poising herself on the threshold, preparing to attack, she suddenly felt foolish. Here she was, a grown woman, acting like a child of six just because she'd heard a few unexplained bumps and thuds. With an uneasy laugh she began to lower the knife. The apartment lights extinguished themselves.

The darkness was complete and solid, like a black wall. She had always hated the dark, ever since she'd been a small child. As she ran across the lounge to the front door her shin caught the edge of the coffee table and she fell sprawling, her knee tearing open on its sharp steel edge. When she reached the doorway to the hall she found Jerry standing there with his finger still resting on the apartment buzzer.

Seconds later, the lights came back on.

The last thing she had intended to do was cry on his shoulder. Perhaps it was a culmination of the month's events that caused her to behave in such an uncharacteristic manner, but she hung on to Jerry and told him all her fears—about her job, her private life, and even the inexplicable problems of her apartment.

When she had finished he smiled and poured her a brandy before taking her to bed and tucking her in. He sat with her for three hours and didn't try to lay a finger on her. It was a side of him she had never seen before.

That night, for the first time in what felt like an age, she slept soundly.

The next night was a Friday, and Laurie returned late from a meeting to find that she had been burgled.

"That's the whole point," she told the officer. "I'm not even sure if there's anything missing." She was standing in the lounge amid the wreckage of the shattered glass coffee table and the stuffing of the slashed sofa. The young policeman picked his way from room to room with a distant, indecipherable look on his face.

"Forgive me for saying so, Ma'am," he said, "but this is kind of a regular problem at the moment, and we don't have too much of a chance of catching anybody. A lot of folks resent the yuppies moving in and forcing up the local property prices."

"I understand what you're saying," said Laurie angrily, "but I've as much right to protection as the next person and I don't think it's your job to make value judgements."

"Listen, I'm just trying to tell you how it is around here." Now armed with a legitimate excuse to lose interest in the crime, the police officer moved away towards the door. "Just make a list of the missing items and bring it down to the station, Ma'am, and we'll do what we can. Also, give me the names of anyone you know who might have done this."

Halfway to the door, Laurie halted. "What makes you think I know anyone who would do something like this?" she asked.

"Well, there's no sign of a break-in. Either you forgot to lock the door, or whoever it was had a key."

"Nobody has a key to this apartment except me."

"Then you left the place unlocked. If it's not one, it has to be the other."

"Terrific. You've been a great help."

After slamming the front door, she returned to the ruins of the sofa, sat down and cried.

She found nothing missing. Her jewelery box was unopened, and some dollar bills lay on her dressing-room table untouched. The damage was less serious than it had at first seemed. Even so, the coffee table and the expensive designer sofa would have to be replaced.

Peter and Fran came by to help Laurie tidy the place up, and suggested that she install a burglar alarm. At least, they said, it would prevent the same thing from happening again. After the last dustpan of broken glass had been emptied into the bin they opened a bottle of red wine and toasted the coming new year.

"You have to get an entryphone to this place, you know that?"

"Jerry, what are you doing here?" Laurie stood in the doorway in her bathrobe, unprepared for visitors. To be honest though, she was pleased to see him. "You'll have to be quick, I'm getting ready to go out to dinner. But while you're here, you can do something for me." She moved aside to let him enter.

As he walked into the lounge he pulled a champagne bottle from his jacket. "To warm the new apartment," he explained. "Better late than never. What do you need me to do?"

Laurie led him by the hand down the hallway and through to the strange crystal-and-mirror bathroom that Ray Bellano had designed for her. Taking the champagne bottle from him and standing it down on the washbasin, she positioned Jerry in the center of the room and held her finger to her lips.

"Listen," she whispered, "and then tell me what you hear."

Jerry cocked his head on one side in an exaggerated gesture of attentiveness. He listened for a while, then shook his head. "Zip," he said finally. "Nothing at all. What was I supposed to hear?"

"I don't know. There's this weird sound I keep hearing at night. Maybe I really *am* imagining it." She shook her head, then picked up the bottle and headed into the kitchen.

"What do you mean?" asked Jerry, following her through. "What are you imagining?"

"Oh, I don't know, rats, mice, you name it. Something. You need a haircut." She reached up and touched the back of his neck.

"This is the Frankie Avalon look. I happen to like it." Jerry patted his hair back in place. "So, have you had a fumigator in?"

"No, it doesn't seem that serious." Laurie found two glasses and opened the champagne. "It comes and goes."

"Forgive my saying so, but it looks like it's keeping you awake at night."

She poured, then touched Jerry's glass with hers. "You know how I always used to worry about little things? I'm just doing it again, that's all."

"You want me to stay with you tonight?" His smile became a sly grin.

"I know it's Christmas," she said with a chuckle, "but I'm not quite that full of goodwill yet."

An hour and a half later, though, she was.

It was the first time she had had sex with anyone since the departure of the master builder, and for a while it was a very different experience to get used to. Jerry was a courteous, considerate, conservative lover. He took into account a woman's needs. He took things slowly. He massaged her body gently. In fact, she had completely forgotten how boring he was in bed.

He lay heavily on top of her, his hands kneading her breasts. His clothes were folded neatly on a nearby chair. The bedroom lights were all turned off. He was moaning softly in what he considered to be a sexy manner. Laurie felt her left leg falling asleep as he shifted his weight, pulling the sheets out again.

Suddenly the room began reverberating with a series of deafening rhythmic bangs. Jerry leapt from the bed with a cry as if he had been electrocuted. As the hammering continued he ran to the wall and slapped on the lights. Immediately, the noise stopped—as swiftly as it had begun. Laurie cautiously removed the pillow she had pulled over her ears to block out the sound.

"That's a hell of a plumbing problem you've got there," he said as soon as his heartbeat had returned to normal. "Jesus, does that happen often?"

"Quite often," replied Laurie.

"Where was it coming from?"

"The apartment," she said, still shaking. "It just comes from the apartment."

"Laurie, you *have* to meet up with me tonight for a Christmas drink. I've a present for you." On the other end of the telephone, Alison already sounded a little merry. In the background Laurie could hear an office party in full swing. She looked from the receiver to the stack of paperwork on her desk and sighed.

"Allie, I'm flying down to spend Christmas with my folks tomorrow night and I have all this work to catch up on . . ."

"Meet you in one hour's time at fourteen, Christopher. If I'm there first I'll have Michael get us a table. Be there or I'll tell everyone that you rekindled an old flame last night."

"How did you know that?" asked Laurie in amazement. "Word sure gets around fast."

"You forget that Jerry still works in my department."

"Yeah, but I didn't expect him to go around telling everyone."

"Not everyone, just me. Oh, about Ray Bellano . . ."

"You managed to get hold of him?"

"No, I didn't. Nobody seems to have seen him alive since you had him, you maneater. Listen, do you still have the blueprints he made up of your apartment?"

"I've got them right here in my desk drawer."

"Good, bring them with you to the restaurant. I have a little surprise for you."

The line went dead.

An hour later in the restaurant at 14 Christopher Street, Laurie and Alison exchanged gifts and drank a toast to each other. Then, at her friend's request, Laurie unfolded the plans to her apartment and laid them flat on the tablecloth.

"Remember the woman who was washed up on the beach? After she died, they put her apartment up for sale," explained Alison, fishing about in her handbag as she spoke. "I applied to the realtors and they sent me a copy of the floor layout." She found the piece of paper she was looking for and studied it carefully. "I thought it might be interesting to see if your suspicions—whatever the hell they're supposed to be—are well-founded."

Laurie leaned forward and perused the two sets of plans. She was disappointed to find, however, that in blueprint form they bore little resemblance to each other.

"Kind of a letdown, huh?" said Alison, draining her glass. "I can't say I understand what you were expecting to find."

"I'm not sure I know any more," replied Laurie as she reached for the wine bottle. "Let's just forget about it. Be happy I was wrong."

On the 28th of December Laurie returned from her parents' condominium in Florida and climbed the stairs to her apartment. As she opened the front door she could see the red light on her answering machine ticking on and off. She put down her bags in the hallway, then went into the bathroom and turned on the central heating. While she waited for the flat to warm up, she played back her messages.

"Laurie, call me the minute you get in. Something awful has happened. It's Allie."

Laurie raised the receiver and speed-dialed the number on the handset.

"Thank God. I didn't want you turning on the TV and hearing about it on some news show."

"Hear about what?" asked Laurie. "What are you talking about?"

"It's Jerry. I don't know how to say this any other way. He's been murdered."

The room dipped before Laurie's eyes. "No, that's not possible."

"Laurie, listen to me. Don't watch the news, OK?"

"When did this happen?" She reached out for the arm of the chair and slowly sat down.

"Yesterday. He was found in his apartment in a very bad way. I really don't want you to hear about it. Stay there, I'm on my way over."

Alison came and stayed at her friend's apartment for the next two days. The police called by a number of times, but only made the situation worse by describing the murder in greater detail. Jerry had been at home sitting in front of the TV when he was attacked by someone wielding a hammer, or a similarly heavy blunt instrument. By the time his attacker had finished, there hadn't been a whole lot left of Jerry to take downstairs. The door to his apartment had been torn from its hinges. There had been no witnesses to the crime, and the police had no direct leads. Was there anything at all she could tell them that would shed some light on his death? Laurie tried to think of something tangible, some concrete piece of evidence that would link the half-formed suspicions in her mind. In the end, though, she settled for promising to call the detective at the station if she remembered any further details of their final meeting.

"You sure you don't want me to stay with you again tonight?" asked Alison for the third time. "Absolutely sure?"

"Go, go, for God's sake, I'll speak to you tomorrow morning." Laurie pushed her friend to the front door and opened it for her.

"All right, but you know where I am if you need me. I'll call you before I leave and we can go to the cemetery together."

Jerry's funeral, delayed by the need for a post mortem, had finally been scheduled for eleven o'clock the following morning. Laurie was grateful for her friend's concern, but was relieved to be left alone for a while. Beyond the windows the river lay in darkness, ebbing sluggishly in the freezing night air.

She went to the kitchen and made herself a cup of herbal tea, then sat in the lounge with a paperback novel. She felt more enervated than she had at any time since moving into the apartment. As she scanned the page and tried to concentrate on the complexities of the plot, her fingers explored the knife-rips in the fabric of the sofa. Because of the Christmas rush, the new covers she had ordered had yet to arrive. The jagged striations across the material which she now absently touched seemed to recall the fine red scratches which had once adorned her back like tribal markings. On a nearby table the telephone rang, making her start. She reached across and answered it.

At first she thought there was nobody on the other end of the line. Then a strange tapping sound began, like someone running a stick back and forth across the bars of a wooden cage. Behind this, she could hear a man steadily breathing, the air in his throat being forced out in a series of sexual spasms.

She dropped the receiver back into the telephone cradle with a gasp of disgust. Now was not the time for someone to be playing practical jokes. She wondered if perhaps she should ring the police and report the call, then decided against it. She had had enough questions from them in the last two days. The only sure way to outwit cranks was to get an unlisted number. She sat back on the damaged sofa and tugged her robe more tightly over her breasts. Slowly but surely the apartment felt as if it were becoming her prison, and the containment of all the unnamed things she most dreaded.

Alison entered the claustrophobic chaos of her Soho flat and headed for the kitchen. Something had been bothering her on the journey back from Hoboken. She pulled out the drawers beneath the cluttered kitchen counter and began to search among the balls of twine and special offer coupons. Finally she located what she was looking for—the blueprints Laurie had accidentally left behind in the restaurant just before Christmas.

Unfolding the plans, she held one end down with a cookie jar and began to study the geometric diagrams inch by inch. Then she took a piece of tracing paper and began to draw.

Laurie reknotted the robe-cord around her waist and headed into the bathroom. Turning on the basin tap, she splashed cold water over her face in the vain hope that it would make her feel less exhausted. She was debating whether to run a bath when the telephone began to ring once more in the lounge. She hesitated, her hand resting on the handle of the door. Her parents sometimes liked to call her at this late hour. She walked across the darkened lounge and picked up the handset.

This time the sound was clearer, a steady clicking, wood on wood, expanding and contracting. And beneath it was the rasping, quickening breath of a man fast approaching orgasm. She slammed the receiver down hard and cleared the line, her heart thudding in her chest. She was about to pick it up and dial the police when it rang again. Gingerly, she raised the earpiece and slowly moved it closer.

This time the voice was a familiar one. It was Alison, probably calling to say that she had arrived home safely.

"Laurie, thank God! Now listen carefully. You must do as I say."

Laurie frowned. The voice at the other end of the line sounded taut and strange. "Allie, what's . . ."

"Shut up and listen! You have to leave the building, right now. Just grab your bag and walk to the front door."

"Are you nuts? It must be minus five degrees out there."

"Please," pleaded the voice, "do this for me. Just get up and go."

"Why?" asked Laurie, puzzled. "Just tell me why."

"Your apartment, I checked the plans."

"So?"

"I kept thinking something was wrong. The way the place looked didn't seem to match the way it was on the blueprint." Alison sounded out of breath. Had she been running? "Ray Bellano, he built it according to the plans that he presented to you, but he built it the other way around."

"What do you mean?"

"If you flip the drawing over, you get a different-shaped apartment. I tried it just now with a piece of tracing paper. There's a second wall running all the way around the place. An inner skin."

"I don't understand," said Laurie, shaking her head as if to clear away her gathering fears. "What are you saying?"

"I'm saying that he's in there with you."

Horrified, Laurie looked up from one wall to the other. Away in the background, the clicking wooden sound had started up again. This time it was not being transmitted over the telephone, but was coming from somewhere within the apartment.

"Laurie, are you there? You see what this means? He's been there with you all the time. He must be watching you right now."

The receiver slid from her hands. She knew that Alison was telling her the truth. Everything made sense. The builder had been controlling her every movement from the start, forcing her to reveal her nakedness in the sudden glare of the bedroom lights, slowly baring her body beneath the drying taps of the shower, sending her from room to room, feeding on her growing anxiety.

She rose and moved into the center of the lounge, searching the walls, listening for the smallest sound. Now other details began to fall into place. She remembered forsaking her blanket and crossing naked to the TV as she tried to fix the picture, a hand touching hers as she emerged from the shower stall, the sense of someone standing over her bed watching her as she slept, the jealous rage which hammered in the bedroom walls because Jerry had made love to her. The burglary had been nothing more than a display of anger at her leaving. How many cracks and crevices, peepholes and passageways could he have built into the apartment?

As the creaking wooden noise became more urgent, she recognized its origin. He was breaking through the slats of the wall in the lounge. No more sneaking from secret openings, the master builder was about to make his grand entrance.

She ran for the kitchen and the knife rack above the sink as he appeared behind her in a showering explosion of plaster and wooden staves. For a second she caught sight of him striding across the room through a spray of dust, and the madness which glittered behind his blood-streaked eyes spurred her on.

"Stay away from me!" she screamed, grabbing a bread knife from the rack and holding it with both hands in front of her stomach. Ahead in the hallway, he paused. His erect, bloodied penis swayed from side to side as he began to move forward once more. She backed against the counter, desperately trying to think above the noise of her racing heart. Turning, she peered ahead through the doorway of the kitchen into the hall, but now there was nothing to be seen. It was as if he had suddenly disappeared.

The apartment had fallen silent. Laurie took a step forward, then another, carefully shifting her weight as lightly as possible. She began to think clearly again. The first priority was to get out of the flat. Her neighbor below worked nights, so she would have to go into the street for help. And to do that she would need clothes. The bedroom was at her back. Her jacket and car keys lay on the bed. She listened once more. There was still nothing to be heard from the lounge or the hall. Out on the river, the sound of a barge-horn was muffled by falling snow. Slowly she lowered the bread knife, then turned and walked into the bedroom. Into his awaiting arms. The power of her scream was matched by the thrust of the knife as she pushed it deep into the master builder's chest.

"You'll feel better if you drink this down in one." The young officer holding out the brandy to her was the same one who had called after the burglary. "Do you have someone you can stay with tonight?"

"I guess so, yes." Laurie accepted the drink and sipped at it. Although the blanket was pulled high around her shoulders she was unable to stop herself shivering. The doctor had told her it was shock, not cold. The officer watched dispassionately as they removed the builder's body from the room. The handle of the bread knife thrust out above the edge of the sheet, firmly wedged between his ribs, just below the heart.

"He designed the apartment, huh?" The officer looked about, approvingly. "He did a nice job. Got a good finish on these units." He ran his hand along the edge of a shelf, then looked back at the blood-spattered body as it went through the door. "Guess he took too much pride in his work."

"Ray Bellano started rebuilding the place right after I broke off with him," said Laurie, unfolding her napkin and dropping it into her lap. "I was hardly ever there, so I never noticed what he was up to. He was able to come and go as he pleased, and I was none the wiser. The police say he'd tried the same thing before on a smaller scale, when he rebuilt Irene Bloom's apartment."

"That poor woman," said Alison, burrowing her fork into a stuffed mushroom. "She obviously wasn't quick enough for him. You're lucky you didn't get washed up on the beach as well. These are delicious."

"All that time spent between the walls, watching." Laurie reached across to Alison's plate and stole a mushroom. "The police wouldn't let me see inside. They said he had—things—in there." She shuddered. "No more fixer-uppers for me. My next apartment is going to be completely ready to move into."

"Just think," said Alison through a mouthful of food, "if you hadn't slept with him in the first place, none of this would ever have happened."

Laurie narrowed her eyes at her companion as she continued eating.

"He knew that you'd never have sex with him again," said

Alison refusing to let the subject drop. "He must have gotten so frustrated."

"That's the worst part of it," said Laurie, slowly lowering her fork to the table. "I have a horrible feeling he never did."

They finished the rest of the meal in silence.

THE BUREAU OF LOST SOULS

IF THE RAIN had been heavier, Daniel Harper would never have located the building at all. Its bleak granite façade functioned as a perfect backdrop to the monotonous downpour. Why was it, he wondered, that Victorian buildings looked so much more appealing in the rain? It was almost as if they had been designed with inclement weather in mind. Stepping into the dark cavern of the doorway, he consulted the slip of paper once more.

6TH FLOOR,
ABADDON HOUSE,
EXETER STREET,
STRAND WC2

Hrs 9:30 a.m.—5:30 p.m.
One-hour lunch
Report Monday 17 November

The idea of going to work for the Civil Service hardly filled him with enthusiasm, but at least it would end the boredom of winter unemployment. He had registered with the agency just a few days ago, and had taken the first position offered to him. The money was reasonable, and he could always leave if the work proved too strenuous. After all, he was only filling in as a temp . . .

Daniel hitched back a cuff and checked his watch. Still twenty minutes too early, despite the fact that a body on the railway line at Baron's Court had caused long delays between the morning's rush-hour trains. Standing on the congested platform earlier, it had been hard to shake from his mind the image of a crushed commuter-corpse lying face down in the gravel between rain-clogged sleepers. Who were these tortured travelers who chose such a public form of suburban suicide?

He raised his eyes to the building before him. At the corners of the roof, squatting gargoyles sprayed thin channels of blackened rainwater into a somber sky. Perhaps it would be a good idea to show willing and head up to the office rather than while away his spare minutes in a coffee shop. Folding his umbrella shut and rattling the rain from it, Daniel stepped into the gloomy marble foyer of Abaddon House and attempted to locate the lifts. His shoes squeaked on the floor and the sound echoed slightly, as if he had entered a church.

High above him unlit strip-lights appeared out of place against the cool cream-colored curves of the ceiling. On his left a tall Formica-topped reception desk stood unmanned, a black tangle of telephones unattended. Within the sepulchral splendor of the vestibule the utility furniture looked tacky and insubstantial.

The door of the lift, like many of the original features of the building, belonged to an earlier, more elegant time. Each one featured an inlaid brass sunrise, the surrounds carved in rich dark wood, like polished chocolate. Here, carelessly taped to the wall, were several typewritten notices informing employees and visitors of the dangers of leaving packages unattended, the times of the monthly fire drills and the availability of new pension schemes.

Welcome to the wonderful world of the Stationery Requisition Form, thought Daniel cheerlessly as he summoned the lift. Already the smart white collar of his newly purchased shirt had begun to chafe his neck, as if constricting in anticipation of the day which lay ahead. Behind him several chattering young women tick-tacked across the foyer and vanished into an infinite corridor beyond the stairs.

When the lift arrived he found it manned by an incredibly ancient one-armed man in pseudo-military regalia.

"Where are you going, sonny?" he asked, turning an enormous crimson-veined nose towards his passenger, and immediately losing points with Daniel, who at the age of twenty-four resented being referred to as a child.

"The sixth floor."

"Ah ha!" cried the superannuated attendant, as if he had suddenly been visited with a heavenly revelation, "Credit Accountables. Mrs. Sharpe's lot. Going to see her, are you? A holy terror, she is, if you'll forgive the pun."

Daniel couldn't see that there was any pun to forgive. As the attendant maneuvered the single brass handle which controlled the lift, his left sleeve fell emptily to his side, the threadbare gold braid unravelling below the cuff buttons.

"Lose that in the war, did you?" asked Daniel cheerfully, pointing at the sleeve.

The old man turned a glass eye to him. In the gloom of the lift it glittered like an angry marble.

"No, it fell off." The glass eye glared before swivelling back to face the doors.

Daniel decided not to say anything else. He stood up smartly, straightened the knot of his tie and waited for the doors before him to open, trying to ignore the smell of disinfectant and damp wood which pervaded the lift.

As the old man maneuvered into position for the third time, he once again failed to marry the floor of the cubicle with the brass-plated step beyond it, and Daniel was forced to haul himself out of the hole by gripping the steel grille of the lift door.

The large-bosomed woman in the gray woollen suit who met him turned out to be Mrs. Norman, the assistant to Mrs. Sharpe. If she possessed a first name, she did not offer it for general usage. She wore gray plastic-framed spectacles whose corners flew up into wings. Her hair and face were as colorless as her clothes, as if her physical attributes had begun to merge with her wardrobe, but she seemed friendly enough, chattering away as she ushered Daniel through the plain oak doors and into a corridor which looked about half a mile long.

As they walked Daniel noticed that the heel of her left shoe was heavily built up in order to match the length of her legs.

"You'll be replacing Mr. Weatherby," she explained as she headed along the featureless corridor, her cumbersome left shoe sounding with a repetitive thud on the linoleum squares. She walked with a slight dragging limp, as if she had trodden in something unpleasant and was looking for a place to get rid of it. "He was with us for fourteen years, you know. Loved it here. Then he had the most awful accident. It left him so that he couldn't really move about by himself, so the management had to let him go. He was recompensed, naturally. He used to be such a nice man, and now he's so terribly disfigured that even . . . here we are, your new office. How would you like to be addressed?"

"I'm sorry?" Daniel turned to face his colleague.

"What shall we call you?"

"Dan, if you like."

"Well, Dan, you make yourself comfortable and Mrs. Sharpe will be along shortly to explain your duties."

Once Mrs. Norman had thumped off along the endless corridor, Daniel removed his coat, hung it on a nearby empty stand and sat down at the desk before him. So far there was no one else in the office. Somewhere in the distance a vacuum cleaner whined as it nosed back and forth. He looked at the desk before him. Someone had taken the trouble to lay out a neat pile of blank forms, a matching Biro and pencil set, in and out trays, a blotter and a booklet explaining departmental policy. At the back of the desk, somewhat incongruously, sat a small computer keyboard and screen.

Daniel raised himself from his chair and walked to the far end of the room. Hands in pockets, he looked out of the single broad window. The panes were nicotine-brown with residue from the traffic-clogged streets, the stunted archway at the top of the window suggesting that the room had been divided in half at some earlier time. On the rain-spattered ledge outside lay a pigeon, little more than a filthy collection of bones and feathers. Its narrow red beak was deformed, its eyes closed in death. It had only one leg.

As he watched, another pigeon, equally as bedraggled, landed on the sill. It stared sideways at the befeathered cadaver of its brother for a few seconds, then suddenly keeled over and fell off the ledge. Daniel furrowed his brow, then peered thoughtfully at his reflection in the glass. He removed a comb from his back pocket and ran it through his cropped black hair. He was just beginning to wonder how much more depressing his welcome could get when a thin, high voice spoke up from behind him.

"You must be our new recruit," it said. "A replacement for Stanley, no doubt." The voice belonged to an attractive young woman with cropped blonde hair, pale staring eyes and an odd sense of dress. She was gazing intently at a point on the wall two feet above Daniel's head. He followed her eyeline in an effort to see what was so interesting about that particular piece of paintwork, but failed to locate anything out of the ordinary.

"Stanley, that is Mr. Weatherby, used to sit at the desk over there, where they've put you." She pointed at a spot somewhere out of the window, then realized her mistake and pointed at the coat stand. "Please don't be embarrassed."

"I'm sorry?"

"I can feel you staring at me. I'm Mary. Mary Summerville."
It took him a few more moments to realize that she was blind.

Mary held out a tiny hand. Daniel maneuvered himself in front
of her and gently shook it. For a blind person she didn't seem
to have a very well-developed sense of direction.

"How do you take your tea?" she asked, feeling around the
edge of the desk in front of her and sidling daintily past it.
"That's a very important question in this office."

"Um, white without, thanks."

"Ginger or chocolate?"

"Pardon?"

"Biscuits."

"Oh, er, I don't really have a preference." Daniel scooted in
front of her and moved a chair before she had a chance to en-
counter the obstacle.

"Thank you, Mr. . . ."

"Daniel. Dan. Dan Harper." Flustered, he had already held
out his hand again before he remembered that she could not see
it.

"I'm new on this floor myself," said Mary. "After my . . .
accident I never really expected to keep the job, but they found
me a new position on one of the computers." She led the way
to a small alcove containing a kettle, a huge battered urn and a
refrigerator.

"But how do you, er . . ." Daniel found his sentence trailing
away as he searched for a way to avoid direct confrontation with
Mary's disability.

"Part of my work is sorting credit codings," she said, sensing
his difficulty and helping him out. "The codes are translated
into my dictaphone in a series of beeps. It's simple once you get
the hang of it. Too simple, really." She reached forward and
turned on a switch at the wall. "But it'll do until I'm ready to
advance downwards. Where were you working before?"

"Oh." Daniel pulled a face. "Well, I was at art college. But
I couldn't find a job after I left."

"That's my desk, over there." Mary pointed—with a greater
degree of accuracy this time—at a gray steel table partitioned
from the others. One side of the partition was festooned with
photographs of famous actors clipped from magazines.

"Oh, I know," she said, forestalling his next question, "I
can't see them but people tell me who they are. It saddens me
to think that I won't know what the next generation of film stars
will look like. I guess I'll have to stick with the ones I remember

from my sighted days.'' Mary looked sadly at the wall. There was an awkward silence while Daniel racked his brains trying to come up with a consoling remark.

"Well, I guess Cliff Richard will be around until the year two thousand," he said finally, then immediately bit his tongue.

"That'll be Mrs. Sharpe," said Mary, suddenly cocking her head to one side like a poodle becoming aware that someone was calling it. "She's the noisiest person in the building. You can hear her on the floor below."

Daniel listened for a moment. "She sounds very cheerful."

"Yes, doesn't she? It's so depressing. I frequently find myself wishing ill fortune on her just to hear the tone of her voice change. Something major, kidney failure perhaps. But of course that wouldn't have any effect." Mary guided milk and tea into two mugs, not very successfully. Daniel wanted to help her but was unsure of the protocol involved. "She's always collecting for Ethiopia. Forget solving world hunger, she won't be happy until they've all got CD players. I'd better get to work. I'll see you later." Mary returned to her desk with her tea. She stopped and threw him what would have been a backward glance had she possessed the gift of sight. "And don't worry, you'll be fine," she said. "Just remember not to think about your situation, and above all not to panic."

The Dead Files

Mrs. Sharpe insisted that Daniel should call her Vera. She was a tall, pale, middle-aged woman with a wide mouth, a tight dress and a firm handshake. She stood for no nonsense. And generally speaking, she stood. She also had an unnerving twitch that caused her left eyelid to close itself in a slow, lewd wink every two or three minutes.

Nobody in the building, she said, had a working record as unblemished as her team's, even taking into account poor Stanley Weatherby's time off after his accident. Planting her ample behind on Daniel's small secretarial chair, she reached across his desk and flicked on the computer. Daniel had assumed that his job would involve minimal responsibility. Indeed, that was one of its attractions. According to Vera, however, this was not the case.

"What we do in the building is process and categorize information about every man, woman and child in the British Isles," she explained in a loud remedial-class voice as she punched a series of digits on to the screen. "As you can imagine, each time Mr. Taxpayer makes a non-cash transaction it is recorded and balanced to provide him with a credit rating. Over the years that rating, together with other statistics like insurance records and medical history help to build an overall picture of our Mr. Taxpayer . . ."

"I thought there was no central system of information in Britain," interrupted Daniel. "Isn't that an infringement of people's personal freedom?"

"I really don't think that the keeping of records infringes anyone's freedom," countered Mrs. Sharpe. "And nor does the government. In this country people are free to do whatever they want. Within reason. Now . . ." She turned her attention back to the screen, obviously not prepared to become involved in a debate. "You'll be working with statistics. Since the start of the computer age it has become easy to store a large amount of information in a very small space. Even so, we cannot retain all of the information that we receive here. Contrary to popular belief, we are not infinite." She gave a small dry laugh.

"In the course of a lifetime, the average person accumulates enough paperwork to fill the Albert Hall. So our job is to decide which files are to be retained, and which are to be wiped."

"How do you do that?"

"Obviously, first of all we wait until they're dead." Vera turned to him as her left eyelid closed in an unfortunately timed wink.

Daniel shifted uncomfortably. His job seemed to be taking on a distinctly necropolitan aspect. Vera jangled a bangle back up her arm and continued to program the computer.

"When a British citizen dies, his file is closed. You understand that some files are worth retaining. Others are not."

"I can see that," said Daniel. "But why retain a file at all if the subject has died?"

"Well, let us suppose for argument's sake that you died tomorrow—fell under a train. There wouldn't be much point in us preserving your medical history, your Visacard allowance limit or your national insurance number, would there?"

"No, I suppose not," said Daniel glumly.

"But suppose you didn't die until you were a hundred. What a tangled web of information you'd be leaving behind! Mortgage repayments, insurance beneficiaries, tax problems . . . and who gets to sort it all out? We, the bureaucrats. The civil servants, the red-tape officials, the butt of everyone's jokes. That's what we are nowadays. Gone is the fear and respect of the Middle Ages.'' Mrs. Sharpe creaked back on the chair, her left eye twitching furiously. She indicated a cardboard box filled with floppy discs.

"These are all recently closed files.''

"Dead people,'' muttered Daniel under his breath. He peered at the box in awe. The entire statistical summary of hundreds of lives, arranged in alphabetical order.

"You job is to sort them out. Those files to be saved on the right''—she tapped one side of the desk with an armored finger—"those to be wiped on the left.''

"How do I tell one from the other?''

"Oh, you'll see soon enough. Half the files have virtually nothing in them. There are a lot of worthless lives in there.'' She gave the file box a damning look.

"I really don't see how you can judge a person's worth by his finances,'' Daniel complained. His sense of discomfort was growing by the minute.

"Really, Mr. Harper, this is no time for metaphysics. Times have changed. I promise you that our sentiments are completely in line with the government's. Read your department pamphlet thoroughly and you'll quickly learn to perform the simple mathematical calculations necessary to determine whether a file is stored or destroyed.''

Daniel sighed and picked up his handbook. It seemed like a strange kind of job. Although he could see now that it might well be a lot more interesting than it first appeared to be. Evaluating the sum worth of people's lives, and deciding whether to preserve them for all eternity, or damn them to oblivion. Why, it was almost . . .

Vera Sharpe suddenly announced that she was taking her leave in order to allow him to familiarize himself with the department handbook more thoroughly. She promised to look in again before lunch in order to check his progress. Daniel began to read.

"In addition to the processing of financial statistics,'' it said, "you must take Personal Achievement profiles into account.''

This was starting to look complicated. He hunched over the book and began to concentrate as, around him, other workers tapped at their keyboards and shuffled sheaves of receipts. Outside, the rain continued to fall in gentle bands across the road and against the windows of Abaddon House. Inside, Daniel was immersed in the art of evaluating the lives of the recently dead.

"How are you getting on?'' Mary stood by the side of his

desk. Her clothes were a glaring mismatch of colors and patterns. She obviously lived alone.

"Okay, I think," he replied with a smile. "This is what I do: plug in a file, boot it up, check the file-holder's financial situation at the time of death . . ."

"They don't like you to say that. You're supposed to refer to it as Closure of File."

"Okay, at Closure of File, then cross-reference it with his Personal History, and if there's nothing remarkable in either I mark the file to be wiped. Condemn it to eternal damnation. Makes me feel like God."

"Silly, only He feels like God. I've never actually seen Him, just a photograph that a friend took on one of the Parade Days," said Mary. "But she wasn't close enough and it didn't come out very clearly. She really caught just the back of His head. No, we're merely Purgationers. You know, receptionists in the waiting room of the dead. It's rather like Passport Control. More tea?"

Barking mad as well, thought Daniel, alarmed. What an incredibly raw deal. He decided to humor her.

"No thanks. Tell me, what happens to all the files that we decide to keep?"

"Oh, I'm sure His clerks just stack them all away in vast libraries to gather dust. And I bet they're arranged in order of privilege, just as they were in life. You know, politicians at the top, working classes at the bottom."

Daniel studied Mary's face. She was staring into the middle distance, a slight smile playing on her lips. The poor girl was obviously deranged. He was surprised that they allowed her to continue working here. He thought of another question.

"And what about the files we wipe?"

Mary suddenly looked uncomfortable. "Well, you *know* what happens to those." She made a pointing gesture at the floor. "Whoosh," she said. "Eternal You-Know-What."

"No, I don't know," replied Daniel, more puzzled than ever.

She raised her finger to her lips, then mimed someone being jabbed with a pitchfork. Then she smiled brightly.

"I expect you'd like to know the lunch arrangements," she said.

In at the Deep End

Daniel stared at the screen and attempted to make some sense of it. The files were written in such heavy code that he had to stop every few seconds and look up an abbreviation in the department handbook. After a while, however, he began to notice that the same codes were cropping up again and again. No doubt he would master the establishment jargon soon enough. He leaned back in his seat and listened. No sound came up from the street, and everyone else was immersed in their work. He looked at his watch and noted that it was almost lunchtime. Apparently there was a canteen on the floor below. He could hear the clatter of crockery now, and there was a familiar savory tang in the air. The sensation immediately revived memories of indigestible school dinners.

"I see you've got your first file up." The shadow that had fallen across his desk belonged to the gray Mrs. Norman. "You'll soon get used to the codes." She eased the weight of her elevated boot by leaning against the desk.

"It seems terribly complex," said Daniel, watching the screen as another string of abbreviations appeared.

"Let me give you some advice. You should do what I do. When you put a new file in—who have you got in there at the moment?"

Daniel consulted the handwritten sticker on top of the file-box. "Templeton, Richard. File Closure twenty-sixth of the fifth."

"Since we had the computers installed, the decision to save or destroy files has become a purely statistical one. It's supposed to save time. But sometimes I still use the old method. It's just as quick, and a lot easier to memorize. You might try it on your Templeton file and see if you prefer to work that way."

At last, thought Daniel, someone was talking sense. "Fine," he agreed. "What do I do?"

"Use your instinct," said Mrs. Norman with a secret smile.

"I'm sorry."

"Instinct. Was he a good man or a bad one? Did he love his family? Was he faithful to his wife? Was he kind to stray animals? The answers should all be on file. You just type your question directly on to the keyboard. After all, you're controlling the destiny of his soul, you need to find out as much about your client as possible. Me, I don't hold with the new system."

"My . . . client?"

"Dead or alive that's what he is, and it's the least you can do to process his afterlife correctly."

Did everyone around here have a screw loose? Daniel looked at Mrs. Norman very carefully. Smartly coiffed, sparkling-eyed, she appeared to be sane enough. Yet, in the conversational sense, he was lifting the receiver and getting no dial tone. Perhaps her neat appearance concealed the kind of philanthropic, obsessive lunacy that usually manifested itself in people like Mary Whitehouse. He decided to humor her.

"I had no idea the position entailed such responsibility. If I'd known that I'd be processing souls on the first day, I might have reconsidered applying for the job."

"You had no say in the matter."

"Excuse me?"

"The decision to come here was out of your control." She regarded him strangely, as if being forced to labor an obvious point. "You were chosen."

"I'm not sure that I . . . ." he began, but faltered, watching as Mrs. Norman leaned over the desk and ran her hands over the keyboard, slowly revealing the secrets held on the floppy disk labeled "Richard Templeton."

"My, where in the world did you get this file from?" asked Mrs. Norman after she had finished studying the data which had unscrolled on the screen.

"It was in the box that Mrs. Sharpe left for me after her briefing this morning."

"Show me the lid. Just as I thought. Someone's throwing you in at the deep end. Well, it's all good practice for you. Let me give you a peek into this man's final days." While Daniel looked on, she began to tap the keyboard faster. Presently she stopped and sat back in her chair, studying the screen.

"Well, well, well," she said, analyzing the codings. "Goodness dearie me." Suddenly she switched on a smile like a torchbeam and shone it at him. "Templeton, R. Thirty-four years old. Divorced—black mark there, for a start. Creative director of an advertising agency, that's another black mark. Got his head chopped off by a lift! Was it murder or an accident? A very determined suicide, even? No, I think we can safely rule that out." She pressed a button marked SCREEN DOWN and ran through the rest of the codings.

"A flat in docklands, a house in Norfolk, healthy bank balance. No charity donations, though, even though they're tax deductible. Ah, here's the juicy stuff, number of sexual liaisons in his last year of life . . .''

"That's listed, too?" asked Daniel, shocked.

"Of course," said Mrs. Norman, concentrating on the screen. "Goodness gracious, what a terrible womanizer! Oh, well . . ." She began to remove the disk from its drive slot.

"Wait, is that it? You've already made your decision? Suppose he really was murdered?"

"Suppose he was?" countered Mrs. Norman. "He led a rotten life. Whoever bumped him off was doing the world a favor. What good was he to anyone? Advertising executive, a flea on the back of mankind. Good riddance." She threw the file into the rubbish bin.

"Doesn't he get a second chance?" asked Daniel, appalled.

"There are no second chances. To coin a cliché, Life is not a Dress Rehearsal. Now you do one."

Daniel was still staring into the bin as Mrs. Norman loaded up the next case history.

Revelations

Daniel had slowly begun to decipher the second disk when Mrs. Norman impatiently moved him to one side and squinted at the lettering which filled the screen.

"Hawkley, Neil, middle initial L. Probably stands for something awful like Lionel. Oh dear, a property developer. Owned a silver Porsche with a car phone. Those facts alone are enough to condemn him to eternal . . . thingie. Came to a sticky end on a beach. Thoroughly nasty piece of work by the look of it, deserved what he got. Not a very nice way to die, though, with his leg stuck in a mantrap." She turned to Daniel.

"Well, what do you think? Save or destroy? A pretty straightforward decision, I would have thought." Mrs. Norman tapped a pencil against her false teeth. The screen was blinking a bright green message—STORE/WIPE? She leaned forward and pressed the letter W, and an instant later the disk was wiped clean.

"Wait a minute, what is going on here?" Daniel pushed his chair back and rose to his feet. "This isn't a branch of the Civil Service, this is . . ."

"Go on, dear," Mrs. Norman encouraged.

Daniel thought for a moment. "You're processing lives . . ."

"Afterlives," she corrected.

"Then I must be . . ."

"Dead?" she suggested helpfully.

"But I can't be!"

"I'm afraid so, dear. You died about three days ago. That's how long it normally takes people to get here."

"But I'm in one piece!" Daniel shouted. Several people in the office turned to look at him. He felt his body. There seemed to be no bones broken.

"And that's how you'll remain until your file is forwarded from your local branch office and we discover the method of your File Closure. Few people make it across the divide completely intact, of course. We all get some knocks and bumps. The journey is rather an unusual one. Unless I'm much mistaken, you fractured your skull on the way."

Daniel gingerly raised his hands above his hairline and probed. He located the cracked bone with the tip of a finger. "God, that feels awful!" he cried, snatching his hand away.

"Oh, it'll settle down in a day or two. You'll be in tip-top shape until your file comes through, wait and see. Can I get you an aspirin, perhaps?"

"No wonder everyone's been acting so strangely." Daniel looked at the others working in the office. "Are they all dead, too?"

"Of course," said Mrs. Norman. "We thought you realized. People normally do, you see. The agency usually only sends us personnel who have been through a basic Afterlife Training Scheme. It must be a bit of a shock for you."

"I'm sure I should be feeling more upset than this. My mum must be beside herself. We were always close." Daniel shook his head, trying to make sense of it all. "How come I'm working here as a . . . what was the word?"

"A Purgationer. Simple. Your file hasn't been processed yet. Eventually it should come into one of the departments in the building to be evaluated."

"So if this is Purgatory, none of the people working here can have had their files processed."

"That is correct." Mrs. Norman settled her spectacles more securely on the bridge of her nose, removed the "Hawkley, N" disk from the console and inserted another.

"But you said my predecessor was here for fourteen years!"

"His file went missing. It happens sometimes. Administration isn't what it should be, even here."

"Didn't it ever turn up?"

"Well, it was all very unfortunate. The Management were

about to issue him with a temporary work permit for the Beyond when someone over at our other department in Holborn found the file. It had been lying in a drawer unopened for all those years. It was forwarded on to Stanley, and when he broke the seal on the envelope he naturally adopted the physical characteristics of his demise, which was a great shock to him because he'd been in a smelting accident. Still, we gave him a lovely send-off." She pointed upstairs. "He got a card, a cake, a jumper and a travel alarm clock." She leaned forward confidentially. "Most of the people in this department have some kind of a problem with their paperwork. I myself have been waiting for my file to turn up for nearly seven years now. Personally, I don't think it will."

"But that's terrible!"

"Oh, I don't know." Mrs. Norman smiled beatifically. "I've grown to like it here. Suppose they found my file and processed me for . . . downstairs? I led a fairly blameless life, of course, so the chance is unlikely, but just suppose. It would be awful. Given the choice, I'd rather be playing a harp in Heaven than an accordion in Hell." She silently mouthed the last word in an exaggerated fashion.

"So you're happy staying in Credit Accountables? Better the devil you know, I suppose," said Daniel with a sigh.

Outside, the rain redoubled its efforts, and Mrs. Sharpe went to the other end of the room to turn on the overhead strip-lights.

Mrs. Norman studied the blue cardboard file-box. "She's given you a right old collection here. Look." She indicated a side panel filled with blurred type. "The people in this box have all died in unusual circumstances. It makes for more interesting reading, but they're tougher cases to classify. You've got time to do a file before lunch. I'll sit in with you for one more."

She punched the Return button on the keyboard with her thumb. A new name appeared on the screen. Together they turned their attention to the file.

"Turner, Bryan. Only young. Fell to his death on a housing estate. Possible drug overdose. Coroner's verdict was still Misadventure, though, so let's give him the benefit of the doubt, shall we? He hadn't had time to clock up any real sins or debts in his life."

The screen blinked STORE/WIPE? Mrs. Norman stored.

"I can't bear to see the little ones suffer," she said with a benign smile as she removed the disk and replaced it carefully in the box.

Daniel decided that it would be a good idea for him to get some fresh air.

Or at least, it seemed like a good idea. The ancient one-armed liftman looked on as Daniel attempted to leave the building. Just ahead of him in the street, businessmen and secretaries, mothers with pushchairs and delivery boys on bicycles passed back and forth. But to Daniel this scene could have been unfolding a hundred miles away for all the good it did him. It was as if a vast, invisible wall had been placed at the foot of the steps of Abaddon House. Daniel banged his nose on it twice before conceding that he was indeed trapped inside—presumably until the end of his allotted time in Purgatory.

This set him thinking. As he stood in the doorway watching the people of the real world go about their business, he began to wonder how he could speed things up and solve his own situation. It all hinged on the file of his death. If he could locate it, perhaps he'd be able to get Mrs. Norman to handle the processing. She seemed fair. Surely she would give him the benefit of the doubt if any borderline incidents emerged from his personal history. The biggest sin in his life had been that of laziness, and compared with what he had already seen on some of his clients' files, it could hardly be counted as a major character defect. No, Daniel felt confident about his eventual destination, and as he had no intention of spending the next fourteen years stuck in a desk job he determined to cut through the red tape and speed things up a little. Abandoning his attempt to leave the building, he set off to talk to Mary Summerville.

Mary was standing in the coffee alcove, pouring boiling water into a bowl of sugar lumps.

"Here, let me give you a hand," said Daniel, carefully taking the kettle from her. "I want to ask you some questions."

"Please, go ahead. Would you like some tea?"

"Er, thank you." Daniel accepted the proffered sugar bowl and set it down. "Tell me, if we can't leave the building, where do we sleep at night?"

"We don't, silly," laughed Mary. "We're dead. We don't need sleep. When one day ends, the next one immediately begins."

"Oh, great," sighed Daniel, "we can't even go over to the pub. When somebody dies and his file is closed, who receives it first of all?"

Mary thought for a moment. "It comes out of the file library and goes for sealing and stamping," she said.

"Which department would that be?"

"Case Verification."

"Have you ever been there to check on a file?"

"No, why should I? It'll eventually come up through the system."

Probably fourteen years later, thought Daniel. "Where can I find Case Verification?"

"In the basement."

"The basement. Thanks, Mary." Daniel gave her arm a squeeze and headed back out of the office towards the stairwell.

There were few unlocked doors in the endless miles of tiled corridor which filled the basement of Abaddon House. Daniel passed by dimly lit signs announcing the whereabouts of Stationery Supplies, File Retrieval, Staff Arbitration Services and Luncheon Vouchers. Finally he came to a stop before a pair of green-painted doors bearing the legend CASE VERIFICATION. He knocked twice, then entered.

Inside the vast green and cream room two elderly men sat behind a long Formica counter reading newspapers and drinking mugs of tea. Neither of them looked up as he approached.

"Excuse me," asked Daniel. "I've come to collect a file for Credit Accountables."

First one old man raised his head, then the other. In matching brown suits they looked like tortoises, virtually identical, as if the years spent working in the basement together had caused them to adopt each other's characteristics. Both of them had an ear missing.

"Where's your requisition form?" asked the one on the left. "We can't give you anything unless it's been requisitioned and authorized by the appropriate departmental head."

Daniel knew that he would never be able to obtain such an item, and decided to bluff his way around the problem.

"That's just it," he said. "We're still waiting for forms to be sent over from Holborn branch, and they're out of stock for the foreseeable future. So I've been told to fill out a chit, which you can hold until we get the forms in."

The old men looked at each other, considering Daniel's strategy. Finally they shook their heads.

"Sorry, son," said one of them. "It's more than our jobs are worth to let you have a file without correct authorization."

"Well, can you at least let me see it, so that I can report back and tell them you have it in your possession? That way, I won't get into any trouble with my boss."

Further consideration brought an eventual nod of agreement. The first old man rose and moved to a vast metal ladder which was leaning against what appeared to be an enormous bookcase filled with shoeboxes.

"What's the name?"

"Harper, Daniel. It should have just come in." Daniel could feel the palms of his hands starting to sweat.

"That'll be under New Arrivals, George," said the second old man as he returned to his newspaper. "That's if it's been filed correctly. If not, it could be anywhere."

George trundled the ladder along the bookcase and began to scale it. For the next twenty minutes he searched the racks, muttering all the while to anyone who would listen about what he considered to be the main defects in the management system. Finally he rummaged about in a box and pulled out an oblong folder.

"Just as well I looked under G as well as H," he said, "because it was in the wrong place. Could have been there for years without anyone finding it. Daniel Harper, due for stamping and sealing." He descended the ladder and passed the folder across to the young man so that he could have a closer look.

With trembling hands, Daniel opened the file and began to search the index for the cause of his death. When he reached the correct page, his eyes widened in horror.

"Burned alive?"

The second old man rose and peered at the upside-down page. Slowly deciphering it, he started to chuckle to himself. "Came home pissed one night and fried chips. Knocked the pan over himself. Burned a hole right through the floor of his flat. Nice one."

"But that means when my file is processed I'll become a charred pile of bones!"

The old men stared at him. "You're not allowed to see your own file!" gasped one of them. "It's against all the rules!"

"Bugger the rules!" shouted Daniel, snatching back the folder and running for the door.

Out in the corridor he quickly realized that he would become lost if he ran into the tiled maze which stretched ahead. Instead, he turned a corner and found himself facing the service lift. He suspected that the staff of the Case Verification department were too old to run after him, but surely they would call someone and try to have him stopped. He stepped into the lift and set off for the top floor. Perhaps there was someone up there with enough authority and compassion to hear his case and help him out.

But as the lift doors opened he realized that it was not to be. Before him stood half a dozen elderly gray-suited executives. It was obvious that they were waiting for him. Before he had a chance to send the lift back down to the ground they reached in and grabbed his arms, hauling him into the infinite corridor which bisected the top floor of the building.

"I demand to see the chairman, or at least the managing director!" shouted Daniel as the gray-suited men all started talking at once. He had nothing to lose by fighting back. What was the alternative? Once his file had been processed he'd look like a walking barbecue. He threw a punch at the nearest suit.

"For Heaven's sake, stop behaving like a child!"

Mrs. Sharpe parted the executives and pulled Daniel to his feet. "You'll never achieve anything like this. Stealing your own file, I've never heard of such a thing!"

"I bet lots of people do it," said Daniel morosely as Mrs. Sharpe removed the folder from his hands.

"They most certainly do not. This is a C of E establishment. If you want to see bad behavior you should visit the Catholic offices in Chancery Lane." She turned to the elderly gray-suits. "It's all right, he's from my department. Just started today. I'll handle it." Slowly they began to disperse. Mrs. Sharpe took his arm and walked him away along the corridor.

"You can't seriously have thought that you'd be allowed to see Him. This isn't Tesco's. It's not like you've purchased something faulty and want to see the manager. This is your Afterlife. Besides, He's never in. He's over at his private club with the other management executives. He only ever sees the workers on Parade Days."

"This is terrible," said Daniel. "Everything's the same here as it was when I was alive."

Mrs. Sharpe's face softened, and she patted his hand. "Did you have any reason to think that it wouldn't be?" she asked. "The only images you've seen of your afterlife have been painted on earth by the living."

"Well, this is all very depressing." Daniel took Mrs. Sharpe's arm as they headed over to the elevator bank. "I thought that when I died there would somehow be less bureaucracy. There's not much liaison between floors, is there?"

"I'm afraid not," said Mrs. Sharpe. "Everything needs a

system in order to function, and therein lie the seeds of its own inefficiency. But perhaps we can work something out.''

Suddenly she reached out and dropped his folder through the bars of the lift trellis. The shaft filled with the fluttering papers as they tumbled to the basement.

''Hey, that was my life!'' Daniel threw himself against the bars and looked into the shaft, but the folder had vanished into the darkness.

Mrs. Norman ushered the young black man into the office and pointed at the empty desk before him. Someone had laid out a pile of blank forms, a matching Biro and pencil set, in and out trays, a blotter and a booklet explaining company policy.

''This is where you'll be sitting, Denzil,'' said Mrs. Norman cheerily. ''Over there is Miss Summerville. Yoo hoo!'' She waved at the blind girl, who looked up from her typewriter and waved back at the hat stand.

''Who's that, over there?'' Denzil pointed at a hunched-over figure almost hidden behind an enormous stack of paperwork.

''That's our Mr. Harper,'' she said, lowering her voice. ''A very dear soul. They lost his file. He'll probably be here for ever.''

They watched as the hunched figure pulled another pile from the stack and threaded it into the console. Without taking his eyes from the screen, he stirred his tea with the end of a ball-point pen and took a sip.

''Don't feel too sorry for him,'' said Mrs. Norman, pulling out a chair and ushering Denzil into it. ''He adores working here.''

In return for her silence, Mrs. Sharpe had asked a small favor of her young employee. That if in his processing he ever came across the files of any other staff members, he would see to it that they, too, vanished discreetly into the liftshaft. It was cosy now in Credit Accountables. A tight ship. Why should anyone want to leave?

''Oh yes, I don't know where any of us would be without Mr. Harper,'' Mrs. Norman said, clasping her hands across her car-diganed bosom. ''Although,'' she added under her breath, ''I could take a guess. Now, who's for a nice cup of tea and a ginger nut?''

ABOUT THE AUTHOR

Christopher Fowler is a former advertising copywriter and drama writer for the BBC. The stories of *The Bureau of Lost Souls* originally appeared in two volumes, *City Jitters* and *Further City Jitters*. He is also the author of *Roofworld* and *Rune*, which is slated for filming, and has recently completed a new novel, *Red Bride*.